HAPPY ARE THOSE WHO MOURN

HAPPY ARE THOSE WHO MOURN

A BLACKIE RYAN NOVEL

ANDREW M. GREELEY

JOVE BOOKS, NEW YORK

HAPPY ARE THOSE WHO MOURN

A Jove Book / published by arrangement with
the author

PRINTING HISTORY
Jove edition / December 1995

ISBN: 0-515-11761-7

A JOVE BOOK®
Jove Books are published by The Berkley Publishing Group,
200 Madison Avenue, New York, New York 10016.
JOVE and the "J" design are trademarks
belonging to Jove Publications, Inc.

PRINTED IN THE UNITED STATES OF AMERICA

10 9 8 7 6 5 4 3 2 1

While Butternut Township, the Village of Woodbridge, and the Parish of Saints Peter and Paul are vivid realities in the world my imagination has created, they do not exist in the world that God has created.

From *Who's Who*

Ryan, John Blackwood. Priest; philosopher; born Evergreen Park, Il., September 17, 1945; s.R.Ad. Edward Patrick Ryan, U.S.N.R. (ret.), and Kate Collins; A.B., St. Mary of the Lake Seminary, 1966; S.T.L., St. Mary of the Lake Seminary, 1970; Ph.D., Seabury Western Theological Seminary, 1980. Ordained Priest, Roman Catholic Church, 1970; Ass't Pastor, St. Fintan's Church, Chicago, 1970–1978; Instructor, classics, Quigley Seminary 1970–1978; Rector, Holy Name Cathedral 1978–   ; created Domestic Prelate (Monsignor) 1983; ordained Bishop 1990; Author: *Salvation in Process: Catholicism and the Philosophy of Alfred North Whitehead*, 1980; *Truth in William James: An Irishman's Best Guess*, 1985; *Transcendental Empiricist: The Achievement of David Tracy*, 1989; *James Joyce Catholic Theologian*, 1992. *Tenebrae in "Finnegans Wake,"* 1995. Mem. Am. Philos. Asc., Soc. Sci. Stud. Rel., Chicago Yacht Club, Nat. Conf. Cath. Bshps. Address: Holy Name Cathedral Rectory, 732 North Wabash, Chicago, Il. 60611.

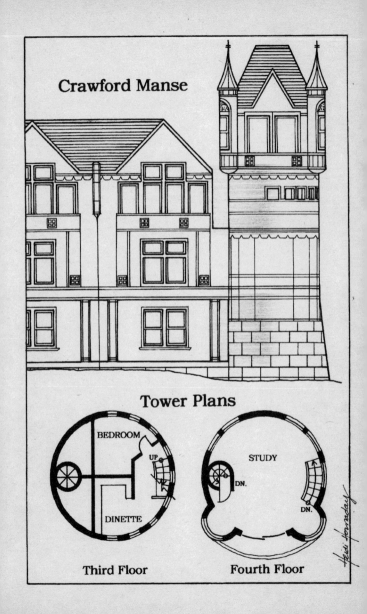

Crawford Manse

Tower Plans

Third Floor

BEDROOM

UP

DINETTE

Fourth Floor

STUDY

DN.

DN.

CHAPTER 1

"THERE WILL BE no haunted rectories in my Archdiocese!" the Cardinal barked as he strode into my study. "Is that clear, Blackwood?"

"Indubitably."

"Much less"—he jabbed his finger in my general direction—"any haunted parishes! Understand?"

"Heaven forfend that there should be."

Approaching his middle sixties, Sean Cronin, Cardinal Priest of St. Agnes Outside the Walls and, by the Grace of God and the long-suffering patience of the Apostolic See, Archbishop of Chicago, looked like a cardinal ought to look. Unlike most of his fellows (bland, dowdy little men), he was tall, trim, passionate, and dramatically handsome with blond and silver hair, an appealingly lined and sharply chiseled face, and hooded blue eyes that occasionally flashed with manic glee. Clad as he was at the moment, in a glittering pectoral cross inlaid with large rubies, crimson cummerbund and zucchetto, with cape trailing behind him, he might have stepped out of a Renaissance painting—though not the one by El Greco.

It was not an altogether uncalculated image.

As for the fiercely disciplined passions that were part of that image, one could only guess what they were, even his humble auxiliary Bishop who knew him better than most.

He was, however, passionately opposed to all psychic phenomena, which led the aforementioned barely noticeable auxiliary Bishop to suspect that he himself was plagued by such phenomena.

"Especially I will not tolerate a haunted rectory in a haunted parish when the parish happens to be that of Saints Peter and Paul in Woodbridge."

The Cardinal, doubtless dressed for some black-tie dinner that was too important to be left to the care of the inoffensive but virtually invisible auxiliary, savagely opened the door of my liquor cabinet, violated the secret compartment, and produced a diminishing bottle of my Bushmills Green Label—a sure sign, as the saying goes, that there was a bee in his bonnet. He poured a far too generous portion of that magic elixir into a Waterford tumbler and passed it over to me. Then he filled a second tumbler much more modestly, presumably the one drink he permitted himself each day, sat on the single uncluttered easy chair in the study, crossed his legs, and sipped from the tumbler.

"Understand, Blackwood?" he said again.

With a loud west of Ireland sigh (which the uninitiated might have thought heralded the advent of an acute asthma attack) I saved the manuscript of my latest scholarly work (*Tenebrae Liturgies in "Finnegans Wake"*) and turned off my new Compaq Pentium computer.

"The parish of the late and barely lamented Right Reverend Monsignor Charles P. McInerny, Protonotary Apostolic."

Both the "Right" and the papal secretary rank have been suppressed in the present allegedly more egalitarian Church, but they were titles that "Charlie Mac," a.k.a. "Jolly Cholly," had claimed for himself. Since the claims incensed Milord Cronin, it seemed only proper that I recall them.

"I will not tolerate that bastard coming back to haunt his

parish." The Cardinal scowled at his drink. "He died in February and I want him to stay dead until the day of Final Judgment."

"He was sufficiently mean while among us," I agreed with another loud sigh, "to attempt just that."

"When the Vatican finally agreed that it was all right to give him the sack three years after he refused to retire at seventy, I sent young Peter Finnegan out there, as you may remember."

"But of course. An admirable if somewhat radical young man. I believe he is on the record as saying that he doesn't believe in rules."

Sean Cronin dismissed that heresy with a wave of his glass. "Who cares about rules! Peter is a zealous and dedicated young man. . . . You teach him in the seminary?"

"A young man not lacking in Irish charm and wit."

"Would you believe that Pete Finnegan thinks he's being haunted by Jolly Cholly's ghost."

"Only if I were told this fact by a prince of the Church such as yourself."

"Those assholes on the personnel board put Pete in third place on the list to be the new pastor out there. They said that they thought the transition from Jolly Cholly to Pete would be too abrupt for the parish. . . . Why is it, Blackwood, that once a guy is elected to the personnel board he begins to think like bishops did thirty years ago?"

It was the kind of Sean Cronin question that did not require an answer. Indeed, it did not admit of an answer. Nonetheless, I always felt an obligation to essay an answer.

"Power corrupts," I murmured.

"So what does Pete do?" he said, ignoring my helpful analysis as he usually does. "In less than a year he turns the parish around. Sunday Mass attendance doubles, parish income triples, the school that was a third empty is filled, and the waiting list is so long that he'll probably have to put on an addition. . . ."

One of the raps against the Cardinal among the clergy of Chicago is that he was so busy running around the world that he knows nothing about the parishes of the city. The reason for this fiction is that priests are terrified of the possibility that he might know everything, which indeed he does. There was not a single fact about a parish that was not recorded in the hard disks inside his skull.

"And Archdiocesan taxes are paid and special collection moneys come in on time, whereas his predecessor of dubious memory never sent a penny downtown."

Again the Cardinal ignored me.

"In Jolly Cholly's day, if you were sick and wanted to receive Communion, uh, the Eucharist, you got it once a month if you were lucky. Now Pete has over four hundred people in the Ministry of Caring and some of them visit the sick with Communion every day."

"Remarkable."

"It shows what the laity can do if you give them half a chance."

He paused to consider the falling level of his drink.

"I don't know, Blackwood, why they endure the assholes we send them."

"Faith," I murmured.

"Woodbridge has never had anything but an asshole as a pastor. I'll not permit a spook to ruin what Pete is doing out there. That parish has been haunted since it was founded by the living dead. No dead dead this time."

"Arguably not. . . . Am I to understand that the shade of the departed Protonotary Apostolic objects to the transformation of his parish?"

The Cardinal swirled the liquid around his tumbler, creating an illusion that there was more in it than met the eye.

"According to Pete Finnegan, Jolly Cholly objects to being murdered in his bed."

"A not unreasonable position to take."

"Pete will give you all the details. The attending physician, a crony of Cholly's, said stroke. Pete says murder."

"Deplorable!"

I knew from the moment of the Cardinal's appearance in my room that I was the designated hitter in this inning. Yet the dynamics of the scenes the two of us created with much relish required that I keep this knowledge to myself.

So I continued the approved scenario.

"The dead do not return, Blackwood. You know that as well as I do. Leaving aside Himself, of course."

"There are," I suggested, "haunted rectories in England."

"As you yourself would say, you have doubtless noticed that we're not in England."

"According to impeccable research two out of five Americans have had some kind of contact with the dead, three out of five among the widowed."

"Nonsense!"

"Unlike the encounters in English rectories and other haunted houses the experiences reported by this valid national sample would appear to be benign. Reassuring not spooky."

"In Woodbridge it's not benign."

"Tim Reardon, who as you know is the best theologian we have, says that perhaps our belief in survival is not based on wish fulfillment as on actual or presumed contact with those who have gone beyond."

"Poor substitute for religious faith!"

I was not about to explain the differences among various kinds of psychic experiences nor to raise the question of whether the phenomena obtaining among the People of God in Woodbridge might fall into the poltergeist category.

"Doubtless. But as William James would have remarked . . ."

"I know. I know. Those who have them do not doubt their accuracy and are not to be constrained to give up their experience by the skepticism of those who don't have them."

"Something like that."

The Cardinal considered me over the rim of his Waterford tumbler. "You're not about to tell me that you've had such experiences?"

The honest answers were that, yes, I have had two such experiences and, no, I don't base my faith on them. However, such a reply would have terrified my ninety-five percent skeptical Cardinal. So I replied, "Some families, my own included, are more likely to report them than others."

Nor would I mention my cousin Catherine Curran's son Jackie, a healthy adolescent and athletic star like his father Nick, with whom all kinds of benign spirits seemed to check in routinely.

The Cardinal did not want to field my ground ball. So he changed the subject.

"I don't want a haunted rectory on the five o'clock news, not in this Archdiocese."

"A reasonable stand . . . Yet who would have wanted to murder a retired pastor, approaching his seventy-fifth birthday?"

The Cardinal shrugged and fiddled with the ruby ring that matched his pectoral cross.

"Who wouldn't have wanted to kill him? What do the pigs say in the Gospel story? Our name is legion?"

"Ah!"

"Cholly McInerny was the meanest, nastiest, most vicious nut in the whole history of the Archdiocese. And, as you well know, Blackwood, that covers a vast area of mean, nasty, and vicious nuts."

"Arguably."

The Cardinal is the only one who addresses me by my middle name, allegedly imposed on me because my mother had made a blackwood convention in bridge the night I was conceived. No one calls me by my Christian name of John either, though my late father normally called me Johnny. I am generally known in the family as "Punk" or "The Punk" and not infrequently as "Uncle Punk." Outside the family the normal and approved form of address is the contraction "Blackie."

As in "call me Blackie."

Not "Ishmael" but "Blackie."

As in the Black Prince and Boston Blackie and Black Bart. But not as in the Black Night of the Soul.

Indeed the name is so pervasive that when I answer the phone "Father Ryan," many of the folk from the Cathedral Parish seem unaware that there is anyone on the parish staff with that name.

Perhaps the reason is that I am such an unremarkable and inoffensive person that when people enter an elevator on which I am being borne earthward or heavenward they do not even notice my presence.

The little man who wasn't there again today.

"You wonder what happens to a guy," the Cardinal said, frowning in reflection on the case of Charles P. McInerny, "a guy becomes a priest with some vague idea of preaching the Gospel and being good to people, joins the Marines during the Korean War and wins the Silver Star, by all accounts seems to be a good guy. Then he turns sour and spends the last three decades of his life being mean to everyone he encounters and his years as pastor reading every book he can find from romance novels to ancient Babylonian history."

"Acedia?" I suggested.

"By the time I arrived at the Chancery he already had developed a reputation as a nasty son of a bitch who loved to raise last-minute objections to requests for marriage dispensations."

"You succeeded him as chancellor, I believe?"

"Yeah, he hated me ever since. Blamed the Cardinal for sending him to Catholic U to get his canon law degree during the war instead of waiting and sending him to Rome where he would have made the connections."

"Yet from the outcome of all but your final attempt to remove him, he was not without Roman friends?"

Milord Cronin drained his glass, looked for a coaster on which to put it and, finding none, placed it on the floor.

"The guys always said it was the clear end of his career which turned him bitter, but he was pretty bitter even before he was dumped."

"He saw you as a rival?"

The Cardinal nodded wearily. "Yeah . . . Dumb. Always felt he could have done this job better than me. Maybe he was right, poor bastard."

A second rap against Sean Cronin among the clergy was that he didn't really believe in God. I would respond by saying that they had it wrong. God was about the only reality in which he did believe.

"Why was he replaced?" I asked.

The Cardinal rose from his chair.

"Why? Who knows? Who gives a damn? The Boss never said. He just told me that Cholly had been appointed pastor in Woodbridge."

The final rap against Sean Cronin was that he was reckless, didn't give a damn in his dealings with Rome and his fellow hierarchs. He had created that illusion with some skill and it was surely true that he was totally unthreatened by the Vatican. Yet he was disrespectful always with the shrewd and ruthless cunning that characterizes South Side Irish politicians—a trait with which my own family is not completely unfamiliar.

"You must have had some suspicions?"

The Cardinal turned and stared at me intently and then shrugged again. "Only he and the Boss knew and neither ever said. Cholly was certainly bitterly opposed to everything that happened at the Vatican Council. As you know the Council was rarely acknowledged in Woodbridge as far as he was concerned. The Boss didn't need a guy like that as chancellor thirty years ago."

"Doubtless."

I waited.

"I sometimes thought that there might be something else, some specific failing or mistake. . . ."

"A woman perhaps?"

"Cholly? Gimme a break, Blackwood!"

I knew Sean Cronin well enough to conclude that he suspected a lot more about the abrupt termination of a promising ecclesiastical career than he was prepared to tell me just yet.

Fair enough. I would come back later.

If it were a woman, there would be a nice irony in his replacement by Sean Cronin whose intense affection for his sister-in-law, Senator Nora Cronin Hurley, was well known. Perhaps the fact that it was well known made it safe.

No one questioned the chastity of that affection, not in the years since he became archbishop. As to earlier years in their lives, I refuse to speculate, it being none of my business and in any case irrelevant. As far as I was concerned it was enough that the good Senator (who has the excellent taste of approving of me) kept the Cardinal alive and that was all that mattered.

"Yet might there not be a connection between the untimely and unwelcome termination of his career and more recent events?"

"Sure there might, Blackwood. It's your job as my auxiliary to find that out. Auxiliary means helper, you know."

"Arguably."

"One more thing," the Cardinal said, pausing at the door as he prepared to sweep out with the same éclat with which he had swept in. "If Pete Finnegan has not lost his mind completely, Jolly Cholly was murdered in a locked room to which he alone had the key."

"Deplorable," I said, repressing the word "fascinating" that would have more accurately represented my sentiments.

"I knew you'd think so." The Cardinal's mad Irish, mercenary warrior grin spread across his gaunt face.

"Indeed."

"Now turn this madhouse here over to one of those bright young guys that work for you and go out to Woodbridge and put an end to all this nonsense before it makes the five o'clock news."

"Naturally."

"Remember, Blackwood: no haunted rectories in my Archdiocese!"

"And no haunted parishes?"

"Precisely! . . . See to it, Blackwood!"

With a rustle of watered silk the Cardinal sped out of my study and down the corridor, his cape trailing behind him like the afterburner exhaust on an F-15.

CHAPTER 2

I SURPRISED WOODBRIDGE the following Sunday afternoon, like a man might stumble into a handsome matron's bedroom and find her in the most minimal of garments. Surprised, she reveals more of her womanliness than she wants revealed. She is lovely indeed, perfection itself perhaps, but yet troubling in her near nakedness, threatening and even sinister in her surprised self-disclosure. The unprepared, nearly naked woman somehow becomes death. Or a threat of death. The man is attracted to her and also repelled. His desire is awakened and also his fears. He wants to enjoy this unexpected tableau but even more he wants to run as Victorian author John Ruskin fled his naked bride because, attractive as she was, her body terrified him. So I felt a powerful impulse to turn my car around and flee under the viaduct and away from the sinister perfection of this community, a perfection that shimmered with a threat of death. For a moment it was as surprised as I was and angry that I had caught it unprepared in its deadly secrets.

You're anthropomorphizing streets and trees and rows of houses, I told myself. You weren't prepared to drive under the viaduct and experience the change from the gas stations and the car dealerships and the convenience stores and the fast food restaurants to this vision of elegant old suburban perfection, this bit of New England in the prairies.

All right, it's still sinister.

Why?

Because it reminds you of a graveyard after all the funeral corteges have left and you're the only live human still around.

The railroad runs at the top of a ridge, sand dunes above the beach off an earlier stage of Lake Michigan (or Lake Chicago as the geologists call it without, as far as I know, permission of the Mayor or the city council). One comes out of the cave of the viaduct and looks down on Woodbridge, only a few feet lower, with the impression that one has come over a mountain range and is looking at a city far below. The gently curving streets were thick with old oak and elm trees, resembling roads in the older sections of graveyards; in the harsh radiance of the afternoon summer sun breaking through the greenery from the west, the stately Queen Anne and Victorian homes seemed perfect, timeless, perhaps eternal, like the tombs in a cemetery. The carefully trimmed lawns and shrubs, bathed golden in the sunlight, were the result of "perpetual care." The famous Frank Lloyd Wright "Prairie School" house on the corner might have been a vast mausoleum. There was no sound, no movement, no other cars, no other living humans. Even the wind had faded to an awed whisper.

My home community on the southwest fringes of the city also possessed the trees and the curving streets and the old homes, but in Beverly there were newer homes too, an occasional uncut lawn or ugly porch and vitality—noise, people, traffic. Here on the fringe of Woodbridge if I strained I might be able to hear the buzz of the Interstate that was the outer protective wall of Woodbridge beyond the railroad, but that was the sole evidence that I was not the only person in the world.

Your imagination is playing tricks on you, I told myself sternly. Because certain easily explained psychic phenomena are occurring in this village, you're permitting yourself a hypogogic interlude, a wide-awake nightmare, in which your preconscious is running wild. Nearly naked women and cemeteries indeed. Your sister the psychiatrist would have a lot to say about that. This is simply a hundred-year-old suburb that for reasons of location and good fortune has survived relatively unchanged. In the nature of things it cannot be sinister, much less haunted. Understand? Start the car—why did you turn off the ignition in the first place?—and drive on to Saints Peter and Paul Rectory.

Right?

Right.

But the image faded slowly. I started the car only after a small boy pulling a red wagon appeared down a side street and reassured me that I was not in a graveyard. The red wagon, like all red wagons that little boys pull, was surely part of this world, wasn't it?

What was all that about? I asked myself as I finally started the car. Premonition? Or what? Jackie is the psychic, not me.

Yet I wanted to get away from the heavy Prairie School pile of bricks only a few yards away as quickly as I could.

In retrospect, psychic or not, I had encountered the barest hint that there was evil in Woodbridge that went far beyond poltergeist phenomena. I should have paid more attention to that waking nightmare.

Before I began my drive "Into the West," into the "Tir-Na-Og" of Woodbridge, I had done some poking around at the Chicago Historical Society and in the archives of the Archdiocese. The village owed its existence to the railroad that a hundred years ago had brought it within thirty-five minutes of the Chicago Loop and its persistence to the tight boundaries that protected it from hostile encroachment—a forest preserve through which flowed a small creek, a country club, two railroad lines, and now two Interstates. Most of the homes had been built before 1920, a few in the brief pre-war prosperity of 1939 to 1941, and a very few after the war. It had been founded by Major General M. E. Crawford, a Civil War general, who had moved to the country from Chicago, bought a large meadow for himself, and built on it a vast Victorian house that he had called Woodbridge because of a bridge in the woods that crossed the creek. Its inhabitants were not the wealthy speculators and corporate executives of the North Shore, but solid and respectable professional men and women, affluent enough but not, in their own judgment anyway, rich. For the first half century of its existence it had been solidly Protestant. After the war Catholics had begun to move in to the village and even found their way into the club. Now Woodbridge was at least half Catholic.

There are no strip developments along its streets and no shopping malls or plazas (though both are conveniently close beyond its boundaries). The "Business District" is a string of high-quality specialty shops and other dignified establishments that stretches from the railroad station at one end of High Street to the city hall and fire station at the other end. There are two public grammar schools and a junior high in the village itself. For those who do not want to send their children to the township high school—Butternut Township North (which is twenty percent "minority")— Woodbridge Academy offers quality private education for a huge price within the safe borders of Woodbridge itself. For Catholics, Benet Academy, Immaculate Conception

High School, and St. Joseph's High School are reasonably close, though many young men and women take buses into the city to attend Fenwick or St. Ignatius College Prep.

There are twenty-one churches in the village, of which the largest by far, according to an old article in the *Tribune* Real Estate section, is Saints Peter and Paul whose white stone Gothic spire towers above the center of the village, only a block from the railroad station.

The *Trib* dubbed Woodbridge "The Perfect Suburb," a title that appeared on the signs at the village limits until the signs were removed in an effort to persuade visitors that the village did not really exist. But those who could afford to buy one of the picturesque old homes (with modern electricity and plumbing of course) still took the title for granted according to a more recent article.

In Woodbridge you could pretend that race, crime, blight, pollution—all the problems of big city American living—did not exist. Woodbridge was an heirloom community, a reminder of a simpler and more elegant past, even if that past existed more in the imagination than in reality.

It was safe from all harm and all evil, except for the misbehaving shades of dead monsignors.

I had returned from the Historical Society to the Cathedral rectory and, with a two-volume history of Chicago parishes on my desk and a phone conversation with one of my ordination classmates who knows the folklore of the Archdiocese, pursued the history, both formal and informal, of the Parish of Saints Peter and Paul in Woodbridge.

The parish was founded in 1902 by one John Laurence Kelly who reigned for thirty-three years, never rising to the rank of monsignor, which was an easy task in those days if one did not mess up too badly. Judging by the picture of

Johnny Kelly, taken on the parish's silver jubilee in 1928 (a year late you will note), he was a gaunt little man with wild eyes. Upon arrival he had purchased a "large Victorian house" near the railroad station, "the oldest home in the village" and adjoining lands. "Even today, this historic house continues to serve as the rectory for the busy parish."

I pondered the picture of the house. It was rococo Victorian, a caricature of the architectural style as if someone had swept all the pretensions of that era into one random combination of components—turrets, gables, eaves, bay windows, balconies, porches, recesses, even a small tower. In the picture it was more comic than foreboding. However, if someone had murdered Jolly Cholly, as Cardinal Cronin had called him, in a locked room I would have to explore every inch of its twists and turns.

Fascinating.

"Johnny Kelly put up that little wooden church you see in the picture," my classmate informed me, "and brought in four 'portable' classrooms. Prefabs as we'd call them . . ."

"Cronin Carts as they are called today."

My friend chuckled.

"You can imagine how the good Protestants of Woodbridge reacted to those eyesores. No wonder someone burned a cross in front of the rectory the week before the silver jubilee."

"Indeed."

"Having established the church and the school and buying a home for the four nuns who taught in it, Johnny Kelly retired to the rectory and did nothing for the rest of his life except drink—and insult people when he was drunk."

The second pastor whose term extended from 1935 to

1966 was one Patrick Flynn, a large, burly man with a fat face and a complacent smile to judge from the history book.

"Paddy Flynn came from a dirt poor Irish family in Canaryville. He literally didn't have a pot to piss in as a kid, only an outdoor privy. But when he arrived in Woodbridge he discovered that he was an aristocrat and spoke only to the wealthiest people in the community and to his gin rummy partners at the club where he played the game for high stakes three days a week, sipping bourbon with his cronies. Showed up at ten in the morning and stayed the day."

"Winner or loser?"

"Claimed to be a winner, but you could never believe a word he said. But give the devil his due. He built that monstrosity of a bastard Gothic church and the parish school and a new convent during the Depression, though they say that the Depression never happened in Woodbridge."

"Also the Monsignor Flynn Parish Center."

"Yeah. They say he locked the door the day it was finished and never opened it again, a tradition continued by his successor. The point is, Blackie, to build a community center as a monument to yourself but not to use it. You let people into it and they make noise and dirt, you know?"

"I believe that I have been told that was the practice of many pastors of his generation."

"He was lord of the manor. His curates chauffeured him around, took his suits back and forth to the cleaners, walked his dog."

"Dog?"

"A Newfie. Can you imagine one of those in the rectory. Paddy spoke only to the top families. The curates did all the work and generally left after two years. He did not want anyone to get too close to his people. A real winner."

"Indeed."

"His bachelor brother 'Doc' Flynn also lived in the rectory and kept an eye on the curates when Paddy took his three months vacation in Hobe Sound every year. The curates ran Doc's errands too."

"A medical doctor?"

"Supposedly, though the word was he rarely practiced medicine. He didn't have to because like his brother he was living off the fat of the land without doing any work."

"A pleasant arrangement."

"Paddy died in the locker room of the club, stark naked in the shower. First Catholic member of the club—he never paid a dime to get in or stay in—and the first Catholic to die in the shower. Poetic, huh?"

"Arguably."

"Then the Archdiocese, having delivered Woodbridge from Annas to Caiphas, proceeded to deliver it to Pontius Pilate."

"The late lamented Charles P. McInerny, P.A."

"Not all that lamented. Jolly Cholly threw Doc out of the rectory, drove off all the curates, hired his own cook and housekeeper, and settled down to being the meanest pastor in the history of the Archdiocese. But you and the Boss know all about him. Give Sean credit. He finally got rid of the guy."

"Milord Cronin does not give up easily."

"That's for sure . . . so the Church has shit on Woodbridge for almost a hundred years. So they send young Pete Finnegan out there and he turns the place around in less than a year. Which just goes to show you, though I'm not sure what it shows."

"Resiliency."

"Something funny must have happened to Cholly back in the sixties. He disappeared from the Chancery overnight and from what I hear he fell off all the lists of potential bishops. There were rumors he was on top of the terna for Joliet when they bounced him . . . the Boss know why?"

"If he does, he's not talking."

"Figures . . . spent most of the time during the last years of his life—when he wasn't feuding with Cronin— sitting in his room and reading all day and half the night. His classmate Joe O'Keefe lived with him all the time. Talented guy but a fall-down drunk. I hear Pete has kept him on and sobered him up."

"Edifying."

"What's going on, Blackie? I heard rumors that Jolly Cholly is haunting the place. Are they true?"

"I think not."

"Yeah, well, he was mean enough to do that. They say the only thing he took care of while he was alive was his own suite of rooms up in the tower and the big lawn across the street. Raised hell if a single weed appeared. Pete has turned it into a softball field."

"Characteristic of Peter."

I had considered the picture of the Right Reverend Charles P. McInerny in the history book. He was dressed in the full choir robes of a monsignor (as such robes were worn in those days) and held the biretta with the purple pom-pom in his right hand. He had been a sleekly handsome black Irishman with the characteristic low forehead, thin lips, and intense eyes of the young cleric on the make. The book also offered a picture of him in his Marine uniform wearing his Silver Star decoration. In this carefully posed formal photograph, he wore the reckless smile of a hell-for-leather gyrene.

There was, I had thought, something of a resemblance to Sean Cronin in that picture.

Interesting.

I had then walked down the street to the Chancery Office and informed our competent and humorless Chancellor that I wanted the secret files on Charles P. McInerny and Peter Michael Finnegan.

He had been reluctant to trust them to me.

"They're secret, Bishop."

"A fact of which I'm fully aware."

"I'm not sure I should show them to you."

"Someone as conversant with the Code as you cannot be unaware that as a vicar general I am a moral person with His Lordship."

I have no idea what that means but I find it a useful phrase to throw at my fellow priests.

"I know . . . do you mind if I ask him?"

"Be my guest."

He had picked up the phone and punched in the number of the Cardinal's office.

"It's not that I don't trust you, Bishop. But one can't be too careful with this stuff."

"Arguably."

"Bishop Ryan wants to see two secret files, Your Eminence . . . yes, that's right, McInerny and Finnegan . . . yes, Your Eminence . . . yes, Your Eminence . . . right away, Your Eminence."

The files had then been promptly delivered into my hands.

Jolly Cholly's file was thicker than a couple of Chicago telephone books. Complaints from the laity. Refusal to permit baptisms, funerals, and weddings. Rudeness to those who wished to contract mixed marriages, which he absolutely refused to permit in his parish. Expulsion of children from the parish school for trivial reasons (skirt too short). Sermons limited to sex—denunciation of birth control, premarital sex, self-abuse, abortion, and too much marital sex. Indifference to spiritual problems of laity. Harshness in the confessional. Associate pastors (as curates were now called in the conviction that a rose might not be a rose if its name were changed) who could not speak English. Money wasted on remodeling his rectory rooms and maintaining a useless parish lawn. Lack of recreational facilities for kids and religious education programs for those who went to public schools.

Not an unusual list in itself. Most of the charges could be leveled against any number of monsignori from that era. But unique to the file of Monsignor Jolly Cholly were both the volume of the complaints and the neat and literate quality of the letters, most of them typed on business letterheads. The People of God in Woodbridge did not accept their ecclesiastical destiny without a struggle.

Then there was the correspondence with the Vatican regarding Sean Cronin's efforts to remove Monsignor McInerny. There were three main charges: failure to implement the reforms of the Vatican Council (the Monsignor continued to say Mass in Latin and facing the altar), failure to pay to the Chancery Archdiocesan taxes and moneys collected in various special collections (he sent a huge Peter's Pence check directly to Rome), and *Odium Populi*, hatred of the people.

Rome had responded by ordering Cholly to implement the liturgical reforms and to pay the taxes. It also granted him an indult to offer one Latin Mass of the Council of Trent every Sunday. Cholly did permit his resident priests— Pakistani, Filipinos, and Croatians as well as his old crony Father Joe O'Keefe—to follow the new liturgy, but he himself refused to do so.

The Cardinal had washed his hands of the Woodbridge affair once it had become clear to him that Rome would not support his removal. "Let the abominations which the people of the parish must suffer at his hands," he had written to the relevant curial functionary, "be on your conscience."

Then, four years ago, the Boss had renewed the battle when Jolly Cholly had refused to offer his resignation when he reached the retirement age of seventy—refusing for the very good reason that he was certain it would be accepted.

The letters from Rome had temporized. The Monsignor had labored long in the service of the Church and was in poor health. Surely another year or two as pastor would not create any great problem.

"If exceptions are made for one man," the Cardinal had replied, "then they must be made for everyone. You either support me in removing him or you'll have my resignation."

The Vatican had backed down. Exit Jolly Cholly. Finally.

He must have had powerful friends in Rome to be able to stand up to a cardinal for so long. And his affluent friends in Woodbridge must have made many gifts to such friends.

The file on Peter Finnegan was much thinner—letters, again literate and neatly typed, complaining about the changes in the parish. With copies to the Pope and Cardinal Joseph Ratzinger of the Congregation for the Defense of the Faith.

The burden of the charges were that the new Pastor was preaching heresy, that the liturgy had become pagan, that the Latin Mass had been moved to six A.M. on Sunday morning, that improperly dressed young men and women were swarming (my word) on parish property, that questionable doctrine was being taught in the parish school, and that the new Pastor was ruining all the good that Monsignor McInerny had done.

While the charges against Pete were grammatical they lacked substance. The nature of the heresy, the paganism, and the questionable teaching in the school were not substantiated—save for the new Pastor's preaching that Jesus was human, a doctrine laid down by the Council of Ephesus unless my memory fails me.

A curialist had written to the Cardinal demanding an investigation of these charges and reminding him of the risk of shocking the faithful with "novel" ideas. The Boss had replied, "I am delighted to learn once again that there are men on the staff of the Roman Curia who understand the problems of my Archdiocese better than I do. I have been monitoring the work of Father Finnegan since he was appointed to a task that was made exceedingly difficult by the Holy See's refusal to permit me to remove a pastor who was openly disobedient to me and cruel to his people. I assure you that Father Finnegan is a pillar of Catholic orthodoxy (he has even restored May devotions to Our Lady, a practice that his predecessor neglected) and is doing excellent work. I see no need for an investigation at this time."

In other words, to heck with you, not to use more scatological or obscene language.

I jotted down the names of the most persistent letter writers—Dr. and Mrs. Stephen Curtin, Mr. and Mrs. Albert Fasio (he an attorney at law), Arnold Griffin, Gerald Reed IV, Mrs. Lynn Reed. These were perhaps the cronies of the late Monsignor, those who had once been winners and now were losers. While their complaints were the most frequent they were also the most restrained.

Moreover they stopped in January, the month before the Monsignor's death.

I buzzed the Cardinal's office.

"Blackie here. Does Pete Finnegan know about these letters?"

"No. He has enough to do. I'll protect him. That's a strange group of people. Many of the writers are Jolly Cholly's friends who moved into the parish after he was made pastor and raised their families there."

"Indeed. Perhaps involved in his, ah, fall from grace."

"Maybe."

He was still not giving anything away.

There was no reason, I assured myself, to consider any of them to be suspects in the murder of their beloved Pastor, if indeed he had been murdered.

I had already arrived at some conclusions about the puzzle of Saints Peter and Paul. They were not, as it would turn out, completely erroneous, but they failed to estimate the depth of the evil that was on the loose in that parish.

"I see," I replied to the Cardinal.

"You'll smoke out what you have to, Blackwood. See to it."

The phone at the other end of the line clicked off.

In other words, if I developed any specific suspicions in the course of my sojourn in Woodbridge, he *might* be willing to confirm them.

Thus armed with as much information as I could garner without venturing to Woodbridge, I packed my clothes and my Compaq Aero notebook and on a hot August Sunday afternoon drove out to the western suburbs, an area as familiar to me as are the back waters of the Congo.

After poking around for a while, I finally found Wood-bridge and experienced my chilling first encounter with its menacing perfection. After the boy with the red wagon had startled me out of my reverie, I drove cautiously toward what I thought might be the center of the town. I evaded a number of cul de sacs, one-way streets, and dead ends, and found myself at the railroad station, looking down High Street, as devoid of human life as had been the streets near the viaduct. The parking at the station and on the street was diagonal—a conceit favored by most affluent suburbs—and sparse. If you provided too much parking, people from outside the village might come in to catch the train and you couldn't let that happen.

Sure enough behind the trees on High Street, the white stone spire of the parish church loomed, a statement that Catholicism was the most important faith in Woodbridge. Regardless.

Regardless of what? Just regardless.

I turned left on the first street I could find that permitted such a turn and then left again on Oak Street and came upon the parish "plant."

Here, thank God, vitality had returned with a vengeance. Throngs of young people were everywhere—a softball game on Jolly Cholly's prized lawn across from the rectory and basketball and volleyball in the school-yard—boys naked to the waist and girls wearing halters, the latter an innovation that I had yet to observe in my own neighborhood and that would doubtless lead to yet more letters to the Congregation for the Defense of the Faith.

The church was indeed a monstrosity, a vast, tasteless white stone, pseudo-Gothic affair that was too big for its site, too big for Woodbridge, and too big for the parish—unless the liturgy and the homilies would reverse the flow and bring people from other parishes into Woodbridge for Sunday Mass.

You can never tell what will happen in these days when the laity think it proper to shop for liturgy and preaching on Sunday morning as though we priests were competing in an open marketplace.

I pulled up in a driveway next to the rectory and thus heeded the warning that cars parked in the street overnight would be removed by order of the Woodbridge Police Department.

The rectory was still a gross pile of random Victorian-isms. Still comic and not threatening. Now, however, with a fresh coat of white paint and bright green trim, it seemed almost bright and cheerful.

If Peter had been tasteless enough to paint a band of orange somewhere the house would have celebrated Irish nationalism.

I opened the trunk of my car and removed my Chicago Bears duffel bag. As I was closing the trunk, the bells in the church tower began to toll for a funeral liturgy. I walked to the street and peered at the front of the church. No funeral cars.

Welcome to Woodbridge, Blackie Ryan. Ask not for whom the bells toll. They toll for you.

CHAPTER 3

"FATHER RYAN TO see Father Finnegan, Megan," I informed the young person who answered the rectory doorbell almost as soon as I had stopped pushing it—a violation of the old Catholic rule of "make them wait."

The blond young person wore a summer suit of light blue, nylons, shoes with moderately high heels, and careful makeup. At first you thought "twenty years old." Then you noticed the mass of orthodontia work inside of her mouth and realized that she was fifteen going on sixteen and had dressed up for her turn at answering the rectory doorbell because either her mother or her Pastor (arguably both) had insisted.

She considered me with grave suspicion. Admittedly in sport shirt, gray slacks, and a Chicago White Sox windbreaker and toting a large Chicago Bears duffel bag (to say nothing of wearing my Coke-bottle glasses), I didn't look much like a priest. Perhaps not much like someone who would be permitted, under normal circumstances, into Woodbridge.

"How do you know my name is Megan?" she demanded.

"At my parish we have four porter persons. They are all called Megan."

I did not add, because it would have confused the issue,

that they were African American, Mexican American, Korean American, and Irish American.

The kid smiled. Perhaps I was all right after all.

"My two associates are not called Megan."

She did say "associate." This after all was Woodbridge.

"Then they are called Lisa and Jennifer."

She gulped. "How did you know that?"

"Elementary, my dear Megan."

"Where is your parish?"

She was not yet ready to permit me into the rectory.

"Downtown."

"Holy Name Cathedral!" she exclaimed happily. "Now we're even! You're Bishop Blackie, aren't you?"

"Arguably."

She opened the door and allowed me to enter. "Father Pete said you would be here this afternoon. You're going to help put the ghost at rest. I'll kind of miss him. He's sort of a cute ghost. Did you notice the funeral bells he just rang? Wasn't that neat? My mom and dad get angry when he rings the peal bells at night. So does everyone else. But we kids still think it's cute."

Thus do the young cope with a haunted rectory and a haunted parish.

"Indeed," was all that I could manage under the circumstances.

"Oooooo, is that your car, Bishop Blackie?"

"You mean the turquoise-green 1955 Ford Thunderbird convertible in the driveway? Not exactly mine, Megan. It belongs to my family and they let me use it in the summertime."

"Co-*ool*!"

"Perhaps while I'm here I can take you and your boyfriend Matt for a ride in it."

"It's *not* his name," she said triumphantly as she showed me into a parlor.

"Then it's Sean."

"How did you know *that*?"

"I just kind of know things."

"*Fersure* . . . Father Pete is playing softball with the guys. I'll tell him you're here."

She picked up a walkie-talkie and pushed a button.

"Father Pete, Bishop Blackie is here. . . . He's kind of neat actually. . . . OK, I'll show him up to your study."

"Busy day here at the store, Megan?" I asked as we climbed a wide staircase to the second floor of the house.

"Totally! Every time it gets this hot, some of the kids show up in halters and we get phone calls about immorality. Like they don't know what immorality really is, you know?"

"And what do you tell them?"

"Exactly what Father Pete says I should," she said in the tone of long-suffering and patient martyrdom that Irish women learn very early in life. "I thank them for their interest, take down their name and phone number, and promise them that Father will call them back. Which he does. Naturally."

"He win some of them over?"

"No way. But he says they have the right to be heard too."

So young Peter Finnegan had learned diplomacy since the days I knew him in the seminary.

"That's Father's room down at the end of the corridor, Bishop Blackie. Hasn't he done like a totally neat job in remodeling this old place?"

"Indubitably!"

The pastel colors and the soft indirect lighting made one forget that one was in a Victorian house of horrors.

Until the irrepressible Megan threw open a door half-way down the high corridor.

"Want to see the stairs up to the ghost's room, Bishop?"

"I suppose I should. . . . Ah! A spiral staircase!"

Not only a spiral but a narrow, tightly wound spiral, filled with sunlight streaming in from a skylight.

"Father Pete put in the skylight so it wouldn't be so dark. But it's like we have to leave it a spiral because there is no way we can get to the top of the tower otherwise."

"Indeed! And have you climbed to the top?"

Is the Pope Catholic?

"Promise you won't tell Father Pete? Or my parents?"

For reasons that escape me I am always deemed by teens to be a truly excellent unindicted coconspirator against "adults."

"Promise."

"Sure, like I've taken up a whole bunch of kids. I think Father Pete knows I do it but he doesn't want to know officially. Right?"

"Right . . . what is it like?"

We continued to stare at the spiral staircase that seemed both too narrow and too steep for an elderly man to climb without help.

"Kind of weird but also neat. Sort of like a hideout on a desert island, you know? At the top is this totally humungous study with oriental rugs and antique furniture and lots of leather-bound books and a sixty-five-inch television screen. Then you go down a flight of steps and there's a kind of kitchen and dining room combined and next to it is this totally luxurious bedroom."

Megan, sophisticated woman of the world that she was, did not seem at all scandalized by the lifestyle implied by what she was describing.

"You have to go up to the top to get down to the bedroom."

"Weird, isn't it? I think he was murdered, Bishop Blackie, don't you?"

"Arguably. . . . Are there any phenomena when you go up there?"

She nodded vigorously. "I won't go up there again. The last time I sneaked up there were, like, crowds of people closing in around me. Then the TV went on. I turned it off. And it went on again. So I'm, like, I'm out of here. This place is, like, history for me."

"A wise decision."

She then conducted me to Pete's room and promised me that "Father will be right up."

His study was done in a kind of refined Swedish Modern and was unconscionably neat. I noted with disapproval that he was still using a 386 computer and a dot matrix printer.

Fulfilling Megan's promise, Peter Finnegan, in sweatshirt and shorts, charged into the room, a bottle of Jamesons Twelve Year Special Reserve (now twice as old as the label promised) in his left hand.

"Welcome to Woodbridge, Bishop!" he exclaimed, shaking my hand vigorously.

"Call me Blackie."

Peter Finnegan had shed his beard and mustache and his confrontational style since he'd left the seminary and become the charming Irish pol that his father and his grandfather before him had been. In his middle thirties, no taller than five nine, apparently in excellent physical condition, and pleasantly exhilarated by his exercise, there was nothing about this handsome priest with thick brown hair and lively brown eyes that suggested he might be hallucinating.

"Mind if I turn on the Sox game?" he asked as he poured me a generous ration of the Jamesons. "I see that even you are supporting the Sox these days."

"More than you would do if the positions were reversed."

"Arguably," he chortled as he turned on the TV. "Bigger one up in Monsignor's room but there are too many interruptions up there."

He pulled a diet Coke out of the refrigerator, popped the top, and smiled contentedly.

"The kids exhaust me. Not sure how much longer I can keep up with them. . . . Do you want to go up to Monsignor's room now?"

"Not yet. I'd rather hear about his last days."

Out of the corner of my eye I noted that an immense African-American man named Frank Thomas had approached the plate. I have reason to believe that he is, perhaps for obvious reasons, called "The Big Hurt."

"Funny thing, Blackie, he was not such a bad guy toward the end. The Boss wanted me to throw him out of the rectory, but I saw that the poor man was on his last legs, so I said, hey, leave him here with his books and his TV. There's no one else to take care of him."

"Except his cronies."

"Creeps." Pete dismissed them with a wave of his hand. "Bet some of them were on the phone to Megan this afternoon complaining about the halters the girls are wearing on the courts and over in the ball field. . . . Toward the end he couldn't relate to most of them and vice versa."

"Indeed."

"There were a few, like Lynn Reed . . . Just a minute, Blackie," he interrupted his memories about the last days of Jolly Cholly. "I want to watch this next pitch."

The hapless pitcher from the Cleveland Indians threw a high fast pitch to the "Big Hurt." With fluid ease the latter swung his bat and sent the ball on its way to the left center field stands.

"How about that!"

"You knew he'd hit a homer?"

"Just a hunch. He was overdue."

Indeed, I thought to myself.

Aloud I said, "As I remember your seminary days, you often had such hunches."

I remembered no such thing.

"As often wrong as right . . . but about Monsignor: he kind of mellowed out when he found that I was not going to evict him. Became sort of dependent on me. Maybe even liked me a little. Told me all kinds of great stories about the Archdiocese in the thirties and forties. Some scandalous stuff about the Cardinal and the Senator, mostly fiction, I'm sure."

"Doubtless."

"He knew that I was taking the parish away from him, but he didn't seem to mind so long as I was respectful to him and pretended nothing much was changed."

"But everything had changed?"

"Oh, yeah. I fired the Croatian, who was a Fascist as well as unable to speak English, and hired a whole new staff from cook to music minister and redid the rectory. . . ."

"Tastefully, I note."

"Interior designer's taste, not mine." He laughed. "But I kept his buddy Joe O'Keefe around. Still is here. Does the Latin Mass on Sunday. And I kept his housekeeper around, so he was happy. She retired when he died."

"He tolerated your new array of various staff persons?"

"He didn't see them, partly because he didn't want to

and partly because I told them to stay out of his way and
humor him if he showed up. I kind of hinted at the same
thing when all the people began coming back here from
the other parishes. There were some bad moments, like
when he denounced our Indian Jesuit anthropologist at the
ten-thirty Eucharist one Sunday as a terrible pagan and
himself with an Oxford degree. But generally things
worked out. He was tired, Blackie, exhausted from all the
years of bitterness and resentment. I felt sorry for him."

The trouble with Peter Finnegan, I told myself, was that
he was a Christian, albeit a politically astute Christian.

"You were able to afford all the expenditures?"

He opened another can of diet Coke and held up the
Jamesons in an offer of more. I shook my head. If one is
about to encounter a ghost, better that one be in total
possession of one's faculties.

"Hell, Bishop, there was two and a half million in the
bank. Not at the Chancery, but at the Woodbridge Bank
over on High Street. When I asked for checkbooks he
meekly turned them over to me. His buddy, the President
of the bank, was not so willing to accept my name on the
account. I about died when I saw how much it was. I called
the Boss and he said I'd need it for the school addition. . . . I don't know how he figured out there was
going to be a school addition that early."

"He gets hunches too."

I note for the record that it is absolutely forbidden for a
pastor to have more than a hundred thousand dollars in an
account from which he can draw money. Everything else
must be remitted to the Chancery where it is credited to the
parish account and used to draw interest that accrues to the
Archdiocese.

"I guess he does. Anyway, we'll be able to put up the
new building and redo the church and still have a lot left

over. Of course I sent it all downtown, but I have a letter
from the Boss authorizing everything."

That way he would not have to struggle with bureaucracy that hated new construction because it deprived the
Archdiocese of interest earnings.

"As far as you know there are no other accounts?"

Peter Finnegan stiffened in his chair.

"Gee, Blackie, I never thought of that. You think there
were?"

"There was doubtless a surplus when he became pastor.
Twenty years of postwar prosperity in an affluent suburb.
Then another quarter century of Sunday collections, however small the congregation might have become. Easter
and Christmas collections too. In that perspective two and
a half million doesn't seem like much."

"Wow!" he murmured softly.

"He submitted no annual reports to the Archdiocese.
Did he keep such reports on file?"

Peter Finnegan frowned. He was out of his depth now.
"I never saw any. I don't think he made any distinction
between himself and the parish."

"Probably not . . . did he leave any personal financial
records?"

"I never saw any. Lynn . . . Lynn Reed . . . cleaned
out all his stuff after he died. I saw her carry away a couple
of boxes of papers. Maybe his records were in there. I
never had a priest die on me before. I didn't know what to
do. I was glad she did."

"Who is this Lynn Reed?"

"She's the wife of Gerry Reed, president of the Bank of
Oak Bridge. Owner of it really. Family inheritance."

"Ah?" I waited for more.

"A nice woman. Very, *very* attractive even if she is in
her late fifties. I think she persuaded the Monsignor that I

was all right after I assured her that I would not throw him out of the rectory."

"Indeed."

"She spent a lot of time up there with the Monsignor, especially when he was sick. She would hold his hand and calm him down. I suppose they loved each other. Not that I think anything ever happened between them, if you know what I mean."

Peter Finnegan had not been in the world long enough to know that much can happen between a man and a woman without "anything" happening. I would have to meet this Ms. Reed.

"What were the Sunday collections when you first arrived?"

"Four thousand, forty-five hundred. Chicken feed compared to most parishes like this one. It's up to ten thousand now."

"Let us assume four thousand. That would mean something in excess of two hundred thousand a year. Subtract some subsidy for the school . . ."

"Hardly any. He didn't believe in the school. Told the sister principal that she had to make do for herself."

"Not much for parish upkeep. Let's estimate then two hundred thousand dollars banked every year."

"Plus another hundred from Christmas and Easter collections. He bragged to me about that."

"All right. Three hundred thousand a year at rock bottom. Probably no less than that in inflation free dollars for a quarter century."

"Seven and a half million," Peter murmured softly.

"At a minimum. Wisely invested, perhaps twice that by now, much more if there were some successful speculation in real estate or, heaven save us, the commodity exchanges. Subtract the millions in the account he turned over to you. Round it down to take into account slippage, mistakes, errors in judgment, and perhaps some malfeasance, deliberate or indeliberate, and there may be ten million dollars floating around somewhere."

"Belonging to the Catholic Bishop of Chicago?"

"A corporation sole."

Milord Cronin would be astonished at these numbers. As well he might be. A man could become rich as pastor of an affluent parish if he had no scruples even if he served that parish badly. His cronies could become even richer.

Fascinating!

"Motive for murder, Blackie?"

"Arguably."

"Gosh."

Peter Finnegan was nothing if not guileless.

CHAPTER 4

"BE CAREFUL, BLACKIE, these steps are kind of steep. And you can never tell when the stuff will begin. I've been through it hundreds of times now and it still scares the hell out of you."

"Doubtless."

Peter Finnegan was leading me up the spiral staircase to the "Monsignor's apartment." He was reluctant to do so, but I insisted that I wished to unpack my bag before supper.

"You're not going to sleep in that room, are you?"

"Of course I am . . . when did the phenomena begin?"

On the way up the stairs, he explained that there were a few strange events immediately after the Monsignor's death and then they seemed to subside. Only in recent months had they begun again. First there were strange noises from the tower—Peter had never moved into the tower suite and had no desire to do so. Then they spread to the whole rectory. The noises turned into other phenomena—objects moved, electronic equipment turned on and off, windows and doors slammed shut or yanked open. Now the "haunting" had spread to the church—sacred vessels overturned in the sacristy, doors that would not lock or unlock, the organ playing without any visible musician, and most recently the bells ringing inappropriately at odd hours.

"The natives are getting restless, Blackie. I'm not sure what will happen next."

"Five o'clock news."

"That wouldn't be good . . . we'd better solve the murder soon."

The young priest had lost all his healthy color. His face was ashen, his body tense. It must have required enormous effort to isolate worry—and fear—about the psychic phenomena from the ordinary parish responsibilities, including playing softball with the "guys" and charming everyone who crossed his path.

"You are convinced that he was murdered?"

"At first I thought it was a natural death. I had no reason to question the doctor's verdict, except I did wonder about the bloodstain on the carpet. Now I think he was murdered. Why else would he come back from the dead?"

"The cause of his death was listed as massive cerebral hemorrhage, was it not?"

"That's what Dr. Curtin said."

"Another one of his close friends?"

"Yeah. I can't figure out why any of them would want him dead or why cover up for a murder."

Money would be a very good reason.

"Yet now you suspect that for some reason they did cover and perhaps are still covering up?"

"It doesn't make sense, but I don't know what else to think."

We had reached the top of the stairs. The door to the Monsignor's suite opened noisily—by itself. The bells in the church tower began to toll again.

"Sure you want to go in?"

"Naturally . . . when did you begin to think that he had been murdered?"

"Not at first, like I said. The doctor said stroke. It

seemed reasonable to me. Then I began to wonder if it might be something else. I couldn't think of a motive. A lot of people hated him, but not enough to kill him. Especially since he was an old man in poor health who would die soon anyway. . . . Now you have come up with a very good motive—ten million dollars."

He was hesitating at the door. I eased him aside gently and strode into the suite myself.

"And while he was alive he might have at any time turned this money over to the new Pastor of whom he was becoming increasingly fond."

A barrage of magic tricks waited for me in the room. The television flipped on. The air conditioner began pumping cool drafts into the stuffy room. Desk doors opened and shut. A crucifix on the wall tilted sharply to one side. Pius XII seemed to grin at me from his painting next to a grandfather clock that chimed manically. Outside, the church bells changed from toll to peal, as if celebrating a wedding or a great victory.

Cheap magic at that. I ignored them.

"As I understand it this door was locked the night of his death?"

"This one and the one down in his bedroom. You couldn't get into either room when they were locked unless you had the key. He was the only one who had the key. Even if you had a key, you still couldn't get in if the catch was set from the inside, as both were that night."

"Indeed . . . Did he lock them often?"

"Sometimes he'd forget. Then when he decided he could trust me he'd forget pretty often."

"Even Ms. Reed didn't have a key?"

"No. She called me that evening. Said she had not been able to reach Monsignor on the phone all day and was worried about him. I rang him on the house phone. No answer. I came up here and pounded on the door. Still no answer. I called Lynn back. In a few minutes she came over with Dr. Curtin and a carpenter who removed the whole lock assembly. We came in here and went down the steps to his bedroom. That was locked too, so the carpenter had to pull out the assembly. Then we went in and found him dead. Dr. Curtin said he'd died in the early morning hours and that there was nothing we could have done for him."

I picked up the remote control of the television and turned it off. It turned itself on again. I went over to it and pulled the plug out of the wall. That should take care of that.

I confess that if it had turned itself on again without electricity my sangfroid would have been shattered.

The study was the most opulent rectory room I had ever seen. It was a big room occupying the whole top of the tower with windows all around its circumference—high ceiling, oriental rug, antique furniture, deep couches, oak paneling, thick maroon drapes. I wondered irrelevantly if the same interior designer was responsible for Peter's new look in the rest of the rectory.

That worthy young priest pulled back a drape and opened a sliding-glass door.

"Here's his little balcony. He used to sun himself out here and admire this park across the street."

Since I do not like unprotected heights I was content to stand at the doorway.

"Now he would be forced to admire the young women in halters playing softball on your field of dreams."

"I thought you'd notice them," he said with a chuckle. His face, however, was still pale.

Would it have been possible for a skilled climber to rappel up the wall and come in this window. Perhaps.

Despite my queasy stomach, the so-called tower was only four stories high, one more than the rest of the rectory. But why would anyone take the risk of climbing the wall, even in the early hours of the morning at a time when the police cars of the village would be prowling the streets looking for vehicles to impound and "undesirables" walking the streets of Woodbridge?

"Scandalous," I replied to Peter Finnegan apropos of the haltered young women, with notable lack of sincerity. "Doubtless when they have children, they will insist on nursing them in public, as did the mother of Jesus."

"Good line."

I sensed a crowd of people in the room, closing in on me from all sides, the same experience as the worthy Megan had reported. If she had not reported it, I told myself, I would not experience it.

"Let me orient myself, Pete. The rest of the rectory is on our left. Your room is at the far end of the second-floor corridor, closest to the church."

"When we get a deacon from the seminary in the fall, he'll have another room on that floor. There's also a big community and conference room. The other three priests have suites on the third floor; they're bigger than the ones on the second floor and they are willing to climb the steps for more space."

"And this floor, which does not connect apparently to the spiral staircase up which we climbed, seems to abut"—I peaked cautiously out the sliding door—"on the rooms below us here in the tower."

"Not quite abut, Blackie. The tower wall and the third-floor wall of the rectory are independent of one another with about a foot of space between them. I thought of that too."

"Indeed . . . well, let us descend."

The magic tricks diminished, though the door behind the drapes opposite the desk flew open as we approached it.

They were still cheap tricks.

The stairway down to the lower floor of the tower was steep, narrow, and dark, like the stairway to the basement in my youth. Pete switched on a light. It promptly went off.

"Damn! Watch your step, Blackie."

He opened another door at the bottom of the steps and light came pouring in. In a moment I was in a sleek, polished combination kitchen and dining room with sunlight pouring through its porthole windows.

"We are, I take it, on the far right-hand side of the building as we face toward the softball field?"

"Right. The bedroom is on the near side, close to the third floor of the rectory."

"Fascinating."

I was already beginning to develop a theory. Later I would test it against whatever evidence I could find.

"I don't know what to do with this place. I'll never live in it and after what's happened here no one else will want to either. It's kind of a monument to Monsignor now."

He pushed against a wide oak door. It did not budge.

"Damn, he's locked it again!"

Peter reached in his pocket, pulled out a key chain (you can't be a proper Catholic pastor without one, which is why the younger priests on my staff say I'm not a proper pastor), fiddled with the keys, and opened the door.

"The latch on the inside is never locked?"

"Twice. I've had to call over the carpenter and the locksmith."

The bedroom, notably smaller than the study on the floor above, was as luxurious but more old-fashioned—

black marble tables, a four-poster bed with maroon curtains trimmed in gold, paneled walls, an elaborately decorated and molded ceiling, leafed in gold, and an oriental rug that might have been worth a half year's salary to a beginning teacher in the Catholic schools.

A crystal vase, filled with cut roses, occupied the center of one of the tables.

"Comfy . . . fresh flowers?"

"Lynn brings them over every couple of days. The kids let her in and she climbs the stairs, leaves the flowers, and goes over to the church to pray. No one even thinks it's strange. I guess the kids like her too. I can't bring myself to stop her."

"Ah."

"It's near that table where we found him."

"So far from his bed?"

"Dr. Curtin says that he had a stroke, stumbled out of bed, collapsed over here, and hit his head against the table, which caused the bleeding on the floor. He died, the Doc told me, from the stroke and not from the blow."

"It would be interesting to know how he knew that. Have you asked him?"

"Only when the, uh, manifestations started. Doc refused to discuss it with me."

"Indeed."

"See this place where the rug has been repaired?"

He pointed at a square patch in the oriental rug that was a bit lighter than the rest of the intricately designed floor covering.

"Very cleverly done."

"Lynn brought in a Persian rug maker to do it. In a couple of years, she says, no one will notice the repair. It's hard even now to pick it out, unless you know it's there . . . You see what is so odd about it?"

"You found the body facedown, with the dried blood next to his head?"

"Yes."

"Then what is so odd is that if he indeed hit his head on the marble tabletop, he fell on his face an improbable distance from the table."

"Got it. I never thought about that until these things started to happen. Now I think someone, probably someone he knew, got into the bedroom somehow and hit him over the head with something, maybe one of those gold candlesticks over there, and slipped out the same way he or she got in."

"Whatever that might have been . . . there was of course no blood on the candlesticks?"

"Not when I got around a couple of weeks ago to thinking one of them might be the weapon."

"And you noticed no blood on the tabletop when you and, ah, Ms. Reed were able to enter the death room?"

"No, but I wasn't noticing anything except a dead priest's body."

"And what was her reaction?"

"She gasped softly and then very calmly said she would call the undertaker while I got the oils to anoint him. She shed a few quiet tears at the funeral, but she is not the kind of woman who expresses much emotion."

"Save for bringing fresh flowers to the room of a man who has been dead for six months."

"I think that is sentiment, not emotion."

"Perhaps . . ."

"Are you really going to sleep in this room?"

"Why not? One must see if the late lamented Monsignor McInerny has any messages for the auxiliary Bishop."

I doubted that he would.

"Do you think he was murdered, Blackie?"

"It is not completely improbable that he was."

I carefully removed my Aero subnotebook and dumped the contents of my duffel bag on the bed.

"Do you think he's come back from the dead to tell us he was murdered?"

I chose my words carefully.

"I find that unlikely. If a terrible crime were committed here, memories of the agony and horror would remain for a time, psychic imprints on the place, if you will. Under the proper circumstances such traces of suffering could be activated to produce a wide variety of phenomena."

"Maybe you're right."

But Peter Finnegan did not seem to think that I was right. Fortunately he didn't ask what the "proper circumstances" might be.

"Well, anyway, here's the key. Be careful. Supper at six."

"I will indeed be careful."

I did not think the haunt would lock any doors on me, however. Computer in hand, I followed Peter Finnegan up to the study, placed the Aero on the late Monsignor's massive desk, and plugged in the power supply to the wall socket. After he had left the room, I plugged the TV back into its proper receptacle and turned it on. The five o'clock news. Nothing about Woodbridge.

Much more random bell ringing and Woodbridge *would* be the lead story. "Was a Catholic priest murdered in the affluent suburb of Woodbridge? Has he come back from the dead to avenge his own killing?"

I shuddered at the thought of Milord Cronin's reaction to that eventuality.

I turned the TV off. It stayed off.

My first phone call was to the aforementioned Cardinal Priest of the Church of St. Agnes Outside the Walls.

"Ten million! Blackwood, you gotta be kidding!"

"Find out from your overpaid lawyers what our rights might be in the matter."

"Tomorrow."

"No, tonight. I am sure the money belongs to the Catholic Bishop of Chicago . . ."

"A corporation sole."

"Precisely. Nonetheless I want to be on safe ground when I go to the bank tomorrow and demand it."

"You're going to do that?"

"Of course. I'll call you after supper."

I do give orders to him sometimes. He always obeys.

I then called my classmate who is the specialist on Archdiocesan folklore and asked him who the last three curates were in Paddy Flynn's day. He told me without a moment's hesitation and reminded me that one had left the active priesthood to marry, one had died, and the third was pastor of a parish in Lincoln Park.

"Indeed."

This worthy, a couple of years older than I am, was one of the two rivals with the Cathedral for the dubious honor of having the most marriages in a single year. Alas for both of us, Old St. Patrick's over on Adams Street had lapped us both.

"Timmy, Blackie."

"Hey, the good Bishop. Am I in trouble?"

"Doubtless, but I don't know what you've done lately and in any case, others make those calls. I need some information."

"Improbable," he said, mimicking me, a seditious form of behavior that showed no respect for the Episcopal purple.

"Arguably . . . nonetheless I need to know whether,

when you were out in Woodbridge, Dr. Flynn, the Monsignor's brother, truly lived in the rectory."

The expected answer was, "Why do you want to know that?"

Instead he snarled, "That sneaky little passive-aggressive bastard with his sick smile!"

"Ah?"

"Yeah, he lived there all right. I wish I believed in hell so I could hope that the two of them would be rotting there."

"So."

"Sorry, Blackie. I forgot how much I hated them both. They almost drove me out of the priesthood."

Not a chance in the hell in which Timmy did not believe that anyone would accomplish that. I let the remark pass, however.

"Yeah, he lived in the rectory, somewhere up in that creepy, frigging tower. The little sneak would appear from nowhere while his brother was down in Hobe Sound. He was as detestable a son of a bitch as I ever met."

"That seems to be the consensus . . . do you know where in the, uh, tower?"

"No. We never got up to that place. Doors always locked. The two could have been having wild orgies up there for all we knew."

"Indeed?"

"No, they weren't the wild orgy type, sad to say. Just fall-down drunks. Best thing Cholly McInerny ever did was to throw the Doc out when he took over the rectory. Nothing good since then as far as I know."

"The Doc is dead?"

"A couple of years after his brother. Left all his money to a young 'companion,' male of course. I bet a lot of it was parish money."

"Arguably."

"Boy, am I angry and bitter! Sorry. Mention Woodbridge and it all comes back. Those poor people didn't deserve the crap the Church gave them. Now, finally, we show some sense and send young Peter Finnegan out there, though I hear those assholes on the personnel board didn't want to do it and the Boss made them."

"Father Finnegan," I said soothingly, "is a talented young man."

The poor lay people of God. Send them one good religious leader after a century of bums and they forgive and forget the past.

I noted after I had hung up that Tim had not wondered why I was asking about Woodbridge. His memories of more than a quarter century ago were so angry that his curiosity had been stifled. It was just as well.

My next move was to creep down the stairs to the second floor and then to the first floor. I wanted to fetch proper priest clothes for my work on the morrow and I wanted to have another conversation with the good Megan.

"Hi, Bishop. Are you really going to sleep in *that* room tonight?"

"No self-respecting haunt would waste his time on a bishop."

She giggled. "Awesome."

"I gather that Ms. Reed goes up there with flowers."

"Isn't that neat? I really like her. My dad's, like, she's the only one of the Monsignor's friends who is not a total creep. Her and that Mr. Griffin who, like my daddy, is a commodity broker. . . . Did she really love him, Bishop?"

"There are many different kinds of love in the world, Meg. On the basis of her devotion to his memory I would say that she did."

"Yeah, I know."

She didn't know of course, but someday she might.

"Indeed."

"She's really pretty, Bishop. My mom goes anyone can look gorgeous at that age so long as they have the right genes, eat the right food, do the right exercises, and wear the right bra."

"Arguably."

"She's awfully nice too. Always stops in here for a chat with one of us. She has teenage grandchildren, would you believe? Anyway, she knows what we're like."

"Never says anything about why she brings the flowers?"

"Not a word, but she always goes over to the church to pray afterward. My mom's like, well, at least the young priest leaves the church open all day, unlike her friend."

"Your mom thinks she loved the Monsignor."

"Totally. She goes she's the only one who ever cared about him. Maybe she'll get him into heaven. The day before the Last Judgment."

So there was some awareness in the parish of the intensity of the relationship. Meg had provided me with more information than I had expected.

"Bishop Blackie . . ."

"Yes?"

"*Well,* Lisa, like, replaces me in a half hour and, *well,* Sean goes he'd like to go for a ride tonight and so . . ."

"It shall be done. Eight o'clock. Are you legal, Meg?"

"*Well,* I've passed my driver's ed but I won't be sixteen till next month and my mom's like don't you dare even think of putting your hand on the steering wheel of the poor Bishop's car."

I am always astonished at the fact that women who do

not even know me prefix my name or an allusion to me with the adjective "poor."

And often add the even more inexplicable adjective "cute."

"Sean, however, is legal?"

"Oh, yeah. For a long time. Since April."

I found my neatly pressed priest suit in the back of the car, along with the St. Brigid pectoral cross my cousin Catherine Curran (mother of the mystical Jackie) had made for me and the ring band with a Celtic cross (sexual intercourse symbol of course) that she had also produced. I might not, even in such finery, look like a bishop. But the cross and ring were proof positive that nonetheless I was one. They were useful when I had my own doubts.

Megan stopped me on the way into the rectory. Her mother had told her to look at my "punctual" cross if I had brought it along because it had been made by a very famous artist. She was appropriately impressed and surprised to learn that the artist was the mother of Jackie Curran who was a classmate of hers at St. Ignatius and "kind of cute."

I had signed up permanently the best intelligence officer in Woodbridge. You can't beat teenage women in their ability to report all the gossip in the community. The ride with her and Sean in the Ryan family's prized T-bird should be most illuminating.

CHAPTER 5

FATHER JOSEPH O'KEEFE, Ph.D., cornered me after supper.

"Can I have a word with you, Bishop?" he asked anxiously, his eyes averted. "Won't take but a couple of minutes."

"Take as long as you want and call me Blackie."

"Not Ishmael?" He chuckled. "That's a dreadfully dull book, isn't it?"

Father O'Keefe's doctorate in American literature was from the Catholic University of America (so-called at any rate), the source of his friend Charles P. McInerney's degree in canon law.

"More than I would want to know about either whaling or obsession."

The supper, nutritious, politically correct, healthy, and unquestionably good for me, had been well prepared and elegantly served. I found myself wondering whether Megan and Sean would mind leaving Woodbridge for a McDonald's or a Thirty-One Flavors "over at the mall" on our excursion at eight this evening.

I had informed Peter Finnegan of this planned trip, since I thought it only fair to suggest discreetly that I might be using his employee as an informant.

He had missed the implication, truly a man without guile.

"That one usually gets what she wants. She took one look at the car, zoned out, and decided she, like, totally *had* to ride in it, maybe even drive it."

"Her mother has forbidden such conduct on the grounds that she does not have a license yet and might do irreparable damage to the poor Bishop's car."

"Yeah, those two bond by fighting, her mother told me. Great family. He's a trader, she's an editor."

"A book editor!"

"Right."

"I shall pray for her conversion to a more virtuous profession."

"The whole bunch of them—three younger kids—are just about the sharpest crowd in the parish. They don't miss a thing. I hire her as much for the gossip as the charm as a gatekeeper."

Really?

If the meal had not been truly satisfying—I am not one of those who thinks because the Church now permits meat on Friday it is legitimate to have fish any other day of the week—the conversation was stimulating.

Father Emil Baptist D'Souza, S.J., who had been forced to abandon his research in India because the government didn't like Catholic priests studying the Untouchables, was now doing his anthropology with the Chippewas, aboriginal Americans as he had called them rather than the politically correct but inaccurate name of "Native Americans."

Father Tom Wozniak, newly ordained, had rejected the title of Polish American for himself. He was, he insisted, a "Euro-American." The Pastor opined that he was probably the only one in his family or neighborhood who thought that. There are no Euro-Americans, Peter contended, save in the seminaries.

Some of the sprightliness of the conversation was doubtless for the benefit of the visiting Bishop, but the team seemed relaxed and at ease with itself, even Joseph O'Keefe who didn't say much but smiled at each alarum and excursion.

"What's your ethnic identity, Bishop?" the Euro-American young priest demanded.

"Call me Blackie . . . and, alas, my identity is so particularistic that I am part of a mini-minority, one might even say an invisible minority."

"And that is?"

He knew he was being setup but he couldn't resist the temptation.

I sighed my asthma attack sigh.

"South Side Irish Cub fan American."

The repartee turned to the Cubs and Sox, a bad subject for my side in this time when the Tribune company was proving that it could destroy a team more thoroughly than the Wrigley Spearmint Gum manufacturers.

I propounded my thesis that God was a Cub fan because She is pure mystery and it was pure mystery why anyone, myself included, would be a Cub fan.

It was obviously a happy rectory, for the first time in almost a century. I would report this to Milord Cronin when I called him after supper.

Then Joe O'Keefe cornered me with his plea for a "word" with me.

"Do you mind a pipe?" he asked me when we were seated in his study, more casual and old-fashioned than Pete's modern hangout.

"No."

I did, but it was essential that he feel relaxed.

He stuffed the bowl of his pipe tenderly, lit it with a

butane lighter, and leaned back in his easy chair with a happy sigh.

"Only one a day. The kid says we have a nonsmoking rectory but that's to keep the dolls at the door from smoking. He told me I have an indult."

He chuckled lightly but studied me carefully over his pipe smoke.

"The kid is not the worst of them, Blackie, in the Irish sense of the words in which that is high praise. In fact, he's one hell of a fine priest. Gives me hope for the future of the Church."

"Indeed."

Joe O'Keefe was a compact, white-haired man in his middle seventies, apparently in good physical condition and excellent health. Only his slightly red nose (and a large nose at that) and a transient lack of focus in his watery blue eyes (behind bifocal lenses that were even thicker than mine) hinted that he was a recovering alcoholic.

I had noted that his fingers trembled as he lit the pipe. Afraid of me? No one was afraid of me.

"He's been very good to me. It's quite a change after being treated like shit for a quarter century. He has never once said anything about my drinking; he treats me like I'm a member of the parish team. I almost died when I got my first salary check from him. First time in almost thirty years. Says I'm a senior priest and that means I get even more money. I didn't even know that there were such things."

"You may depend on it that there are."

"Hell, he's even got me giving a course in American literature one night a week. First course since I was thrown out of the seminary."

Joe O'Keefe had come back from Catholic U in the late

1940s with the reputation for a brilliant dissertation, a profound disregard for rules, a strong radical streak (with overtones of Marxism it was said), a dangerous habit of drinking too much, and an almost infinite capacity for self-pity. He became a popular teacher at the seminary and at labor schools in which he tried with some success to bring literature to the working stiffs. Unfortunately the labor schools closed during the 1950s and his radicalism became passé. By the time of the Vatican Council he was a fall-down drunk and known as such to everyone in the Archdiocese. The seminary rector was glad to use this as an excuse for firing him from the faculty. He spent the next couple of years in various clerical centers for drying out. No one wanted him in a parish until his old friend Charles P. McInerny had been appointed to Woodbridge and took him in as a kind of household slave. There had been reports of many falls off the wagon in the subsequent quarter century. At first his fellow clergy lamented the loss of a great talent (though if he had exercised the talent by writing they would have damned him), then they ignored and eventually forgot about him. Finally a new generation had appeared that had never heard of him—priests Peter Finnegan's age.

"I thought sure that Pete would throw me out. I figured he kept me around just to placate Cholly. I was ready to pack my bags when Cholly died. Turns out he wanted me to stay all along. A real surprise."

His voice trailed off as his eyes seemed to lose their focus.

I said nothing.

"I guess I'm happier now than I have been since that damn General was elected President."

"Forty years ago."

"Right." He shook his head sadly. "Maybe it was a

mistake to come out here. I don't know. I needed a place
to stay and Cholly was the only one who wanted . . . not
a day passed when he did not impress on me that I was a
drunk living on his sufferance. The guy was a master of
cruelty. He beat me into the ground so there was nothing
left."

"A strange kind of friendship."

He puffed reflectively on his pipe. "He was a bitter and
angry man. Strange. We were really good friends growing
up and great drinking buddies at Catholic U. Nicest guy in
the world. Lots of fun. Generous. Sensitive. I guess that's
what happens when you get in the race to be a bishop and
lose."

"Arguably."

He grinned impishly. "No offense, Blackie."

"None taken. I didn't know I was in the race until I
won. . . . What do you think changed him?"

"The Marines, Korea, I don't know. He had some rough
times over there. Never did seem quite the same when he
came back. Seemed to love lording it over everyone when
he was chancellor. Then the Council. Funny thing, he was
one of the founders of the Vernacular Society back in the
early fifties."

"A liberal of a sort?"

"Labels didn't fit him, Blackie. He had a lot of charisma, even at his worst. There was a whole crowd of
young priests around him at the Chancery before he got
the sack, guys you'd expect to support the Council; but
they admired Cholly so much that when he had a stom-
achache, they belched."

"So."

I assumed that eventually Joe O'Keefe would get to the
point.

"Same thing here. He had maybe twenty couples that

adored him and he didn't give a shit about the rest of the parish. One day he charmed them, the next day he was cruel to them. Had them eating out of his hand. Just like I was. As I said, he didn't pay me a regular salary—told me that I was a drunk and didn't earn my room and board. Then the next week he'd slip two hundreds into my hand.

"One never knew which Cholly you'd meet on any given day. He'd tell me that I was worthless and that if Cronin finally got him, I'd starve to death. Then he'd promise me that he had left money for me in his will and I'd never have to worry about a thing. There was no will, of course."

"That we know about anyway. You make him sound like a lord of the manor?"

"Liked to play that role but he was erratic. The only person in that whole crowd he wasn't cruel to when the mood was on him was Lynn."

"Ms. Reed?"

"She's a real sweetheart, Blackie. The only one of them ever noticed my existence. She's the only one of that crowd who was nice to the kid at the beginning. She and Griffin. Most of them like him now. A real beauty even today. A quarter century ago she'd stop traffic in the street. Even a guy as self-centered as Cholly could fall for her."

"He was self-centered?"

"The most self-centered man I've ever known, even before Korea. Had to be the center of everything. Lynn may be the only one he ever cared about and probably not all that much."

"Indeed."

"Don't get me wrong. I'm not suggesting he slept with her: that would have been quite impossible."

Why was everyone so eager to dismiss the possibility that Charles P. McInerny might have had a love affair?

Perhaps because if one knew him one felt that there wasn't even a remote possibility of his being that human.

"It might have been a good thing for him if he had slept with her," Joe continued. "Bring him back into the human race."

"Ms. Reed brings fresh flowers to the site of his death I am told."

"You don't miss much, do you? There were special feelings there, that's for sure."

"Do you think he was murdered, Joe?"

"That's what I wanted to talk to you about, wasn't it? . . . Yeah, I thought that from day one. The kid was too shaken to think about anything. I wouldn't believe that quack Steve Curtin even if he said the sun was coming up in the morning."

"By whom?"

"One of them. Anyone but Lynn."

"Why?"

"Money maybe."

"Whose money?"

"The parish's money. Cholly never paid any attention to money. Beneath his dignity and importance. Other people were supposed to provide for him. So his friends took care of his money, parish money I mean. He never sent any of it downtown. Griffin is a trader, Reed is a banker, Fasio a real estate developer, Curtin a blowhard investor. It would have amounted to a lot over the years. Cholly paid no attention to what they did with it. They're all capable of 'borrowing' some of it when they needed a few extra million. Maybe someone told Cholly and he threatened to call in the cops. So he got killed. Funny thing is he probably didn't mean it. But his erratic irascibility finally caught up with him."

Alliteration. What one might expect from a professor of literature.

"Arguably."

"Don't ask me how it was done. Pretty damn clever killer."

"Do you have any suspicions?"

"Not Lynn, like I said. Probably not Griffin, though with a quiet guy like that, you can't be sure. He's been in love with Lynn for a hell of a long time. Can't tell what she thinks about him."

"Dux femina facti."

"I'm probably the only priest in the Archdiocese besides you that knows that quote from Virgil. *Cherchez la femme,* huh?"

"Possibly."

"Some *femme,*" he sighed, knocking the spent tobacco out of his pipe. "If you ask me, I'd bet on her husband Gerry Reed. He's a pompous little creep. I don't know what she ever saw in him."

Joe O'Keefe had provided me with a motive and a list of suspects. Perhaps his exclusion of Lynn Reed from the list was intended to make her especially suspect. Perhaps not. Whatever his intentions, however, his suspicions seemed reasonable, especially since I had already made tentative conclusions of the same kind.

"What do you think about the, uh, haunting?"

"Damned if I know, Blackie," he said, scratching his head. "It sure is scary though when you're about ready to start the early Mass and the organ starts playing Bach—without any visible organist—and someone grabs a chalice out of your hand."

"Indeed!"

"Yeah, it's a great organ too. Cholly installed it so he could play on it. Loved Bach for some reason. Mathematical order I suppose. He also put in the new electronic chimes in the tower."

"Is the organist as good as Cholly was?"

"I'd say better. But maybe that's part of being dead— you do the things you did when you were alive only better."

"Arguably."

"Are you going after the money, Blackie? I guess it belongs to Cronin."

"In fact, it belongs more to the people of this parish. I propose to get it back for them."

"Good hunting."

I thanked him for his analysis. He waved it aside as if it were nothing much. I took my leave, vaguely uneasy. I was not inclined to suspect a poor old man whose life as a priest had been intolerably difficult. But there was something important missing from the puzzle he had assembled for me, one which I was in the process of assembling myself.

Moreover, the person and the character of Cholly McInerny was becoming fuzzier rather than more focused. I would have to meet this Lynn Reed person and listen to her version. But she would not be the first one to whom I would speak.

Back in my tower suite, I phoned the Cardinal.

"Cronin."

"Ryan."

"Indeed."

"My line."

"Arguably," he chortled. "Anyway, the lawyers tell me the courts have been very favorable to us in these kinds of cases. Usually there is an out of court settlement with the heirs. We get most of the money back and save the cost of the suit. . . . Is there a will?"

"None has been found."

"How do you propose to get the money?"

"To demand it from those who have it or had it."

"Just walk in and demand it?"

"Why not? The threat of a suit will terrify them."

"I hope you know what you're doing."

"You did not tell me about the documents you took out of Monsignor McInerny's file."

Dead silence on the other end of the line.

Then, "I won't ask you how you know that. I don't think I want to know."

"A ghost told me."

"Very funny. . . . I came across these two documents when I was doing a routine scan of the secret file for the Boss to see what we ought to discard. I showed them to him. He said by all means destroy them."

"They were?"

"Letters. Signed ones at that or the Boss would have thrown them away."

"And they alleged?"

"That Cholly was involved with a woman, on the basis of having been seen twice at lunch with the woman."

"In these days that would not even be considered a venial sin."

"The Boss told me that he had shown the letters to Cholly out of courtesy. Cholly was apparently completely unruffled and explained that she was a very troubled young woman he had counseled in Korea and that there was nothing more to it than that. He had directed her to an appropriate counselor in Chicago."

"It had nothing to do with his subsequent removal?"

"Maybe in his mind; certainly not in the Cardinal's mind."

"Then why was he removed?"

"I asked the Boss that. He hesitated and then told me the whole story. He didn't fire Cholly. Cholly offered his resignation."

"Indeed! Why?"

"He knew the Boss had been getting a lot of complaints about him, especially about his treatment of priests who wanted dispensations to get married. He told the Boss that he was not in sympathy with the changes in the Church and wanted to leave him free to choose a man more in sympathy with the times. Even mentioned me as a possible replacement."

"Fascinating."

"The letters did not come up in the discussion. The Boss thought they might be on Cholly's mind. He also thought that it was a pro forma resignation and that Cholly was surprised and disappointed when it was 'reluctantly' accepted."

"Astonishing!"

"He was a strange man, Blackie. Gifted, charismatic but strange. . . . Is his ghost haunting you?"

"There are phenomena occurring which are fascinating but not particularly inexplicable. And, no, I am not being haunted. A ghost would know better than to endeavor to haunt me."

"Inarguably. Keep me informed, Blackwood, and don't take any unnecessary chances."

The phone clicked off before I told him that I was not one of those in danger.

I sat there in the tower for some minutes contemplating the new data. The picture of Charles P. McInerny, P.A., was becoming even fuzzier. Perhaps he was indeed a great man with a tragic flaw. Or who had made a tragic mistake. Or perhaps was haunted by a tragic guilt.

The house phone beeped. Megan telling me that her

Sean was here. I apologized for being late, donned my dubious White Sox windbreaker ("Good Guys Wear Black"), and descended.

Sean was a massive and gentle black-haired giant who, since St. Ignatius College Prep did not indulge in football, was captain of the wrestling team.

The two of them marveled at the T-bird and entered it with the same reverential awe with which Sister Sacristan used to enter the sanctuary in the old days.

"I'm going to our family place in Green Lake week after next, so, Bishop Blackie, you must totally solve that mystery by a week from Sunday."

"That is not an impossible goal."

"Do you go up to Grand Beach like Jackie and his family?"

"Soon," I replied. "Very soon. . . . *Ille praeter omnes orbae terrarum mihi angulus ridet.*"

"Horace," Sean responded. "That corner of the world which delights me above all others."

"Impressive."

"He's a keeper, Bishop Blackie."

On that remark I did not choose to comment.

The parish parking lot was crowded. One of the best signs, I had long argued, of a thriving parish was the number of cars in its parking lot on a weekday night.

But after we had driven away from the parish buildings, there was only a little more life in Woodbridge than there had been earlier in the day—other teens cruising in convertibles, a few kids playing on the sidewalks as the darkness encroached, some older people sitting on the porches. But still only little more than a cemetery at the same time of the day.

"Let's go over to the mall," Megan urged. "This place is so creepy."

"Thirty-One Flavors?"

"Neato!"

On the way to the mall, Megan informed me that she had not liked Monsignor very much. He had totally ruined their whole eighth grade by denying them a graduation ceremony because someone had thrown an empty six-pack on his lawn, now the softball field. And the six-pack had belonged not to their boys but to the sixth-graders.

Invariably when something scandalous occurs in a Catholic parish, it is the sixth-graders to whom everyone else assigns responsibility. Automatically.

"I think he's haunting us," Sean observed, "because Father Pete has turned the lawn into a softball field."

"That surely is a tenable position."

I tended to agree with the ineffable Megan that the Butternut Mall was infinitely preferable to Woodbridge. It was crowded, garish, and ugly, but it was also part of the human condition.

I also heard colorful thumbnail sketches inside of Thirty-One Flavors of all the close friends of Monsignor.

Mr. Reed was reputed to be a wimp. His bank was surviving only because of the success his son had made of the banking facility at the mall, which was called the Butternut Bank so the uninformed would not link it with Woodbridge.

Ms. Reed was totally gorgeous but the women of the parish were split on her. Some, like Megan and her mother, thought she was neat and totally gorgeous. Others thought she was a trollop.

Dr. Curtin was a loudmouth and a blowhard who enjoyed killing animals on his hunting expeditions more than he had ever enjoyed keeping humans alive.

Mrs. Curtin was an incurable busybody who pried into everyone else's business so they would not pry into hers.

Mr. Griffin was a nice man and a great trader, but a little too quiet to be trusted and a little too obviously in love with Ms. Reed.

Mr. Fasio had made millions on his real estate developments but he was rumored to be "in bed" with the Mob, though people said that about every Italian who made any money.

Mrs. Fasio was Sicilian in origin and everyone knew what that meant. However, she was a pleasant enough woman and good to her children, even if she was not terribly bright. Everyone thought that Mr. Fasio played around, but not in Woodbridge.

All of them thought it was prestigious to hang around Monsignor but that was an old-fashioned idea. A lot of people resented them because Monsignor paid no attention to anyone else in the parish besides a few families. They were glad that the new Pastor treated these people like he treated everyone else.

There were some comments about Ms. Reed bringing flowers to the rectory every couple of days, but nobody really thought that she and the Monsignor had been lovers. In Megan's opinion, seconded by Sean, it might have been a good thing for the Monsignor if they had been lovers.

As for the Monsignor, he was a strange person. Sometimes he was very friendly to the kids, smiled at them, even stopped to talk to them just like Father Pete was doing now. Other times he did not seem to notice them. And yet other times he compared them to the corrupt and immoral young people at the time of the fall of the Roman Empire.

"Everyone knows," Sean commented, "that the Roman Empire fell because there was too much lead in the water supply of the city."

Such are the results of a Jesuit education these days.

Megan had high praise for "Father Pete."

"I mean, like you know, he's so sensitive. He's not just a totally good guesser like you are, Bishop Blackie. He really *knows* what you are thinking and feeling when you're totally bummed out."

Good guesser, huh?

"Remarkable."

"Like this one time he goes you're really bummed out today, Megan, aren't you? A fight with your mother, a fight with the teachers in school, a fight with Sean, and you're wondering whether you're worth anything, right? And I'm like awesome and then I break down and cry and he's like, well, you're wrong. They all love you, even that ape, and he talks for a while and I talk and I feel totally better."

"I'm the ape, just in case you had any doubts, Bishop."

"Being a good guesser, I know that."

"He's that way with everyone. That's why the parish thinks he's so great, even those that were close to Monsignor. Well, most of them. Even Lynn thinks he's wonderful."

"You call Ms. Reed Lynn?"

"Well when she talks to us in the rectory she's like, you know, one of the kids."

Yet she wrote a letter of complaint to the Cardinal with a copy to the Congregation for the Defense of the Faith. As I remembered, it was a harmless letter, touching a base perhaps because she had to.

"Do you happen to know the names of her children?"

"Sure, like her son who is the youngest is called Junior, a name I bet he totally hates. The two girls are Jill—she's the doctor—and Evie, who teaches college. Because, like, Lynn's real name is Evelyn. Kind of an old-fashioned name, you know?"

This woman I would have to meet. Because she was

apparently a nice person it did not follow that she was not a killer. A lot of killers are nice people.

I dropped Meg and Sean at her house and was introduced to her parents who were waiting on the porch for their turn to ride in the T-bird. While I drove them around a couple of blocks, they assured me that something terrible had happened in the parish at the time of Monsignor's death and money was probably the cause.

Back in my rectory tower, I considered what I had learned in the first day. There was a lot of data, almost too much data. Then I poured myself a substantial amount from the bottle of Baileys Irish Cream that a thoughtful Peter Finnegan had left in the tower and made some explorations of the suite with a measuring tape I had brought along. I found what I thought I would find.

More data, but no key to the puzzle.

I then retired for the sleep of the (relatively) just man, convinced that there would be no haunting there that night.

There wasn't save for the time when I awakened and became aware of a "presence" lurking at the side of the bed.

"Go away," I instructed the presence. "I have a busy day tomorrow and need my sleep."

It went away.

CHAPTER 6

THE ORGAN BEGAN a Bach chorale just as Peter Finnegan emerged for the eight o'clock Eucharist. Peter sighed and continued with the Eucharist as the music continued. It stopped just before he went to the ambo to read the epistle.

From my position in the sanctuary where I was assisting at the Mass, it seemed that the two score or so participants took the music for granted. Haunting was a familiar phenomenon that people almost expected.

The five o'clock news couldn't be far behind.

"That happen every morning?" I asked him in the sacristy.

"A couple of times a week. You get used to it after a while. . . . Any troubles last night?"

"Certainly not. Shades leave bishops alone."

There was no reason to mention the "presence" that had tried to interfere with my sleep or my success in telling it to get lost.

Duly instructed the cook produced my usual breakfast—raisin bran with raspberries and blueberries, waffles and maple syrup, bacon, and hot, very hot, coffee.

"What's on the agenda today, Blackie?" the Pastor asked.

"Talk to people."

"His clique? I suppose they would be the prime suspects."

"I am unable to get a focus on him. Perhaps they will enlighten me."

"They are a strange bunch. All they have in common was their affection for him. As strange as it may seem, they adored him. Most of them still do and so they resent me, though a lot less now than they did at first. I suppose they've been writing to the Boss about me, but otherwise they're no real problem."

"Even Ms. Reed?"

"I may have made a convert there, but she's unfathomable. She's certainly friendly. Irresistibly friendly. Yet I'm not sure what she's thinking most of the time."

He paused for a moment's thought.

"There's a lot of passion pent up in that woman, has been for a long time."

If I were to believe the admirable Megan, Peter Finnegan was skilled at reading souls. I filed his comment for future reference.

And, before I donned my priest suit and bishop jewelry, I made another call to the Lord Cardinal in his suite at the Cathedral.

"You remember the content of the letter of complaint about our late friend the Protonotary Apostolic?"

"It was a long time ago, Blackwood."

"I am not unaware of that fact."

"As I remember, it was from a nurse at the Public Health Service Hospital up on Marine Drive. Used to be the United States Marine Hospital."

"Indeed."

"She said that Monsignor McInerny was having an affair with a slutty nurse she had known in Korea."

"Fascinating. Did she reveal the name of the alleged slut."

"I think so. But I can't remember it."

So, as one who does not read souls, but is, like, a totally good guesser, I guessed.

"The first name perhaps was Evelyn?"

Silence.

"Yeah . . . I think it was. How did you know that?"

"A young person told me last night that I was an awesomely good guesser."

"Doubtless," he agreed.

Fascinating, I thought to myself. More data, but no hint of how it might fit into the puzzle. I must confirm that the much admired Lynn Reed was a nurse and had served in the Korean War.

My first stop, however, was at her husband's bank. Under the blazing summer sun and through thick curtains of humidity, I walked down the street past the church, turned the corner on Pine Street, and walked the block to High Street. Then I turned left again in front of the railroad station and worked my way up High Street, looking for the bank that I had missed the day before when driving into Woodbridge.

Smaller wonder that I had missed it. The Woodbridge Bank was nothing more than a storefront. Or rather three storefronts, hardly distinguishable from the boutique on one side and the gourmet food store on the other side. It did not look much different on the outside than the banks the James boys and their allies had knocked over in the movies. What if they had come here instead of Northfield, Minnesota?

Inside, the bank was not quite as primitive as the banks in the western films, but still seemed very old—lots of brass railings, rolltop desks at which men and women were working at something at less than frantic speed, and an old-fashioned cage protecting the tellers. No spittoons, however.

There were, nonetheless, computer terminals on some of the desks and the bank was air-conditioned. Thank goodness.

"May I see Mr. Reed?" I asked the uniformed white guard (no affirmative action in Woodbridge!).

"Who should I say is calling, Father?"

"Bishop Ryan."

"Just one minute please, Bishop."

In a few moments Gerald Reed appeared, both arms outstretched in greeting.

"You're most welcome, Bishop," he said enthusiastically as he pumped my hand with both of his. "I don't believe we've ever had a Roman Catholic bishop in this bank."

He thereupon attempted to kiss my ring. Though it is an obsolete practice that I detest, I permitted him to do so.

Gerald Reed was a short, pudgy man, with no more hair on his head than Michael Jordan, darting eyes, a round, bland face, and a high piping voice. Despite the summer heat he wore a three-piece black wool suit, a pristine white shirt, and a conservative dark blue tie.

"My great-grandfather founded this bank after the Civil War when much of the land around here was prairie. We try to maintain something of the physical appearance that it had then, though this is obviously a newer building."

He led me through the bank to a small office in the rear. It too had a rolltop desk, larger than those in the lobby of the bank.

"No spittoons."

"We had them till 1953 when I came home from Korea, though no one was using them anymore. I persuaded my father that some of our newer customers found them repulsive."

He sat next to the desk on a wooden chair and waved me to another of the same sort, the only other chair in the room. A devious ray of sunlight slipped into the room from a single, high barred window.

"We try to keep the bank old-fashioned to remind our customers that it is an old-fashioned bank, owned by the family, with all the old-fashioned virtues of stability, probity, absolute reliability."

He rubbed his tiny hands together in satisfaction.

"Fascinating."

"Of course we must modernize some things. Hence the air-conditioning and the computers. We change in order to remain the same."

"I see."

"Our facility over in the Butternut Mall, which my son administers brilliantly, is as up-to-date and as modern as a bank could be."

"The Butternut Bank?"

"It is generally known that we own it, especially with my son managing it. But we still find it proper to make a distinction between the two banks because their respective clienteles are so different."

"I understand."

"We are one of the few family owned banks remaining in the Chicago metropolitan area, though it is difficult out here to think of ourselves as part of that profoundly troubled city. We intend to remain a family bank because we find it profitable to do so. A number of major banking chains have attempted to buy us out with very large offers, but we are content with the profits we make. In fact, NBD recently made us a very large offer."

He continued to rub his hands. A muscle in his cheek was twitching.

He was frightened.

Good.

"Your clients here in Woodbridge would hardly want to deal with a neighborhood bank from Detroit."

"They are," he replied blandly, "a very successful and progressive chain. But they are expanding too rapidly for our tastes. We are confident that the loyalty of our customers will outweigh the blandishments of the chains."

"I see . . . that is your son in the picture?"

"Yes, indeed."

He passed over to me for inspection a formal portrait of himself and his wife and three children. Two tall and attractive young women, a handsome son who had a hard time repressing a grin, and another woman who must be the fabled Lynn, perhaps née Evelyn.

"Your wife is a very lovely woman."

"Yes indeed," he sighed. "She seems to grow more beautiful with the years rather than less."

"I knew she was the wife only because like you she was sitting down. Otherwise I would have thought she was a daughter."

"Many people think that . . . we are very proud of our children. Gerald Junior is a brilliant young banker. Evie— she's the oldest—teaches at Northwestern. Jill is a medical doctor at the University of Illinois hospital. All three are happily married and we have six grandchildren, two in each family. We are very happy with our family."

"I don't doubt it."

"We are very much a traditional family, you see. About the only change is that my father became a Roman Catholic when he married my mother. So we're Catholics now and combine Protestant probity with stern Catholic ethical standards. The best of both."

"Indeed."

"All of us have attended Illinois Wesleyan, though my children went to Catholic high schools. We also have a tradition of military service. My great-grandfather was one of the first Illinois volunteers in the Civil War. Fought at Shiloh and Vicksburg, was mustered out in Washington as a full colonel, and settled here right after General Crawford. My grandfather climbed San Juan Hill with Teddy Roosevelt. My father served in the First World War and returned to a staff position in the Second. I myself was involved in Korea. Pusan. My son missed Vietnam, thank God, but he is a member of the reserves and was mustered into active duty during Operation Desert Storm though the war ended before he had to go overseas."

I almost asked him how many of these men of the family had actually seen combat. Neither he nor his son, for sure. Pusan was down at the tip of the Korean peninsula and as far away from combat as you could be and still be in the country. I also did not tell him that my late father had been on the *Arizona* at Pearl Harbor and commanded a division of destroyer escorts at Leyte Gulf.

"You were in Korea?"

"Oh, yes. I always regret that we didn't bomb the enemy back into the stone age. We wouldn't have the trouble with them now if we had done that."

And all of us might be dead. Probably not, but maybe.

"It was a tough, nasty war."

"Police action which that damn fool Harry Truman called it . . . still one good result came from it for me personally. I met my wife there."

"Indeed?"

"Yes. She was a very young Navy nurse. We were married in Pusan actually by a Navy Chaplain."

"A wartime romance?"

"And unlike most wartime romances, it survived and flourished when we came home to Woodbridge."

One more piece of the puzzle locked into place. But what did it mean? So far it meant only that the relationships among Monsignor McInerny and his friends were a good deal more complicated than they seemed.

"Your wife is from Woodbridge too?"

"Oh, no." He waved his hand dismissively. "She's from somewhere in Nebraska. But it's home to her now . . . we both value the Catholic Church highly. We were very close to the late Monsignor McInerny and valued his friendship too. He was one of the few priests who grasped what a threat all this modernization is to the strongest assets of the Church. Catholicism ought to return to its old modality and become once again a pillar of stability and tradition in a world which increasingly values neither. The late Monsignor perceived that quite clearly."

"Perhaps."

"Now what can I do for you, Bishop. I presume the Cardinal has sent you out here because of the manifestations in the parish?"

"Among other things."

He leaned back on his wooden chair, tilting the front legs off the floor, doubtless a familiar gesture, and hooked his thumbs in the pockets of his vest.

"In my considered judgment," he said solemnly, "these phenomena are nothing more than pranks, most likely caused by the new priest for reasons of his own. They ought not to be taken seriously."

"Indeed."

"You can take my word for it, Bishop. Monsignor was

not murdered. My wife found the body and promptly called Dr. Curtin who diagnosed it as a death from a massive cerebral hemorrhage. Both of them admired Monsignor McInerny enormously. If they did not believe he was murdered, then he certainly was not murdered."

"Yet his spirit might come back, might it not, to demand that the money taken from the parish be returned to the Church to whom it rightfully belongs?"

Direct hit!

Gerald Reed stiffened and paled as would a man who had just heard his own death sentence.

"I don't know what you're talking about, Bishop," he said, his eyes darting wildly. "There is no missing money. I believe that before he died he turned the parish bank account over to the new priest who I assume has been using it to pay for the rather large expenditures he has been incurring."

I put on my sophisticated, urbane bishop persona, always a difficult task for someone who is South Side Irish.

"Come now, Mr. Reed. As you and I both know, two and a half million dollars is only a small portion of the moneys which have accrued to the Parish of Saints Peter and Paul during the last quarter century. We estimate that the total would amount to at least ten million dollars, in addition to the money actually in the parish account."

"That's absurd!" he sputtered.

"We are not sure where these funds are," I went on implacably, "though we assume that wherever they are now they went through this bank. We want them back."

"You have no records to establish that."

"We do not because your wife removed the records from the Monsignor's room shortly after he died. We want those records too, all of them."

"You can't prove that she did."

"Quite the contrary, we have witnesses. She could easily be charged with a criminal offense."

"You wouldn't dare do that," he screeched like a seabird warning of a storm.

"And we will sue you and your bank for the funds. It will be the end of your reputation for probity and reliability and those other virtues which you claim to value."

"Monsignor was not a rich man."

"That may well have been the case, though we do not know it. In the absence of a will we cannot be sure. But we do know that this is one of the richest parishes in the Archdiocese, that he never sent parish funds to the Chancery which he was required by canon law to do. Therefore we wonder where this money might be and, as I say, we want it back. All of it. The interest on ten million dollars could keep a dozen inner city schools open."

"If there were such moneys, they belong in Woodbridge not in some crime-ridden slum."

"I won't debate that with you, Mr. Reed. Legally, as you know, the moneys belong to the Catholic Bishop of Chicago, a corporation sole. And as you also know they will remain in the Archdiocese's account collecting a modest rate of interest for the Archdiocese."

"Very modest. Too modest."

"That is up to the aforementioned Catholic Bishop of Chicago to determine."

"I repeat, Bishop"—he stood up as if in angry protest—"that I have no idea what you're talking about. I remind you that if you should sue this bank you would create a huge scandal here in Woodbridge which would drive many Catholics out of the Church."

I rose from my chair with all the hierarchical éclat I could muster.

"And you out of business, Mr. Reed. We do not want to sue. But we do want the money and the records. Our lawyers will be in touch with you."

I turned to leave.

"You have no evidence, none at all."

"You have all the evidence, or at least your wife does. We want it. If it should be destroyed there would also be the possibility of an obstruction of justice charge against you and her. You can ask your lawyer what chance you would have in a court in this county in such a legal action against a complaint from the Catholic Church. I'll tell you his answer: not much!"

I glanced at him as I left the office. He had sunk back onto his chair. His face was ashen, his fingers trembling. I felt sorry for him. But he was a crook and we both knew it.

Moreover, his wife, whom everyone seemed to adore, was arguably a crook too.

CHAPTER 7

TO REACH THE condo of Arnold Griffin, I had merely to walk back to the railway station and cross the tracks. On the street beyond the tracks there was a row of town houses for those citizens of Woodbridge who, for one reason or another, did not want to or did not need to own a large home. I wondered if a phone call from the bank would warn him.

If I had known what would happen before the week was out, I might have modified my "in your face" strategy. But there was no way of suspecting how intricate and potentially deadly was the corruption surrounding Monsignor Charles P. McInerny.

Arnold Griffin opened the door almost as soon as I had rung.

"Bishop Ryan," he said dryly. "I was half expecting you."

A tall, slender man with silver hair, a hawk nose, questioning blue eyes, and smile lines on his face, he did not offer to shake hands. Nor did he produce any smile to fill the lines.

"Just a moment, I'm engaged in a little speculation and it's time to stop before I violate the adage that bears win, bulls win, and pigs lose."

In his spartan parlor a computer rested on an old and

81

chipped end table, an impressive computer, a Pentium like my own.

"Globex?"

"Yes. It's not the wave of the future but it's the best we have. I'm retired but I can't resist the temptation. The game is too much fun."

"So I'm told."

I looked around the room, plain beige walls, plain beige carpet, plain beige chairs. Two prints of mountains hung on the walls and over the fireplace a dramatic, impressionistic painting of the Matterhorn. Good taste in paintings and computers anyway.

"You climb mountains?"

He glanced up from the computer.

"Only a climber would have a painting like that, eh? Indeed I do. I climbed that one with the Reeds ten years or so ago. A bit long in the tooth for it now, though I still give it a try now and then."

"Both Reeds?"

He typed in a command, smiled complacently, and turned off the computer.

"I see you've met Gerry. Well, he watched while Lynn and I climbed to the summit. Kind of a close one at that. A storm came up that the forecasters seemed to miss. For a few minutes I didn't think we were going to make it. But, as you can see, we made it."

"Indeed."

"I might as well tell you, Bishop"—he turned toward me—"that I'm not a practicing Catholic anymore."

"Once a Catholic," I said automatically, "always a Catholic."

"Maybe . . . but do you realize what you guys have done to Catholicism."

"We guys?"

"You and the Pope."

"I'm not the Pope," I said firmly. "They are not ready for Cook County Democrats yet."

"It would be an improvement," he admitted. "Thirty years ago, that fat, wonderful old man brought hope to everyone in the world. The two idiots after him killed the hope and turned everyone off. All they're interested in is their own power, especially over the sex lives of the laity. It makes me sick to my stomach."

"Yet you were close friends of a priest who supported that old order."

He shrugged. "I liked the man. And I saw his point. If you have change without discipline, the whole thing will fall apart. The idiots who run the Church tried to stop the change and thus lost control of everything. So order collapsed. Monsignor used to say that the change should have been spread out over thirty years instead of five."

"You agreed?"

"Maybe not. But I saw his point."

"Interesting."

"I suppose I was the most radical of his friends. But we still got along. With all his rigor and his obsession with law and order, he was often surprisingly compassionate and understanding. . . . I suppose you're out here because of these odd things which are happening over at Saints Peter and Paul."

"Among other things."

"You know the literature on such phenomena?"

"Backward and forward."

"Make you a cup of coffee?"

"Tea?"

"Sure, even better."

He returned in a few minutes with a teapot, two cups, and a strainer. "How strong?"

"Too strong only when the spoon bends."

"Way I like it too. . . . What was I saying? Oh, yeah, you combine a residue of memories of tragedy with one or more psychically gifted people and things like that will happen. They stop eventually. Usually the person or persons who set off the events have no idea that they are doing it."

"None or very little."

"Right, Bishop. None or very little."

"You believe they will stop?"

"As I read in the books, they always do."

"For a time . . . Do you think the Monsignor died a natural death?"

A quick grimace raced across his face.

"Do you mean do I think he was murdered. Frankly I don't know. The way the scene was described to me he might have been. Dr. Curtin said it was a stroke. He had no reason to make that up, but he's not the sharpest doctor in the world. I don't know who would have wanted to kill him. He made a lot of enemies around this neighborhood, God knows, more than he needed to make. I often thought he was afraid to be as charming in public as he was private."

"Afraid of what?"

"Break down of order, something like that . . . but I don't think anyone hated him enough to kill him. Still there are a lot of crazies here in Woodbridge and he was the kind of man who could stir up violent hatred."

"Indeed."

"The new priest seems to be a pretty good guy by all accounts, although a lot of my friends didn't like him when he first came here."

"Yet you wrote a letter to the Cardinal with a copy to the Eminent Joseph Cardinal Ratzinger condemning him."

His eyes flashed a warning.

"You read those letters, do you?"

"When the Cardinal gives them to me to read. They are not exactly marked 'eyes only,' you know."

"If you remember what I wrote . . ."

"I do remember it exactly. You protested his lack of emphasis on the good work his predecessor had done."

"I wouldn't say that anymore, Bishop. He has a Mass for him every month and promises to name a wing of the new school after him."

Leave it to Peter Finnegan to think of something like that.

"It might not be a bad idea to write another letter, cc: Joseph Ratzinger, in which you retract what was in the first letter."

"You're right. I'll do that."

He reached over to the end table and made a note on a small piece of paper.

"I don't suppose it will do much good. Cronin probably wants to get rid of him anyway."

"You could not be more in error. Peter Finnegan will be here as long as he wants to be."

"Yeah? That's interesting. Good thing for the parish, however."

"It would seem so."

"But I bet Cronin will get rid of him just as he threw Monsignor out of the Chancery twenty-five years ago."

"It was the previous Cardinal who accepted Monsignor McInerny's resignation."

"At Cronin's suggestion."

"Not at all. Monsignor offered his resignation so that the then Cardinal would feel free to appoint someone more in agreement with the Vatican Council changes. It may have been a pro forma resignation and he may have been shocked when it was accepted, but no one asked for his resignation."

Griffin pondered this information.

"I have no reason to doubt you, though that's not the impression one got. Still, it's the kind of gesture he would make all right."

"Actually I'm here to find and recover the money."

"Money?" He raised an eyebrow.

"We calculate that there are at least ten million dollars of parish funds that are missing. He seems to have kept no accurate records of parish income. He sent none of his surplus money to the Chancery. He signed over one account to Father Peter Finnegan when the latter arrived. We know nothing about where the rest of it might be."

I waited while Griffin digested this information, which seemed to be a surprise to him.

"Are you saying he made no distinction between his own money and parish money?"

"Apparently not. Moreover it would seem that he had very little of the former."

He pondered the implications carefully before he spoke again.

"I was unaware of that."

Was he really? How could he have been?

"You of course invested some of it for him?"

"Hell yes. Lynn would come to me from Gerry with a check he had signed and asked me to invest it. I would do so, usually in a fairly short-run position, and then write a check to him for the profits."

"There were always profits?"

"A lot more profit than loss. There are no sure things on the board of the Merc."

"Surely not."

"I have all the records of his investments in the market,

Eurodollars mostly, some S and P index contracts. A few forwards—what people call derivatives—before they went sour last spring."

"How much would you estimate his profits were?"

"Oh, a couple of million anyway . . . and you are saying that was Church money?"

"Some of it, surely. Most of it probably."

"You want it back?"

"Legally such money belongs to the parish and to the Catholic Bishop of Chicago, a corporation sole."

"I understand, Bishop Ryan. What a terrible mess."

"You have no funds in his account with you at the present."

"Not a penny. I'll produce the records for you."

"Our lawyers will be in touch with you."

"Tell them I will voluntarily turn over all records. I might not be a practicing Catholic but I surely don't want to steal from the Church. . . . Why did he do it, I wonder."

"Probably because he didn't trust the Church to invest the money wisely and because he didn't trust either of the last two cardinals and because he thought he would live forever."

"Don't we all?" he said grimly. "He was an odd man. But I don't think there was any deliberate evil in him, not the way he saw the world."

"Normally, as I understand it, when these things happen, there's no ill will intended. Moreover many pastors have been known to withhold funds in S and L accounts so they will enjoy some independence from the Chancery—just as some associates filch money from the Sunday collection so they won't have to ask their pastor to pay for the basketball team uniforms."

He chuckled. "Everyone has their angle, I guess, and sometimes with good reason."

Well, I had made this somber man laugh.

"Did Lynn know?" he asked, suddenly grim again.

"Presumably she did. By all accounts she had the power to sign his checks."

"She certainly seemed to have that power all right. But I think she was a signer and a messenger and nothing more. Her experience growing up in the Depression made her wary of the world of investors and speculators."

"Moreover," I continued relentlessly, "she appropriated his financial records immediately after his death."

He seemed surprised. "Not a very wise thing to do. Possible obstruction of justice."

"We do not want to undertake civil action, to say nothing of criminal action."

"I understand that. . . . Look, I've known Lynn for a long time. She adored the man. He was very good to her when she had her breakdown in Korea. But she's not a fool, much less a thief."

"You would make the same assertion of others who were close friends to the Monsignor?"

He answered without hesitation.

"No," he said flatly. "I would not."

He considered what he had said. "It does not follow that in this particular case they have been either foolish or dishonest. . . . Have you talked to Lynn yet?"

"Not yet."

"You'll like her. Everyone does."

"I have been assured by some very perceptive teenagers that she's, like, one of the kids."

He laughed. "I've seen her with kids that age. She's wonderful with them."

He paused to consider the situation.

"Tell you what, Bishop Ryan. I'll make a deal with you."

"I should risk a deal with the king of the Eurodollar pit?"

"Not that kind of deal. . . . Look, you promise me you'll keep an open mind on Lynn and I'll promise you that I won't tell her a word about this conversation. That way you'll get a spontaneous response from her."

"You have a great deal of confidence in her, don't you?"

"Absolutely."

I almost asked him if he loved her, but that was an unnecessary question. The answer was already obvious.

"It's a deal."

I reached out my hand and he shook it firmly.

Only when I was outside once more, wilting in the heat and humidity, did I wonder if an experienced and sophisticated trader could be so naive about the source of Monsignor McInerny's funds.

I asked myself therefore whether I had gone long when I should have sold short.

CHAPTER 8

PETER FINNEGAN AND I were the only ones at lunch. Father D'Souza was teaching at Loyola; Father O'Keefe had taken Father Wozniak to the Woodbridge Country Club for a game of golf.

"Joe still plays golf?" I asked as I wolfed down a fruit salad with cottage cheese, hardly proper nourishment, but the best I was likely to get unless I was willing to risk another drive to the mall.

"Nine holes one day a week. He goes over twice a week to play gin rummy. Penny a point. Gives him a thrill."

"Indeed."

"Who did you see this morning?" Peter Finnegan asked.

"Gerald Reed and Arnold Griffin."

"Your impressions?"

"I can't believe that Reed is that dumb, but he is. And I can't believe that Griffin is that naive and I'm not sure that he is."

"Don't bet against it. Get Arnie off the trading floor and he's an innocent."

"He's in love with Reed's wife," I suggested.

"Sure he is. Most men who know her are."

"More intensely than most I should think."

"Probably."

"She may have married the wrong man," I continued to

probe, realizing that the young priest was determined to protect Lynn from my inquiries.

"I wouldn't say that she's passionately in love with her husband," he said thoughtfully. "But she's fond of him. He's good to her and the three kids."

"Griffin never married?"

"A long time ago. His wife died in an auto accident a couple of years after the marriage. He never remarried."

For a relatively new man in town he knew his parishioners pretty well.

"So he's not just a crusty old Irish bachelor?"

"For all practical purposes he is. I think he likes being a loner."

"You don't think he and Lynn are lovers?"

He paused to consider my question, understanding perhaps that I was not gossiping but probing the death of his predecessor.

"Hard to tell, Blackie. He adores her. It's much more difficult to tell what goes on in her head. She could have him anytime she wants him, but I'm not so sure she wants him or anyone else. She's as cool and concealed a person as I've ever known. I don't think either one of them would kill Monsignor, however."

"But they might know who did or might think they know?"

"That's not impossible."

"And what are the parish rumors on Gerry and his bank?"

"All kinds of them. The poor man was so browbeaten by his father until the old man died twenty years ago that he never gained any self-confidence. The word is that accounts are disappearing from the bank. They don't even have an ATM over there. Fortunately for him young Gerry, Gerry V, I guess, is doing a bang-up job at the Butternut

Mall and, according to the stories, may pull the bank out of danger. Or at least force his father to sell it to NBD, which is hovering anxiously waiting for something to happen."

"Why no ATM?"

"Because his great-grandfather didn't have one or so people say; and because there should be no ATMs in a village like Woodbridge. Can you imagine how much action there would be at an ATM right across the street from the railroad station?"

"Poor man."

"That's what everyone says. They know he's an incompetent weakling but they blame his father and don't despise him so much as feel sorry for him."

"What did his parents think of Lynn?"

The young priest was mopping up his cottage cheese.

"Don't you want your cottage cheese, Blackie? I love the stuff."

I willingly passed my plate over to him.

"The fresh raspberries were excellent," I said. They were. Only there had not been nearly enough of them.

"About Gerry's parents: I don't know what they thought about Lynn at first. Your only son shows up with a Navy nurse from a small town in Nebraska as a bride, of course you'd be suspicious. But apparently she won them over. They left a ton of money to her and big trust funds to her kids. Gerry got the bank and change. She's completely independent, if she wants to be. It is said that Arnie invested her money in silver just before the Hunt brothers tried to corner the market and got her out of the market when it was at its high."

"You haven't missed much in this parish, Peter Finnegan."

"It's a pastor's job to know his people."

"If Milord Cronin tires of me and wants another detective on his staff, or arguably a different one, I shall recommend you without hesitation."

He chuckled.

"He wouldn't dare. Besides, I'm not tough enough for the job."

Which response demonstrated impressive self-knowledge?

After lunch I drifted into the parish office, assured Lisa, the porter person in charge, that she and her boyfriend (this one truly named Matt) were entitled to a ride in my "fabulous" convertible, and began to poke around in the parish records. Whatever else might have been said about Charles P. McInerny, he kept good parish records.

He had become even more fuzzy in my picture of him, fading into the past like someone you knew long ago but whose appearance you did not remember. He was a name and a puzzle and nothing else.

But it was the almost illegible records kept by John P. Kelly that interested me. After searching through a couple of years I found that Gerald Tonner Reed IV had been born to Mary Ann Tonner and Gerald Reed III in 1927 and that he had been married to Lt. (j.g.) Evelyn Elizabeth Keating, U.S.N.R., in Pusan, Korea, in 1951 by Commander C. P. McInerny, U.S.N.R.

I sat up straight in the chair into which I had slumped in my early afternoon sleepiness.

Had anyone else noticed it? Had Charlie himself bothered to search for the record? Why should he? He knew presumably that it was there. He had sent the notice of the marriage to the parish of the groom's baptism as canon law required but as many priests, particularly busy service chaplains, did not bother to do. A strict canonist then, even with himself.

Did he remember the marriage? Was the Lynn of those days the kind of person who would be easy to forget?

Or was I making too much of what might be a coincidence?

I searched the records in the handwriting of one of Paddy Flynn's curates, the one who had died. Evelyn Elizabeth Reed had been born to Evelyn Keating and Gerald Reed seven months after the marriage at Butternut Community Hospital, though the baptism was nine and a half months after the marriage. The appearance of a premature birth had at least been maintained. The mother was only twenty years old. And a lieutenant junior grade already?

There was a hiatus of ten years before the birth of Mary Anne Reed, presumably now known as Jill, and another two years before the advent of Gerald Reed V.

Yet more data. Was there a ménage à quatre in Saints Peter and Paul—Lynn Keating Reed and three men who loved her, each perhaps in his own way? Or possibly all in the same way?

She was doubtless a formidable woman. One would be well advised to be careful in dealing with her.

Musing on these complexities, I made another inspection of the rectory, this time from the outside, with special emphasis on the tower.

In fact the tower was part of the house for the first and second floor, nothing more than a circular extension at the end of the house. It became distinct from the rest of the house only at the third floor. So the door leading to the spiral staircase that the virtuous Megan had opened for me, in fact, was still in the rectory proper.

Why did one have to climb to the fourth floor to be able to climb back down to the third floor? Why was the circular staircase so narrow? What was beneath the tower on the first floor?

As I considered the balcony of the tower from the ground, I noted that one could scramble up toward it if one was willing to climb over and around a turret and a bay window to the third floor of the house and then make an easy jump from the third-floor roof to the balcony—easy if one were confident and a good jumper. Neither one of which would have applied to me.

But with a ladder braced from the third-floor roof to the side of the tower, one could schlepp to the balcony with very little difficulty—though anyone in a passing car might be able to see you if there was enough light.

Access then could be easy from the third floor if one had a ladder, was not afraid of heights, and willing to take the risk of being seen. One would have had to gain access to the rectory with a ladder and then found a way to the roof of the third floor, however.

I returned to my tower suite and discovered that, sure enough, there was a latch on the inside of the sliding glass door that provided access to the balcony. It was unlocked, however.

Had anyone looked at it on the morning the body was discovered. Not Peter Finnegan who was still paralyzed with shock. But the cool former Navy nurse?

I then went back to the first floor and asked the housekeeper about what was under the tower access on the first floor.

She showed me a combination linen closet, storeroom for food and cleaning materials and supplies, and laundry room. The walls were newly painted, but then so was every wall in the rectory. The washer, the dryer, the vacuum cleaner, and everything else were new and herself was very proud of them. Father had permitted her to buy them because she was the one who had to use them.

In the basement, dark and dusty and as yet untouched it seemed by the Peter Finnegan reform, the foundation stones under the tower section of the rectory were damp and dirty and problematic, but then so were most of the other stones. Presumably the new Pastor had an evaluation that suggested that no immediate crisis threatened. In a year the place would doubtless be transformed into another meeting room, with indirect lighting and pine-paneled walls. I noted four drain pipes that came from the direction of the tower and merged in the basement.

At some point in the investigation I would probably have to insist on removal of a number of walls.

I returned to the third floor, the associate pastor's wing of the rectory. Father D'Souza was teaching and Fathers Wozniak and O'Keefe were playing golf. I had free run of the place.

I could not find any secret access to the tower, not even in Joe's closet that abutted the third floor of the tower. Indeed there was no trace in the plastered walls of even the circular outline of the tower. From the third floor you could not even tell there was a tower save by looking out the bay windows.

There was, however, at the far end of the corridor evidence of a trapdoor that surely provided access to the roof. Since the ceilings of the rectory rooms and corridors were at least twelve feet above the floor one would need a long ladder to take advantage of the access. Presumably such ladders existed somewhere in the parish plant. But I had no intention of seeking one because then I would have no excuse not to climb to the roof.

I returned to the second floor and examined the Pastor's suite and the currently unoccupied guest suites, which would doubtless soon be filled with visitors coming to learn from Peter's pastoral style.

I found nothing unusual, although in the one at the far end of the corridor, right at the head of the stairs up which the ineffable Megan had brought me the first day, the closet abutting the tower had a solid oak back wall that would nicely deaden all sounds coming from the tower.

I had formed the basic outlines of a theory that would explain the locked room aspect of the puzzle. In due course we would move the masonry to test the theory. However, even if the theory were verified, it would not by itself solve the mystery of how the late Pastor of the parish had died.

It was time to pay a visit to Dr. Curtin and accuse him of a false report on the cause of death.

But before I strolled, in the heat of the day, to his house, I made a stop at the office, three doors down from the bank, of *The Bridge*, the community weekly paper.

The elderly woman who presided over its chic and modern office (designed one might suspect to look something like the newsroom of the *Washington Post* in the Watergate film) was happy to let me look at *The Bridge* for 1951. She produced a microfiche and directed me to a reader. No fear of the rough equivalent of an ATM here.

It took only a few minutes to find an account (on the front page) of the wedding in Korea of Gerald Reed IV and Evelyn Keating. The headline announced:

WAR HEROES MARRIED NEAR FRONT

The picture of the two, both in full uniform, caught my attention before the story. Evelyn Keating was beyond all doubt the most beautiful twenty-year-old woman that a man could reasonably expect to meet in the course of his life. On her white jacket there were two ribbons, one a campaign ribbon and the other looked familiar, a dark ribbon with a white stripe in the middle.

I printed out the page and looked at the picture with a magnifying glass. No doubt about it. The Navy Cross, second highest of the Navy's decorations.

Most interesting.

The article was devoted mainly to Gerry Reed and his family and his achievements in the supply center at Pusan.

The last sentence confirmed my suspicion:

"Lieutenant Keating has been awarded the Navy Cross for gallantry in action."

CHAPTER 9

AS I WALKED two blocks south toward Dr. Curtin's house on Elm Street, I pondered the article I had read about Lt. (j.g.) Evelyn Keating, U.S.N.R. In those days the Navy, even more contemptuous of women than it is now, was not inclined to give nurses combat decorations. Lynn Reed, as she was now, must have done something truly spectacular.

Oh, yes, very formidable indeed.

I stopped at a telephone kiosk outside the railroad station. One could use credit cards but not coins, doubtless because the village council decided that if you possessed a credit card you might be tolerated in Woodbridge for the time it took to make a phone call.

I dialed a number I knew in D.C., though actually it was at a place technically in Virginia. One of the Admiral's aides answered, a Marine major.

"Tell the Boss that Blackie is on the phone."

"Yes, sir. Sir, is there any rank I should assign?"

"There's only one Blackie."

In Germany, a bishop ranks in the government payroll with a general. But I wasn't German.

"Blackie," the Admiral said, "how the hell are you?"

"Steaming all ahead full despite the torpedoes . . . you guys gave a Navy Cross to a young nurse in Korea a couple of decades ago."

"I doubt it. In those days we thought women didn't deserve that quality medal."

"You did all right. A j.g.—though possibly she was an ensign at the time of the award—named Evelyn or possibly Lynn Keating."

"If you say so, then we did."

"I want to find out what she did."

"Is she in some kind of trouble."

"If the locals are to be believed that is unthinkable. I want to make sure it's authentic."

"Right. Next week?"

"I'll call tomorrow at ten your time."

"Oh, low priority. You don't want it today."

"Tell your aide that Blackie always gets put through to the Admiral. Right away."

"Yes, *sir*. My best to your family, especially your stepmother."

"Thank you."

I walked on under the heat of the afternoon sun. Why, I wondered, wasn't I at Grand Beach where I belonged.

The Curtin house was almost as big as the rectory, though not so gross in its Victorian pretensions. It was painted gray with rose trim, however, which made it even funnier than the rectory.

I pushed the doorbell several times. Finally, the massive door opened a crack.

"Yes?" said a squeaky voice.

"Bishop Ryan to see Dr. Curtin."

"Just a minute."

The door closed in my face.

A few moments later it swung open again. A large and ebullient man with long white hair and beard and a florid face filled the doorway and reached out with a massive paw.

"Steve Curtin, Bishop. Welcome. Come on in. Good to see you."

Dr. Curtin was perhaps six feet five inches tall and weighed between three hundred and three hundred fifty pounds. Not all of the weight was fat, though much of it was. He was wearing khaki slacks and a bush jacket that would have been appropriate for a trek across the Kalahari with a white hunter fifty years ago. All he lacked was a pith helmet. He was carrying the detached double barrel of a shotgun in one hand.

"Just polishing and cleaning my guns," he explained. "I expect to be leaving for India soon. Tiger hunt. I've got just about every kind of big game in the world except tiger. I want one before they become extinct."

"Indeed."

He showed me into his "game" room that was truly a game room in the sense of "big game." The heads of a lion, a black panther, a rhino, and a water buffalo stared balefully at me from a solid oak wall. On a similar wall a variety of antelopes considered me lugubriously. Against yet another wall, a full-size grizzly and a mammoth polar bear stood ready to pounce. Above me a fan spun slowly, even though the air-conditioning condenser was chugging away outside. Bamboo shades intercepted most of the sunlight that was attempting to enter through the glass doors overlooking a garden of tropical flowers—in a greenhouse.

The illusion, crude but expensive, was that we were in some kind of hotel on the edge of an African jungle in the time when Ernest Hemingway prowled around playing big macho hero. Come to think of it, Dr. Curtin might have thought himself to be a Hemingway impersonator.

"Sit down, Bishop, sit down," he bellowed. "This is my

wife Margie. Margie, Bishop Ryan. He's out here investigating the strange events over at the parish."

"Good afternoon Bishop," she said flatly. "Would you like some iced tea?"

"I would, thank you."

She was a tiny woman, thin and haggard, her gray hair tied in a bun behind her head, her eyes probing, her frown suspicious, her long nose an accusation. Her brown slacks and print blouse suggested compromise with her husband's white hunter illusion. But she didn't seem happy about it or about anything else.

She departed to obtain the iced tea.

"I'll have another stinger, Margie, if you don't mind. Sure you don't want one, Bishop?"

"Thank you, no."

I did not want to fly out of the house and disrupt the traffic patterns over O'Hare.

I noted with unease that some twenty weapons of individual if not mass destruction were stacked behind his worktable, arguably oak also, at which the doctor was working on his impressive shotgun. Two faded pictures of young men hung on the wall behind him, presumably the sons who had long ago left Woodbridge for New York.

"I've hunted game all over the world, Bishop," he roared. "Alaska, Indonesia, the Rockies, East Africa, West Africa, you name it I've been there. And I've killed just about all of them. Most dangerous kind is the North American cougar or mountain lion. Pound for pound they are the strongest predators in the world. They're on top of you before you even see them."

"If you're in their territory."

"Well, sure . . . and they're increasing in this country. When I get back from India I have half a mind to help the government harvest some of them. They're not an endangered species yet. If you ask me, humans are the most endangered species of all."

"Arguably."

"A lot of people think the rhino is more dangerous. They're big and dumb and can't see very well. But they charge you, they come fast. If you don't have your wits about you, they'll smash you. You get one chance to shoot and then they're on you. I got that fellow over there with this custom-made six-gauge shotgun. Smooth bore of course like all shotguns. Deadly at close range. But that's the way to hunt rhinos. Both barrels right between the eyes. Stopped him like he'd been hit with a howitzer shell. Most exciting moment in my life. Can't beat it."

His wife served the iced tea. Noting the venomous look in her eyes, I wondered if by mistake I had wandered into the house of the Borgias. In fact, while the tea was probably not poisoned (as I am still alive), it was the most foul-tasting iced tea I've ever tasted. One sip was enough.

"See my name on the stock, burned in by the maker. Not another one like it in the world. You could blow a man's head off with this. Not that I've done it, though sometimes I've felt like it."

He began to sip on his drink with exuberant delight.

"Can't beat a stinger when you're thirsty on a hot summer day. Has a kick in it like the stock of this gun."

"You're out of medical practice now?" I asked, wishing that I was equipped with a real shillelagh, an Irish war club and not a thorn stick cane.

"Oh, I still keep my hand in it now and then over at Butternut Community. I retired from St. Luke's years ago. Government had ruined medical practice in this country. Government and health insurance. Too many forms to fill out. Too many half-assed young specialists who think they know everything. Too many academic doctors who couldn't maintain a practice so they teach instead. Margie and I would rather travel and hunt, wouldn't we, Margie?"

She offered no response.

"Do you engage in other forms of recreation?"

"Some deep-sea fishing with harpoons. That's exciting too. Used to ride in white-water rafts. That's not as much fun as hunting, so I gave it up."

"Mountain climbing?"

He put down the barrel and began to polish what looked like the firing mechanism.

"Used to. A bunch of us from the neighborhood went over to the Alps, oh, maybe ten, fifteen years ago. Arnie Griffin is a great one for climbing. Only thing in life that excites him. Lynn Reed, Gerry's wife, you know, the banker, she's a good climber too. Gorgeous woman, isn't she, Margie? Sexiest woman her age I've ever known."

Margie offered no reply, but her face twisted with dislike, whether for her husband or Lynn I did not know.

He waved his drink at me and drank another huge sip.

"Anyway, the two of them went up this crazy Swiss mountain one morning. Perfect weather. Nothing to be afraid of, they told us with a laugh. The rest of the group were interested only in the scenery. But I'd done some climbing in the Rockies and knew the basic stuff. Said the night before what the hell I'd go along with them. But that day didn't seem just right somehow. I'm that way, Bishop, I can smell danger when everyone else misses it, can't I, Margie?"

Her answers were apparently neither expected nor required.

"So doesn't a big snow squall hit about one in the

afternoon and fog in the whole upper half of the mountain. We're sitting in the sunshine and sipping lager outside the lodge, some good-looking women in the swimming pool. And up there Arnie and Lynn are caught in a blinding blizzard. I heard an experienced climber say that anyone up there now was doomed. Too exciting. I promised myself then I'd never try to climb mountains again. Poor Gerry was sobbing. Never could stand a man who cries, know what I mean, Bishop?"

My answers were no more relevant than those of his wife.

"Anyway, he's having hysterics all night long and I have to sedate him. A woman like Lynn deserves someone who is more of a man than he is. Knock her into shape when she goes into one of those moods of hers. Gerry is afraid to lay a finger on her."

"Interesting."

"Well, the next morning the sun is up early. Remember this is Europe in the summer and even as far south as Switzerland you get long days. The mountain has a whole layer of thick snow. Not a mark on it. Rumor goes around that two Americans died up there in the storm. The place gets kind of somber, a lot of natives hanging around like they're getting ready for a wake. Gerry is out of bed too and screaming like a banshee. I have to sedate him again."

He paused to inhale another long draft of his stinger.

"Great stuff. Sure you don't want some, Bishop?"

I declined with thanks.

"So where was I? Oh, yeah. About two in the afternoon, Arnie and Lynn came down the side of the mountain, both looking pretty bedraggled, but alive. Arnie is limping a little because he hurt his ankle up there. Turns out they found a shelter just before the storm roared down on them.

I'm thinking they probably shacked up in the shelter for some hanky-panky before the storm started."

"Stephen!" his wife protested.

"Can't help thinking about it, Margie. He's always been sweet on her. I don't know how anyone could resist her, there up on a mountain with her. So they ride out the storm and then go on up to the summit, just to teach the mountain a lesson. Arnie twists his ankle on something coming down and she has to drag him in. I put some ice on it and he's all right in a day or two. She hugs poor old Gerry and calms him down. She were my wife I'd drag her off to bed and teach her not to scare me that way and have some fun doing it. But not Gerry. He's the most pussy-whipped man I've ever known."

"Stephen!" Her voice leapt out at him like a coiled snake.

"Can't help it, Margie," he said agreeably. "The man's a coward and a fool. Doesn't deserve a woman like her. Anyway, I made up my mind that day to stay away from the mountains. Unless I'm flying over them or watching them from a hunting blind down at the bottom."

He finished his stinger with a grand flourish.

What was the point in the story, which now I had heard twice from two different viewpoints? To cast suspicion on Lynn Reed and Arnie Griffin? There was something wrong here. He probably knew what I was looking for and was setting up a smoke screen.

But to protect what? Or whom?

"I suppose you're out here investigating this strange stuff going on over at the church. Probably the new priest is behind it. Maybe it's something strange. A witch at work or something like that. Out in the bush in Africa all sorts of strange things happen. I've experienced them myself.

Makes the blood run cold first time. Then you kind of get used to it and it goes away. The trick is not to pay any attention to them. If you leave these things over at the church alone, mark my words, they'll stop."

"Arguably."

"That leaves them unexplained, but then a lot of things are unexplained, aren't they?"

"Cheap magic trips."

He jabbed his glass at me. "Now you've got it. And if you ask me, I'd say Lynn is the witch behind all these things. She's a luscious tidbit all right, but I've always thought she was a little strange, kind of uncanny, know what I mean?"

"I haven't met the woman."

"When you do meet her, you'll agree with me that there's something uncanny about her. She has no business having the body she has at her age," he insisted. "Out in the bush you run into women like that. Great tits and asses and they're over seventy. Seductive bitches like she is. The men warn you to stay away from them. They live off men like vampires. Screw them and you begin to die and they begin to look younger. Look at Lynn and look at Gerry and you'll see what I mean."

"She's a witch all right," Margie sneered, "and a trollop too. Someone ought to stick a pin in her."

She grabbed a long African spear—not unlike the ones used in the film *Zulu*—off the wall and waved it in the air. Truly the woman was mad.

"Put it back, Margie," the doctor said wearily, "or I'll belt you one."

She put it back. Docilely enough and then, like a wounded dog, slunk out of the room.

"She's harmless, Bishop." Dr. Curtin waved his hand negligently. "Has these little spells occasionally, especially when it's hot. Happens all the time to women in Africa. If a man is firm with them, the spells go away."

I did not like Dr. Curtin. He was a loudmouthed braggart and a bore. His macho pretense and his obsession with guns and killing suggested a man whose virility was weak and who was able to engage in sex only when excited by a lot of extracurricular activity.

So I hit him straight in the gut. Figuratively.

"Why did you falsify the cause of death of the late Monsignor Charles P. McInerny?"

"What!" he bellowed.

His face turned from red to purple and he clutched the stock of his shotgun like he might just hit me with it.

"It is clear from the scene that the Monsignor was hit over the left temple with a very blunt instrument, arguably one of the heavy candlesticks he kept in his study bedroom."

"Nonsense! He had high blood pressure for years and I warned him he'd have a stroke unless he took the medicine I prescribed for him. He was on his last legs anyway. The cut on his head was incidental.

"Very high blood pressure," he snapped.

"I have every reason to believe he was murdered and for the obvious reason that a large amount of money was at stake. I have no doubt that for reasons of your own you falsified the death certificate. Either to protect yourself or others and doubtless for a price in the latter case."

"That's a goddamn lie!" he roared, shoving the pieces of his dismantled gun back together.

"We will exhume the body shortly to determine whether your diagnosis was correct. If it turns out that you signed a death certificate that was a lie, you will be in very deep trouble."

I had not thought before about an exhumation, but at the moment it seemed a very good idea.

The color drained from his face and he laid the shotgun back on his worktable.

"Moreover we have reason to believe that many millions of dollars of parish money have been appropriated by some of his close friends, yourself included. In the absence of the return of the money we are prepared to initiate both criminal and civil action."

I would not tell Milord Cronin of this interlude in my investigation. He would accuse me of recklessness, of taking unnecessary chances, of foolish bluffing, especially if I told him about the spear-wielding wife. In truth, however, I felt I had Dr. Curtin pretty well figured. In the event, I was right.

All the fire seemed to go out of him. He sagged in his chair. His complexion lost its healthy glow and turned ashen.

"Get out of here," his wife snarled.

She had slipped back into the room, so far unarmed.

"Not quite yet, Ms. Curtin."

Stephen Curtin rubbed his hand over his face.

"You wouldn't do those things," he said anxiously.

"Why not?"

"You'd create a terrible scandal. You'd ruin the Monsignor's reputation; you'd destroy the neighborhood; you'd do great harm to the Church."

"Tell me why?"

He shook his head. "You'll have to figure that out for yourself. But I warn you, that's what you will do. It's not worth it."

"A murder has been committed and a huge sum of money taken from the Church."

"It's still not worth it. Believe me."

"Get out of here!" his wife screeched.

She was moving toward the Zulu spear, I thought.

"In a minute, ma'am."

I no longer had any doubt about a conspiracy, a intricate, serpentine conspiracy. Dr. Curtin was not denying it. Rather he was begging me not to reveal it because so much harm would be done if I did.

"You still stand by your diagnosis?"

I stood up to leave.

"It looked to me like a stroke. I knew one was coming. It was only a matter of time. What else could it have been? I disregarded the cut on his head. It seemed obvious he had fallen against something. I saw no point in a postmortem. Who would have wanted to kill Monsignor? Everyone loved him, didn't they, Margie?"

"Everyone who had any sense."

Her hand rested on the spear.

"Have it your way then. Good day. Thank you for the iced tea, Ms. Curtin."

I retreated to the heat, well aware that two sets of eyes were fixing me with burning hate and somewhat uneasy about where the Zulu spear might be at the moment.

Back in the rectory I phoned my cousin Mike Casey the Cop, sometime commissioner of police for the city of Chicago.

His wife, Annie, answered the phone as she usually does.

"Reilly Gallery."

"Blackie here. Annie, is himself in?"

"He's painting."

"It's important."

"I'll get him right away."

There are those who, in the patently mistaken notion that I am Father Brown, insist that Mike the Cop is my Flambeau or that if perhaps I am M. Poirot, he is my Captain Hastings. Nothing can be further from the truth as Annie will be the first to tell you. The comparison overlooks the patent truth that neither M. Flambeau nor Captain Hastings had ever written the standard textbook on police detection.

"What's up, Blackie?"

I briefly summarized the situation.

"You've got yourself into a mare's nest this time."

"Or in more politically correct language a viper's tangle."

"You want me to come out there?"

"Not yet. Do you have any clout with the local cops."

"Hicks. Dumb."

"I feared as much. Then perhaps some of your more skilled associates should appear out here or rather not appear."

"To guard?"

"From my point of view most importantly to guard me. Also perhaps a certain Ms. Lynn Keating Reed."

"You think someone might try to kill her."

"Arguably. She's at the center of the viper's tangle. There are almost certainly some people who would rather that she be dead than alive. Perhaps that is something she deserves. Perhaps not. But we need her alive if this puzzle is to be resolved."

"You've never asked for protection before, Blackie."

"There's always a first time . . . also find out all you can about the financial situations of Albert Fasio, Stephen Curtin, Arnold Griffin, and Gerald Reed IV. And their families. My guess is that they're all in trouble."

"I'll do it right away. Be careful. And call me before you need me instead of after."

"Wise advice I propose to follow."

I did follow it eventually. Alas, after it was too late.

I then phoned a veteran commodity trader who is an excellent source of information.

"Profile on a certain Arnold Griffin, please."

"The Silver Fox?"

"Presumably."

"One of the sharpest traders of the half century. Mind like a steel trap. Instincts like that of a dangerous predator. Nerve like Joe Montana. And yet innocent as a four year old. Also as honest as they come in this business."

"Sounds like a contradiction."

"A couple of them all rolled up into one mysterious but likable guy."

"Lost his wife young, did he not?"

"Some of us think he never recovered from that. He dated a number of gorgeous women. But couldn't quite settle down. The rumor is that he's been in love for a long time with a married woman and is waiting for her husband to die."

"Doesn't sound like a good investment to me."

"Maybe not. But Arnie is the kind of guy who sells long and then hangs on."

"Love is not like the corn pit."

"Geez, Blackie, are you sure? I've always thought it was just like the corn pit."

I then descended to Peter Finnegan's room to meet a promised rendezvous for a pre-prandial sip of Jamesons.

"You look wilted, Blackie," that worthy said as he pressed the goblet into my hand. "Would you like some ice in this?"

"The weather is no excuse for blasphemy . . . and as you no doubt notice on the weather segments of the news, it is always cooler near the lake."

"How did it go with Steve Curtin?"

"The man is around the bend."

"A couple of times. But his wife is ahead of him. She's the crazier of the two. Was a nurse a long time ago. I never could figure out what Monsignor saw in him. He seemed to like his vigor and energy."

"Am I correct that he is virtually impotent unless he plays a very macho role in lovemaking?"

"I wouldn't have thought so, but now you mention it, I wouldn't be surprised. Though he wouldn't dare beat up his sweet little wife. She'd cut him up with one of those bolos knives of his."

"He is alleged to pursue other women?"

"Most everyone believes he fools around, as the saying goes."

"Interesting."

That would presumably mean assaulting and beating women, presumably raping them. Nice man.

At the Butternut Mall that night this suspicion was confirmed by Lisa and Matt.

"My mom, like every other woman in the village, is afraid to be alone with him. She says he's abused and molested a lot of his women patients. Some of them may have wanted it but most didn't have any choice. That's why he had to stop practicing medicine. Some of the men in the village told him that if he didn't they'd have him sent to jail."

"Yet Monsignor liked him."

"My daddy is like Monsignor, only saw in people what he wanted to see. He didn't want to see that Gerry Reed was a dumb incompetent, that Doc Curtin beat up on women, that Albert Fasio was a crook, and that Lynn was a whore. . . . I don't think she is, Bishop Blackie. What do you think?"

"I doubt it," I said.

But I wasn't so sure.

CHAPTER 10

AT NINE O'CLOCK the next morning, after the organ played "Somewhere Over the Rainbow" during the young priest's Mass and the bells (which had produced Christmas hymns during the night) rang out the *Regina Coeli* (an Easter hymn to Mary), I phoned my friend at the Pentagon.

"Holy shit, Blackie, she was some woman."

"Ah?"

"She was on night duty up at a small field hospital in X Corps. Twenty wounded Marines. A squad of North Korean guerrillas—six of them—who had infiltrated under the lines through the tunnels they were always digging, pushed their way into the place by slashing holes in the tent—it was only a big tent—with machetes. They cut the single guard to pieces and started to work on the Marines. She picked up the guard's automatic weapon and killed them all. A nineteen-year-old kid. Some of the brass didn't want to give her the medal regardless, but no way they could stop it. A good-looking kid too, to judge by her picture."

"She killed six Korean guerrillas!"

"Someone had taught her how to use one of those things. She must have taken them out in less than thirty seconds. A few of the patients were cut up pretty bad, but they all made it. The guard too."

"Astonishing."

"I guess it was pretty hard on her afterward. They had to calm her down. They gave her some time off because she was having terrible dreams."

"Small wonder."

"She still alive, Blackie?"

"Very much so."

"Any chance you'd give us her address? She's entitled to some attention from us. Dropped completely out of sight. Should have received the Medal of Honor. A man would have. Maybe we can make it up to her."

"I don't know. I'll see."

"You'll make our case?"

"I see your point and I'll try."

Oh, yes, a *very* formidable woman. I would put off till tomorrow (Wednesday) any attempt to contact her.

Peter Finnegan and the very young priest were waiting for me at the breakfast table.

"Waffles, pancakes, and bacon?" Peter protested.

"I don't put on weight and my genes guarantee that I will have no cholesterol problem," I explained. "And besides, I'm always hungry."

"Just now," Tom added, "you look like someone hit you with a club."

"In a manner of speaking they did." I began to devour the bacon.

"The disturbance at Mass?" Peter asked.

"Oh, no, those magic tricks don't bother me."

"I hope you can stop them, Bishop, uh, I mean Blackie," the very young priest said. "They're getting to people. We had lots of calls last night."

"Unplug the electricity to the bell tower."

The two priests looked at one another. "Not a bad idea, if we could figure out where the electricity comes from."

"The Church has bishops," I observed, "because every once in a while they come up with good ideas."

"Not very often," Peter Finnegan said with a wide grin. "A broken clock is correct twice a day."

"A second good idea: disable the organ except when the organist is going to use it."

"We don't really know how to do that either," Peter said. "I've played organs but I'm no expert on them."

"I'm sure that Father O'Keefe does. . . . By the way, is he a good golfer, Tom?"

"Really good, especially for someone up there in years."

"And he fits in at the club."

"Fits in perfectly. Everyone seems to like him. He has lots of close friends over there. A really wicked gin rummy player. Knows all the gossip. They were saying yesterday that Mr. Reed's bank is in deep trouble and that if they don't sell soon, it will drag down the Butternut Bank too. Mr. Reed's son wants to sell to NBD and his father won't let him."

"And Joe thought this likely?"

"He said he was sure it would happen."

"Fascinating."

"Joe relaxes over there," Peter Finnegan added. "All the members of his AA group belong to the club, so he figures he's in pretty good shape for overcoming temptation. Some of them even show up for his Wednesday night lectures, though I don't think they know what he's talking about."

I changed the subject.

"Is anyone in the parish aware that Ms. Reed won the Navy Cross in Korea?"

"For what?" the Pastor exclaimed.

"She killed six Korean guerrillas who were attacking her hospital tent in the dead of night."

"Wow!"

"With an automatic weapon."

"I can't believe it, can you, Tom?"

"She's so sweet and gentle."

"Blackie," the Pastor continued, "she's a strong woman, but I'd bet anything she's not a killer."

"She killed six Koreans who must have been age peers of hers. Obviously she did it to save her patients and richly deserved the award. Yet one cannot assume that she is not capable at the present time of killing again in what she thinks is a good cause."

"You gotta meet her, Blackie."

"Only after I've met everyone else who seems immediately pertinent."

Before leaving for the Butternut Mall and the real estate offices of Albert Fasio, I called Mike the Cop.

"Any more data for me?"

"Doc Curtin is in over his head at the Merc. Was involved with some very kinky traders in the S and P market. And some very dangerous forwards in the derivatives game. Has made most of it back, but the Feds are supposed to be snooping around him."

"Is Arnold Griffin involved in this affair?"

"No way."

"Or other dubious matters?"

"No one has anything on him. Feds went after him once because he'd made so much money, but couldn't find a thing."

"And Gerry Reed IV?"

"He's hanging on by a thread. The state banking regulators are lurking in the background. They suspect that some of his loans, including those to Dr. Curtin, are problematic to say the least and that he may have been taking bank money for his own uses. Everyone seems to think that he'll have to sell to NBD, as his son wants him to. Still, they say things have been looking up for him during the last six months."

"Interesting. And the son?"

"Clean apparently, but the old man could drag him down too. If he did know that there were any irregularities and didn't report them, he'd be guilty of a crime. If he didn't know, he might not have exercised reasonable oversight."

"Ah . . . and the wife and mother?"

"On whom we now have a guard . . . did you notice the men we have on you?"

"I haven't and don't want to," I said with my patented loud sigh. "But I am grateful for them."

"As to her, she has a pile of money that *his* parents left her, which is kind of odd. She has invested it wisely, and if she's up to anything, it is completely concealed. However, if the Feds and the locals close in on him, they're going to want to ask her a lot of questions too."

"Fascinating."

"Albert Fasio has made and lost a couple of fortunes in real estate development. He may have on occasion bribed a contractor or two or accepted bribes from them, but he has covered his tracks pretty well. Otherwise he's been squeaky clean which is not easy to do in that business. Of course he is 'connected' as is every Italian in that business. Nothing illegal. Some guy comes to him and says we see you have a good thing going. We want to support you. So we're going to invest in forty percent of your holdings. You got no choice. As long as they make a profit on their investment you're all right. They start to lose money, you take out life insurance. Right now he's sitting pretty. He owns most of the stock in the Butternut Mall where he has his office. He's making loads of money off it and spends a lot of his time in Amalfi in the summer and in Cortina in the winter. His three kids all went to Notre Dame."

"That will not be held against him. His wife?"

"Supposed to be the brains of the team, which is often the case in both their ethnic group and ours."

"Except that theirs generally conceal the fact."

Mike the Cop laughed.

"Are you sure you don't want me to come out there?"

"Not yet, but perhaps soon."

On the way out of the rectory, I encountered Joe O'Keefe. He seemed tired.

"Good day on the links yesterday, Joe?"

He laughed wearily.

"Not bad for an old-timer. That big Polish kid can hit a golf ball a country mile. Can't putt worth a damn. Yet."

"What did your friends at the club think of the late Monsignor?"

He frowned, as if considering the question.

"Well, he had a lot of admirers of course. His gin rummy cronies, ultra-conservative Catholics. But a lot of other people thought he was an asshole, especially the Catholics who were going to other parishes. There were some comments about his relationship with Lynn."

"Ah?"

He shrugged.

"Whenever she appears at the club, there are a lot of guys who experience what Jimmy Carter called lust in the heart. Everyone knew she was close to Jolly Cholly and they kind of wondered. I told them they were full of it."

"What is their opinion about his death?"

"Most of them think he died a natural death."

"Indeed."

"If you get a chance, come by my lecture tonight. We're talking about Robert Penn Warren. Seven."

"A.k.a. Red Warren. I'll be there. Wouldn't miss it."

With his friends at the club, hitherto unmentioned to me, it was just possible that Father O'Keefe's lot at Saints Peter and Paul had not been as grim as he had portrayed it.

Fascinating.

As I left the rectory I was constrained to promise the Jennifer porter person that indeed I would, in the interest of justice, equity, and fairness, take her and her boyfriend (whose name I had accurately asserted was "Mark") for a ride in my hoary T-bird that evening. After Father Joe's lecture.

I was told that everyone thought Father Joe was so cute.

Albert Fasio looked like Giuseppe Garibaldi as that latter worthy was depicted in his portraits, solid man of medium height with a high forehead, fierce mustache, and burning brown eyes. However, in the Fasio Real Estate office in the Butternut Mall, he seemed casual and relaxed.

"Come on in, Bishop Ryan." He eased out of his immense "judge's chair" and extended a neatly manicured hand. "The lovely dame, so you get the right idea from the beginning, is my wife Nella. She'll deny it all day long, but she's the brains of this operation."

"Irish women never bother denying it."

We all laughed. Nella, however, in the presence of a bishop did not deny she was the brains of the operation.

Nella was a tall woman in her middle forties, perhaps ten years younger than her husband, ample of build but by no means unattractive with long black hair, black eyes, a face that Raffaello would have liked, and a summer-weight black mini dress that left no doubt about the elegance of her legs as she sat down on the sofa in her husband's office and crossed her legs. Clearly she was an attractive and intelligent woman, yet no one had said a word about her and everyone could hardly contain themselves on the subject of Lynn Reed.

The Fasio Real Estate office was on the top floor of an office building at one end of the Butternut Mall. It consisted of three rooms: an antechamber, in which there was no secretary, and adjoining offices of equal size for Albert and the "brains" of the firm. All three rooms were small and, while comfortable, were hardly luxurious.

"I know what you're here for, Bishop Blackie," Albert began easily, "and I can answer your questions right up front. I assume that the Monsignor died a natural death and I know nothing about Church moneys which might have been retained illegally. However, I wouldn't buy anything that had Steve Curtin's signature on it and I wouldn't be surprised at anything which might have happened in that rectory."

"Indeed!"

"Except," Nella added in a deep voice that sounded something like that of the wondrous Marissa Tomei, "both of us know that Lynn Reed would not do anything wrong."

"Nella is very close to Lynn," her husband explained.

"As far as anyone can be close to her."

"Ah."

"You see, Bishop Blackie, even if she is mysterious, she's a straight-arrow Navy nurse."

"You were aware that she holds a Navy Cross?"

"Lynn!" Nella gasped. "Why?"

"Perhaps I should not say, since she has not told you about the award."

"Typical though," Albert Fasio observed. "She is a very modest person."

Nella laughed knowingly. "He's not talking about the way she dresses, Bishop."

"That's modest too"—her husband winked—"but in a different way. . . . However, Bishop, in case you wondered, this mall, unlike some others in the western suburbs, is a gold mine. The mixed usage, which as you know dates back in Chicago to the Auditorium down on Michigan Avenue, is a concept which should have been applied to malls a long time ago. We have offices at this end, condos in the twin building at the other end, and everything from Nordstrom to Thirty-one Flavors, including art galleries, movie theaters, a dinner theater, and pizza parlors, in between. Something for everyone."

"I confess that I have contributed to your income at Thirty-one Flavors the last couple of nights."

"Try the chocolate chip with cookies and cream," he suggested.

"With raspberry sauce."

"Great idea. . . . Anyway, we may extend this place cautiously. Put in an adult education center and a family counseling center and a Waterstone's Bookstore, plus maybe a Filenes's Basement and a Ghirardelli Chocolate place, maybe even some kind of nondemoninational chapel, but only when I can find my capital contribution from revenues. No more big loans for the rest of my life. Sitting here and collecting rent is the best job I've had all my life."

"And gives you time to travel and to spend with your grandchildren," his wife added. "Do you know Amalfi, Bishop?"

"Splendid place indeed. . . . Were any of your loans from the Woodbridge State Bank as I find it must be called?"

"Are you kidding, Padre, er, Bishop? That guy wouldn't know a good investment if it hit him over the head. His kid downstairs in the mall bank is a smart young fella, but his old man screws up a lot of good possibilities for him."

"I hear that NBD is casting covetous eyes on the bank."

"On the one here, sure. They'd be welcome as far as I'm concerned, though I might jack up their rent a little. They're smart enough to keep young Gerry on their staff if he wants to stay. They might take the crap house over on High Street as part of the bargain, but they'd probably put an ATM over there and maybe add a teller or two and build a drive-through if they could get away with it. Certainly not a loan officer. They couldn't care less about the 'Woodbridge tradition' that poor dumb Gerry IV or whatever number he is cares so much about. I can't see why a woman like Lynn would marry a creep like him."

"Yet she's loyal to him," his wife said firmly, "and faithful."

"I suppose so," her husband conceded.

"She seems to have had a special relationship with the late Monsignor."

"She was very good to the poor old man." Nella continued to defend her friend. "But if she loved anyone out here it would be Arnie Griffin. And she's not sleeping with him either."

"A pity it seems to me, Bishop," Albert said, "though I suppose you'd disagree. Nella thinks that they'll marry once Gerry dies, which by the looks of him should be pretty soon."

"Are opportunities for development limited out here now?"

"You wouldn't think so if you saw the stuff going up all around. But I wouldn't put a penny of anything I have into any of the junk they're building. All right, the housing market has improved since that asshole Bush was Presi-

dent, though poor Bill Clinton won't get any credit for it.
If a young guy wants to take a risk, all right put up a high
quality subdivision near Oak Brook. But it takes more than
low interest rates to make a boom and the Fed isn't going
to let the rates stay low for long."

"A reasonable position."

"If there's any money to be made in this part of the
world, it would be in Woodbridge itself."

"You shouldn't even be thinking of that, Al," his wife
said bluntly. "You don't need another project at this stage
of your life."

"Yeah, I know. I've talked to Arnie about it and he's
interested too. Thinks it would be a lot safer than the stuff
he does down at the Merc. It would take a hell of a lot of
money, though."

"You know what Will Rogers said," Nella warned him.
"All horse players die broke."

It was actually Damon Runyon, but I saw no need to
correct her.

"I know, I know . . . but I'd better tell you about it,
Bishop Blackie. It's going to affect the Catholic Church
out here in a big way. There's going to be a big change out
here in Woodbridge and it will be the result of religion and
race and education."

His eyes glowed with a love of adventure and risk and
the expectation of a sure thing. His face narrowed into a
shrewd, indeed ruthless, grin—a cat ready to pounce on
the proverbial canary.

"Fascinating!"

"Most people don't notice what's happening out here.
The district school board over north of here decided that
ten percent minority students weren't enough for the Hillside
High School. So they changed the boundaries and kicked

the proportion up to thirty percent. Everything I've ever read says that once you go over twenty percent, you're going to have white flight. Well, the goo-goos on the school board say that won't be true out here. It's seventy-five percent now and the school district is finished. People with high school age kids are moving out. You know who's moving in?"

"I'd guess Catholics."

"I see why Cronin made you a bishop. Sure, Catholics. They have other schools to go to. First people move out and the real estate market goes down. Then Catholics see they can get a nice home in a great place at a bargain price. So they move in. Somebody who buys the homes at basement prices is going to make a lot of money as the market goes up to almost where it was and maybe even higher. He's doing the neighborhood and the Church a favor."

"Arguably."

"Church has to be willing to put up new grammar schools and expand or even build a new high school. I told that to the late Monsignor and he told me that there'd be no school construction in Woodbridge while he was pastor. It would not be keeping faith with the community."

"The same phenomenon would occur in Woodbridge?"

Nella, who had disappeared silently, reappeared with a teapot and cups.

"Irish breakfast tea," she announced in a stage whisper.

"You bet your life it would!" Her husband continued to talk. "And will! Within the next two years, the Butternut Township school board will fiddle with the boundaries and Butternut North will reach what the guys who study these things call the tipping point. There'll be too many kids for the Academy to cope with and people will begin to move to Hinsdale and Lake Forest. This smart young priest sees it coming, he'll build. He's already planning an addition to the grammar school. If he wants to, he'll have the money to build a high school. When our kids were that age, they rode the train down to Ignatius. Now some of them go to Fenwick which has turned coed, but neither school will have enough room for all the Catholics who are going to move out here."

"What would you say if I told you there was ten million dollars missing from the parish accounts of Saints Peter and Paul Parish?"

"Ten million!"

He rubbed his hand across his face.

"At a conservative estimate."

"Where are they?"

"That's the question."

"If I had to guess, the money would have gone through Woodbridge Bank. . . . Did McInerny know about it?"

"Debatable. He sent nothing down to our bank at the Chancery Office. He seems to have commingled his funds with parish funds. What would seem to have been a large sum was turned over to Father Finnegan before the Monsignor died. In fact a few simple calculations demonstrate that it was only a small part of the money."

"A lot of people could kill for that kind of money," he murmured softly. "So maybe the Monsignor was killed."

"How horrible!" Nella whispered.

"So the question is where the funds might be now," Al Fasio said.

"If anyplace."

"Right. If anyplace. . . . You going after Reed's records?"

"If we have to."

"He'd be involved naturally. And Doc Curtin for sure. Not a chance of Arnie being in on it."

"Lynn wouldn't do a thing like that," Nella insisted. "I absolutely refuse to believe she would."

"I agree." Al Fasio nodded his head. "She wouldn't knowingly do anything wrong. She's smart and does a fine job at that art center she runs. But I don't think she has any business sense."

"Except in protecting the money her father-in-law left her."

"That's true," he admitted.

"She'd never steal anything from the Church," Nella argued. "Never!"

Neither of the Fasios had found it necessary to deny that they were involved in the use and possible misuse of Church funds. Presumably they thought that it was evident that if you owned a gold mine like the Butternut Mall, you wouldn't have to steal anything. It did not follow that no money had been lent to them by the Woodbridge Bank out of the McInerny funds.

What if you needed money to buy up a quarter of the homes in Woodbridge?

"Are you going to exhume his body?"

"Perhaps."

"Doc Curtin must be scared shitless. Watch him, Bishop, he goes crazy when he thinks he's in danger. Those who threaten him become rhinos charging him."

"So I would assume. . . . How did you become involved with the group around the Monsignor."

"Bunch of weirdos, right?"

"Arguably."

"When we moved out here from the West Side we weren't exactly welcome . . ."

"Too Italian," his wife interrupted, her eyes blazing. "And we were supposed to be connected. Same old lousy stereotype. We were turned down by the club and Al is a better golfer than any of them. Won the cup last year."

"I was lucky. . . . Well, anyway, the Pastor seemed to court us. We were flattered because in our own parish, the Pastor wouldn't talk to us because of the rumors about the outfit. . . ."

"Shanty Irish bigot!" Nella snapped.

"Nella," he said mildly, "we don't want to offend the Bishop."

"I know the type all too well!" I said.

"I suppose he took the initiative because Lynn asked him. She and Nella had become great friends playing tennis."

"She still beats me most of the time. . . . Besides, the Monsignor liked to stare at my boobs."

"Which only proves that he was a normal human male . . ." her husband said gently. "So we kind of drifted into that crowd."

"Into the center of it because Lynn and I were friends. She's such a fine woman, Bishop. Not just beautiful, though she surely is that. Men have a hard time keeping their hands off her. Women stare at her in the shower room. Pretty, pretty boobs. Best I've ever seen. My husband will tell you that I'm the farthest thing from a lesbian that a woman could be. Yet I look forward to staring at her. She's like an expensive work of art. She knows it but she ignores it all. Whatever they tell you, she doesn't fool around."

"Have you spoken to her yet, Bishop?" Albert asked.

"No, but I will soon. She is clearly the key to the various mysteries."

"I'm not as enthused as is my wife, though I agree that there isn't a man in Woodbridge who can resist fantasizing about her. But I agree with Nella that she's a fine woman.

I'm not sure, however, what she might do if the Monsignor or Gerry or Arnie were in trouble. She's so fiercely loyal, you'd almost think she was Neapolitan."

"Or Irish." Nella laughed.

Had she not gunned down six Koreans to protect wounded Marines who were in her charge?

"We began to realize just how weird it all was," Al Fasio said carefully, "only when we got to know the new priest. Nella and I realized that the letters we wrote about him were pretty dumb and that the whole thing with Monsignor was kind of sick."

"He was a powerful and appealing man, Bishop," Nella said. "He controlled you by mixing charm and meanness."

"Like Mike Ditka," Al agreed.

"Who organized the letter writing?"

They looked at one another, puzzled for a moment.

"Gerry, I think," Albert said finally.

"I know that he and Lynn disagreed because she sent her own letter," Nella said. "Do you think we ought to write letters of retraction?"

"That would be very helpful, especially if you copy the letter to Joseph Ratzinger as you did your first letter."

"We'll do it this morning," Nella said, with the firm tone that indicated that she had made up her mind and therefore her husband had too.

"Can I make a suggestion, Bishop?" Albert said cautiously.

"Of course."

"Be careful. If all you say is true, you're contending with dangerous and possibly demented men. And women. If I were in your position, I'd have someone watching my back. If they've already killed one priest, they wouldn't hesitate to kill another."

This time I didn't say "arguably."

Rather I replied, "That sounds like very good advice."

"Hey," he said, abruptly changing the subject, "if you like Thirty-One Flavors, take this book of gift certificates. They send one to me every month. In addition to the rent. They're a constant temptation to me."

How could I have refused his generosity?

As I was leaving, with appropriate thanks for the Irish breakfast tea (of which I have often said that it is useful for cleaning spark plugs), I asked one more question.

"What do people think of Father O'Keefe?"

They both smiled.

"Everyone likes him, both the Monsignor's friends and the new priest's friends," Nella replied. "He's a pure delight."

"He kept a lot of people in the parish who otherwise would have left because they didn't like Monsignor," her husband added.

"When the Monsignor began to fail and the Cardinal tried again to remove him, Father was afraid that the new priest would get rid of him. We were all pleased that Father Finnegan decided to keep him. Both of us go to his lectures. Will you be there tonight?"

"Naturally. . . . How would you describe his relationship with the Monsignor?"

Again they glanced at one another.

"Ambivalent," Al said finally.

"Sometimes they seemed like buddies. Other times they barely spoke to one another. Monsignor never invited him in when his group of friends were at the rectory."

Driving back to Saints Peter and Paul Rectory, I thought about the Fasios. They were as sane and as reasonable as the Curtins were wild and erratic. Yet they were tough and smart people who had climbed together up the ladder from a step above poverty to affluence. Before Austin, they probably lived on Taylor Street. Now they lived in Woodbridge and had sent their children to college. Despite initial resistance they were now accepted members of the Woodbridge community. Despite their charm and their obvious affection for one another, they could be ruthless if the world they had created for themselves seemed to be threatened. Or if they decided to take one more leap on the ladder—from affluence to great wealth.

As I was pulling up to the rectory, my car phone beeped. The young priest I had left in charge at the Cathedral reported that there had been the death of a long-time parishioner. I should come in for the wake, say the funeral Mass the next day, and go to the cemetery.

Glancing at my watch I told him to take the wake service that night and I would show up at the funeral home before the Mass tomorrow.

I suddenly realized how much I missed my own parish and my own people.

I might be able to make an appointment to speak with La Bella Evelina this afternoon. Otherwise I would have to try for Thursday morning, since I did not want to face such a fabled woman after a long car ride from a cemetery in Evanston.

I told Peter Finnegan that I would drive back to the Cathedral after Joe O'Keefe's lecture and come back tomorrow afternoon.

Actually I meant after my expedition with Jennifer and Mark.

"Any conclusions so far, Blackie," he asked nervously.

I hesitated.

"In some sense I find myself more confused than when I came out here on Sunday, Peter Finnegan. But I expect the pieces will fit together before the week is out."

"The haunting is getting to the staff. Some of them are

saying that as much as they like the place they may have
to quit."

"Give me to next Sunday."

Little did I realize how explosive the end of the week
would be.

CHAPTER 11

"MAY I SPEAK to Ms. Reed?"

"This is Lynn Reed."

I had dialed the home phone of Ms. Reed. A light, musical feminine voice on an answering machine instructed me to try the Woodbridge Gallery and gave me the number.

So, always one to follow suggestions, I had dialed the number of the gallery.

"This is Father Ryan calling, Ms. Reed."

"Oh, yes, Bishop, I was expecting to hear from you."

Were you now?

"I wonder if I could make an appointment to talk with you."

Why was I feeling diffident? After all I was a bishop, was I not, the legate of a Cardinal Prince of the Holy Roman Church? Was I permitting this by all accounts remarkable woman to bemuse me even before I met her?

"I'd be delighted to talk with you, Bishop Ryan."

"This afternoon?"

"My daughter is visiting me from far away Evanston this afternoon and tomorrow. Would Thursday be convenient for you?"

"Surely."

"Ten o'clock? At my house on Maple Street. We are less likely to be disturbed than here at the gallery."

"Of course."

"I'll be looking forward to it, Bishop Ryan."

"As will I," I admitted.

Why were my hands sweating when I hung up? Can a voice on the phone convey that much intensity? Or had the aura that had already been spun around the person affected my reaction?

I would have to be very careful. She was a primary suspect because she was the key person in the group that had formed itself around Charles P. McInerny. My hopes of resolving the puzzle rested to a considerable extent on what I could learn from her.

I then ambled over to the convent, which now housed two nuns and a pre-school facility. Sister Mary Rita McGee was in her office in the school, I was told. So I doubled back to the school where construction work involving the heating and ventilation system had created a mess of ducts and pipes that would be unacceptable in most Catholic schools I knew.

Sister greeted me politely but not with an overabundance of respect. Her office was hot enough to serve as an antechamber of purgatory in the old conception of that place.

"You must excuse the mess, Bishop," she said. "The new Pastor is installing air-conditioning so the school can be used in the summer."

Sister was wearing lay garb, naturally. An ill-fitting, sacklike summer dress. She was in her middle fifties, medium in height, and stern in expression. Her thin face seemed drawn in a permanent frown of disapproval. Yet Peter Finnegan had assured me that she was a gifted educator and an effective school administrator. She was the only person held over from the previous administration. Moreover she had renewed her contract for only two years so that she could make up her mind at the end of the coming school year whether she would stay at Saints Peter and Paul. She was what you would call, with considerable understatement, a "no-nonsense" person.

"You don't approve of air-conditioning in the school?"

"It will certainly make life in the school more comfortable. But ought not the money be better used for schools in the inner city where they need to have school in the summer to keep kids away from gangs?"

I might have remarked that the record of schools in struggling against gangs provided little grounds for hope that the schools had much of a chance.

"Ah."

"The new priest is spending money like a child who has just received his allowance."

"There is much work which must be done to counter the neglect of the last twenty-five years."

"I would hardly deny that, Bishop," she said tersely. "The new priest is a considerable improvement over his predecessor and not bad as pastors go. Nonetheless I find his energy excessive. It often seems to me unfocused, like that of President Clinton."

Thus was the case of Peter Finnegan settled definitely.

"Yet you elected to stay here?"

"Only to put the school back on the right track before I leave. It is proving a very difficult task. The children are generally spoiled by their rich parents, the parents in their turn make excessive demands on my staff who are not paid a living wage despite the affluence of this community, and the parish suffers from a quarter century of administration that was both capricious and indifferent."

She tapped a ballpoint pen on her desk as she talked and spoke in a flat monotone that hinted at repressed—and mostly angry—emotions.

"That sounds somewhat less harsh than other descriptions, Sister."

"I try to be careful in my use of words, Bishop. The late Monsignor McInerny could be charming and generous. He redecorated the convent for us a number of years ago. The improvement was long overdue. But the results were far too elaborate for women dedicated to evangelical poverty. Moreover, although there were only four of us at the time, he redecorated all twenty rooms. You may have noticed that the new Pastor has turned most of those rooms into a preschool for two-income families."

I was not about to get into an argument about two-income families.

"Monsignor was a difficult man to work with?"

She sighed loudly. "In all candor, Bishop, the best a principal in a Catholic school can hope for is a pastor who will leave her or him free to do the job. Monsignor's indifference was a blessing. Unfortunately he was not indifferent all the time. He would impose inappropriate punishments on the children for real or imagined offenses and appear unannounced to deliver lectures on sexual behavior which were as opaque as they were angry."

"I see. . . . How do you explain his, ah, pastoral style?"

"He was insane," she said tersely. "Quite mad. Untreated manic depressive syndrome, probably inherited. The insanity was doubtless aggravated by a rigid family life and by the failure of his ecclesiastical career. Monsignor wanted unconditional love, yet was afraid to risk the vulnerability of being open to human affection."

Sister had doubtless taken summer courses in psychology, perhaps even had a degree in educational psychology. Hence her diagnoses would always be confident if unnuanced: her personality did not dispose her to nuance.

Nonetheless, she probably was accurate enough in her evaluation of the late Pastor.

"Cronin should have replaced him long ago," she continued.

"It was not for want of trying, Sister. Rome kept overruling him."

"Cardinals can get whatever they want."

"Would that they could."

"He was able to select you to be auxiliary bishop, was he not?"

Her lips tightened, hinting perhaps that Milord Cronin had been ill-advised in the matter.

"Only by not putting me on his *terna*, Sister. The Vatican imposed me on the People of God only because they thought he did not want me."

"Is that true?"

"Absolutely."

Her lips moved in what might be a smile. "Clever of him."

"You know why I'm here, Sister?"

"Of course. You are supposed to get rid of this ghost which is haunting us. I hope you can do it soon. The ghost will disrupt the school year if he is not banished by September."

"I think he will be gone long before then."

"I would have thought Cronin would have sent an exorcist instead of an auxiliary bishop."

"My visit is an exploration. Should an exorcist be needed, we will send him."

If we can find one.

"Do you believe that we are truly haunted, Bishop?"

"Candidly, Sister, I doubt it. I think there's a perfectly natural explanation for the phenomena. When we solve the puzzle of the Monsignor's death the phenomena will stop. . . . What is your opinion about his death, Sister?"

She hesitated, for the first time in our conversation.

"It is not required that I have an opinion, Bishop. Nonetheless, I accepted at first the report that he had died of a cerebral hemorrhage. On reflection I'm not so sure. He came to see me the day before he died to ask about school funding. I showed him our books. Since there was never a parish subsidy—which I would rather call an investment—in the school, we financed ourselves with tuition, special parental contributions, and the usual raffles and festivals. On occasion he would give the teachers a Christmas bonus, but one would never know until Christmas Eve whether he would on any given year. You can imagine what that did to teacher morale. In any event, he found the books in order. He asked whether anyone had tried to obtain funds from the school. I assured him that they had not. I would add that while he was clearly upset, he did not seem in particularly poor health."

So. A new datum and one by no means unimportant.

"He seemed to suspect someone was taking parish funds?"

"That was my conclusion. On reflection after his funeral I thought that this might be grounds for murder. I presume that he routinely sent excess funds to the Chancery?"

"No, Sister. He did not."

"Oh, my." She was ever so faintly flustered. "That would mean a rather large sum of money, wouldn't it?"

"Very large, Sister."

"If I were in your position, Bishop, I would suspect the woman. She had access to everything. The sisters often referred to her as the associate pastor."

"The woman, Sister?"

"Ms. Reed of course. She had the Monsignor wrapped

around her little finger. Virtually every other man in the
parish as well. Men make fools out of themselves over
beautiful women, especially when there is an aura of the
mysterious and sinister about them."

"Indeed."

Sister was warming to one of her favorite subjects.

"I taught her youngest child when I was here the first
time. He was a nice enough boy and has grown into a
splendid young man. Despite her. She was a smothering
mother, Bishop. She made a nuisance out of herself in
worrying about the boy. She was always pleasant of
course. Oh, so sweet. She never mentioned her influence
with the Pastor, but there was never any doubt about it. I
was forced to spend time with her, lest there be a serious
problem should she complain to him. I'm sure the money
she spent on her physical appearance and clothes would
have paid the salaries of several of our teachers. She is the
vainest woman I have ever known."

"Ah."

"Monsignor had his emotional problems to begin with.
She certainly made them worse. He was seeking uncon-
ditioned love, as I have said, from a mother substitute. She
provided the illusion of such love, though the strings she
attached made him more uncertain of his own worth rather
than less. Moreover, as I have said, she had access to
everything, including, I have no doubt, parish funds."

"You're not suggesting they were lovers, are you,
Sister?"

"She is a thoroughly amoral woman, Bishop. If money
or power was involved, she would stop at nothing."

"A bit of a hooker?"

"Precisely, Bishop. Though sex worker is the politically
correct word."

She smiled again.

"However," she continued, "she does not deserve the sympathy that word implies. The usual sex worker plies her trade because she has no other way of surviving. That woman engages in her seductions because she likes the game."

"The other sisters who were here with you at that time agreed?"

"Of course . . . she's the key to the puzzle, Bishop. There's no doubt in my mind about that."

"Arguably."

It was a very different picture of La Bella Evelina than that provided by Nella Fasio.

"If she had left Monsignor alone, he might have been a much better man. He needed love, as we all do. He needed it more than others. He would have been much happier and I think more reasonable if he had permitted the people of the parish to love him, which they are always ready to do if they are given half a chance."

"An astonishing truth, Sister, but the truth nonetheless."

"The only point in celibacy, if you ask me."

"One of them at any rate."

We shook hands, I wished her success in the coming school year and asserted that women like her not only kept the schools going but had been and still were the best hope of the American Church. She smiled in agreement and I left. I stumbled only twice as I walked down the corridor filled with air-conditioning ducts. However, I narrowly escaped serious injury only the second time.

I find it very hard to ponder a puzzle and watch where I'm going at the same time.

Sister's attitude at the end of our conversation strongly implied that like all other stupid men (and all men were by definition stupid) I would fall victim to the deadly charms of Ms. Reed. I rather doubted this, but I told myself that I must be wary.

Jolly Cholly was worried about parish funds just before his death. If he was talking about such things, he may have alerted those who had reason to wish him out of the way.

Nor should I dismiss the Sister's image of Ms. Reed out of hand. She did have some sort of relationship with the Monsignor that probably did involve access to if not control of parish funds. She signed some of his checks, did she not? Did she use sex to maintain her control of him?

That was not the way to phrase the question. Sex and its appeal is always present in the relationship between a man and a woman, especially if the woman is attractive. The late Monsignor McInerny certainly did need tenderness in his life. Doubtless Ms. Reed provided tenderness. Whether that would involve sexual intercourse was another matter. Sister McGee was the first one to suggest that they might have slept together. It seemed to me likely that the two of them were more intimate with each other than my other interviewees had suspected. I was one of the only ones who knew that their friendship antedated Monsignor's appointment to Saints Peter and Paul and perhaps even his return from Korea.

Why had no one checked the baptismal record of her husband?

Or had they?

Back in the rectory with a couple of hours before supper, I continued my explorations of the locked room puzzle. I was able to confirm my suspicions about that aspect of the larger puzzle with surprising ease. However, that discovery provided no solution, only some hunches, to the larger mystery of who used the locked room dynamic to escape from the murder of Monsignor Charles P. McInerny, P.A.

I had to admit that some of the clues pointed directly at Lynn Reed.

At supper I remarked over the carrot salad, with apparent innocence, that I had spoken with Sister McGee that afternoon. Everyone laughed.

"She's a tough one," Peter Finnegan said. "Very strong opinions and a quick hater. But she's a wonderful principal. I'm glad I was able to talk her into staying for two more years. We had to have some continuity in the school. At the end of next year she'll leave, angry at me and everyone else no doubt, and I won't miss her. But the whole parish will be grateful for what she's done."

"Often in error and never in doubt," Joe O'Keefe said with his usual chuckle. "She never liked me, not from day one. She thought I was a bad influence."

"And as the very young priest," Tom Wozniak added, "I don't exist. She does not want me in her school disturbing good order in the classroom."

"I would assume that she does not approve of the carryings-on at the basketball courts and on the softball field."

Again there was laughter.

"You'd better believe it, Blackie," Peter Finnegan said. "She thinks the young women are shameless teases. Which I suppose they are, in a way. But it's an innocent and harmless tease. Boys will have lustful thoughts about them no matter how they dress."

"I believe," Father D'Souza observed in his clipped Oxford accent, "that despite her feminist principles, Sister has a negative breast fixation. She thinks it a mistake for women to have breasts and even more of a mistake for them not to pretend they don't have them. Such an attitude exists among many primitive tribes, even those who wear few clothes, though I think it is rare among the Irish."

His perfect white teeth glinted in a quick smile as he glanced around the table at the rest of us.

"That is an accurate observation, I believe," I replied. "And evidence that despite their many problems there are some signs of mental health among the Irish."

Much laughter.

"She also told me that the late Pastor was deeply concerned about the misuse of parish funds shortly before his death. She asserts that he came to her with a request to inspect the school financial records. Though he no longer had the right to do that and apparently never did it before, she complied with his request."

Dead silence.

"I wouldn't think of questioning her about how she spends the money," Peter said slowly. "I suppose I should check every once in a while for the record."

"Did Monsignor give any hint at that time to either you, or you, Joe, of such a concern."

"I can't recall . . ." Peter began. "Well, I think he asked me how much the improvements were costing and I showed him the books. No harm in humoring him, I thought. He seemed very interested and remarked how much prices had gone up since the old days. He also wondered about the money in the account he had given me. I told him again how much it was and he grunted. I wouldn't say he seemed upset or anything like that, but it was the only time he showed any interest in money. What about you, Joe?"

Father O'Keefe frowned thoughtfully.

"I can recall him being very upset about the 'flow of money,' as he called it sometime after Peter came here. He was muttering about stanching the flow of blood. But he wasn't very coherent. I thought he was talking about all the repair work and redecorating and the softball field and all the expenses Peter was incurring. I said that the Cardinal had approved them."

"And he said?"

"I'm trying to remember, Blackie. I think he said that the Cardinal had not approved of these expenses. But he didn't say what they were."

"Do you think he found out someone was on the take?" Tom asked innocently.

"Arguably he thought he did."

"You can have an accountant look at all the books," Peter protested.

"Don't be defensive, Peter Finnegan," I said. "I'm sure he didn't have you in mind."

"Do you think that is why he was killed, Blackie? It seems like more than a coincidence that he would be killed at that very time."

"Or it might only have been a coincidence," I said soothingly. "We have no evidence yet that it was any more than that."

The rest of the dinner conversation was subdued and somber.

The shade, however, celebrated my suspicions by ringing the peal bells for twenty minutes. I packed my priest suit as neatly as I could, donned my White Sox jacket, sport shirt, and gray slacks, left the duffel bag in my tower suite, and put the suit in the trunk of the T-bird, having assured Jennifer that I'd take her and Mark for their promised ride after Father Joe's lecture.

The humidity was thick, the sky was darkening, the smell of rain was in the air. That would make for a slippery ride on the Congress Expressway (as we Democrats still call the Eisenhower) later on in the evening.

Joe's talk on Red Warren was dazzling. He titled it "Poet in Search of God," and in language that would have been clear to any high school kid (and many of them were there, including the other two porter persons and their knights) traced Warren's search through the years of his long life, a search that at the end had seemed more confident, if still uncertain.

The audience, perhaps two hundred people, applauded him enthusiastically. The teens, clutching notebooks, swarmed up afterward, doubtless seeking books—short books—for their term papers.

"Guy's really got it, doesn't he?" Peter Finnegan whispered to me.

"Indeed."

"The Church gave him a bad deal."

"A wise shrink once said to me that the first signs of maturity in a troubled priest is when he is willing to admit that the Church is only the occasion of his problems and that the roots lie in his family life."

"Well, the Church didn't help him much."

"It did what it could by its own lights."

Peter thought about that for a while and then nodded in silent agreement.

I did not learn much from Jennifer and Mark that I had not already learned from their age peers. Mark did say that his mother, who liked Lynn Reed a "real lot," was convinced that there was some deep mystery in the woman's past, a mystery that made her aloof and reserved sometimes.

Yeah, she killed six Koreans when she was nineteen and had a baby conceived out of wedlock when she had just turned twenty.

"And sometimes so very sad," Jennifer added. "Like she's about ready to cry and never does."

I displayed my Thirty-One Flavors gift book and duly impressed my young friends. It was raining when we left the ice cream store, so they helped me put the top on the convertible, a task at which I would have had little hope for success. I dropped them off at Jennifer's house, greeted her parents, and then, with considerable relief despite the fierce rain and crackling lightning, drove under the viaduct and out of Woodbridge and back to Chicago.

CHAPTER 12

THE CARDINAL WAS waiting for me in my study, sitting on my computer chair and leafing through the pages of my work on *Finnegans Wake*.

When he has nothing else to do (except as in this case of waiting for my return), he will pick up any reading material at hand and absorb it.

"Interesting stuff, Blackwood." He put the paper aside. "This guy was a genius all right, and a Catholic one at that, maybe despite himself."

"Arguably," I agreed, as I poured myself my allotted ration of Baileys Irish Cream—having forsaken a drink before supper because I would be driving later in the evening.

"Why no apostrophe in the title?"

"Because the first word in the title is the vocative case, a typical Joycean play on words. He is calling all Finnegans to awake, lauding the hotel at which his wife Nora worked, and honoring the old street song of the same title. Perhaps also he assumes that Finnegan is everyone, and is calling on all of us to wake from our discouragement and guilt."

"I hope young Peter Finnegan is bothered by neither phenomenon."

"Not in my observation."

I discarded my wet White Sox jacket, slumped into my official easy chair, put my feet on my appointed ottoman, and began to sip the Baileys, which would surely cure me of any lurking elements that had found their way through the leaky roof of the T-bird.

"What's going on out there?"

I told him in full detail, omitting only my theory (as yet untested) as to the origins of the phenomena and my discovery of the locked room secret—that would have to wait till the grand denouement.

"Hmm," he said thoughtfully.

He was dressed informally, that is to say in a collarless white shirt with a collar button attached and black trousers.

"It is a most unpleasant affair."

"I draw one conclusion at any rate, Blackwood. You ought not to interview this woman." He picked up the printout from *The Bridge* I had given him. "She's much too dangerous."

He replaced the picture on my desk. I knew the game we were playing, but I saw no harm in playing along.

"Who then should interview her?"

"Why the Cardinal Archbishop, naturally!"

We both laughed. No way would he interview her.

"Let us wait till the occasion when she formally hands over the ten million dollars to the Catholic Bishop of Chicago, a corporation sole."

"You think she has the money?"

"Almost certainly. Or knows where it is."

He looked at the picture again. "I guess like you, I go for happy endings, Blackwood. I hope she's innocent."

"Innocence is a complex characteristic. And finally we make our own happy endings. . . . Nonetheless I too hope that all ends well for her. There is too much vitality in that picture and too much courage in the reason why she won that piece of blue and white ribbon to think that somehow it has been snuffed out."

"What do you make of the other lead character in this little morality play? Give me some of that Baileys. It really doesn't count as a drink."

I complied as instructed.

"Irish milk shake costs have gone up?"

I added another few drops.

"That's better."

"As to the late parish priest of Woodbridge, I confess he becomes more obscure rather than less. A deeply troubled and erratic man but not without certain generous instincts or charisma."

"I suppose the Ryan family did not force you to become a priest?"

"As the Prophet has written, gimme a break! When I announced my intention they thought it was a wonderful idea. But my late parents thought everything one of their children did was a wonderful idea. They disliked the Boston Irish with an intense passion. Yet when the good Mary Kate succeeded in capturing Dr. Joseph Murphy, you would have thought it was the greatest thing that ever happened in the family. Similarly they hated journalists, and not without reason. Yet when the virtuous Eileen married Red Kane they bragged of his Pulitzer Prize. Either way the possible future priest wins."

"Yet even in your days there were men in the seminary whose vocation was their parents and not their own, were there not?"

"To my astonishment. I would have thought that would have ended decades ago. Most of them have since left the priesthood of course. I continue to be baffled by the psychology of both parents and sons."

"There were many in my day too. Some of them, oddly enough, turned out to be excellent and happy priests."

"The Holy Spirit has ways of Her own."

"I spent some time during the years I've been fighting with Jolly Cholly trying to figure him out. His father was a clerk for the Pullman company. They lived with all seven of their children in an apartment in Rogers Park. St. Jerome's. They never owned a car. Cholly, who was the oldest, was destined to be a priest from the day he was conceived. He was too busy helping with the household chores and then working when he was growing up to have any serious friendships or participate in any sports. When he was at the high school seminary he was something of an unnoticed loner."

"Fascinating."

"Then at the major seminary he was caught up in the Jesuit star system. You know how it works. In the old days, the Jebs used to select someone in the novitiate who, in their view, had extraordinary if unrecognizable abilities. They promoted him as a spectacular find and it became an obligation of loyalty to the Society that everyone sing his praises."

"I'm not unfamiliar with the practice."

"Some of their stars really turned out to be brilliant. Others were duds, but you could never get the Jebs to admit it even to themselves. Hell, they still celebrate some of the guys who have left the priesthood."

"Such as the excellent Paul Featherweight."

"Well, in the generation before mine, they chose Cholly to be a star. Promoted him so much that everyone, including the rector, believed him to be someone special. From being in the middle of the class at Quigley, he rose to the top at Mundelein and stayed there. Even in his own class there was a lot of pride in his success, though some of the guys, not without envy I suppose, said it was all fraud and the grades the Jebs gave him were faked."

"Perhaps not intentionally."

"Sure. They believed in their own brilliance at selecting stars. So after ordination he was shipped to Catholic U with Joe O'Keefe who was an authentic genius and who had apparently resigned himself to being number two."

"Why no parish experience?"

"The Cardinal then thought he needed another canonist in a hurry; and Rome was still behind enemy lines. You can imagine what happened at C.U.?"

"The late Monsignor was in the mediocre middle of his class and Joe was hailed as the genius of the two."

"It was a terrible blow to Cholly. His success and fame at Mundelein had brought out the charm and what we now call charisma. The Cardinal recalled him after a year and put him in the Marriage Tribunal. He hated it so much that he joined the Navy Reserves for weekend duty, an activity he seemed to enjoy."

"Anything beats the Matrimonial Tribunal."

"So he ended up in Korea where he apparently met this lovely young woman, vulnerable after the trauma of the guerrilla raid. Probably fell in love with her. It would be easy enough to do."

"Indeed it would."

"The point in all this is that Cholly wasn't happy being a priest, not ever. If you like being a priest and they stick you in a tribunal, you can always throw yourself in weekend parish work. You don't have to choose the Marines."

"Which were as rigid as his family life."

"Make him twenty years younger and he probably leaves the priesthood. If he met young Evie here in

Vietnam, he would have married her and they would have lived happily ever after."

"I doubt that."

"I doubt it too. But you see my point. He realized at some level of his soul that he wasn't cut out for the priesthood. But in those days you couldn't leave. He probably wouldn't have left anyway, come to think of it. It would have killed his mother who was still alive then. Probably didn't think about it even. By the time the mother was dead and it was easy to leave he couldn't admit his mistake."

"Sublimate sex into a power urge," I said. "Besides the woman was already married. And the Archdiocese, unaware of the situation, sends him to the parish in which she lives. I'm not sure what the scenario is after that. Though by now he's probably too locked up inside his fears and his pain to think that they would sleep together."

I helped myself to another tumbler of Baileys, arguing that in the rush to avoid the storm I had failed in my duty to Thirty-One Flavors.

"You never can tell, Blackie. But one way or another, it means a quarter-century of agony and frustration."

I filled the Waterford old-fashioned tumbler to the top. It is inappropriate, I have always felt, to put Baileys in a cordial glass.

"With alternatives always present and available, yet unavailable," I said.

"A wasted life, he must have often felt, though I doubt he could say that to himself."

"A sad and tragic life with only one light of joy in it."

"Yes, Blackwood, La Bella Evelina."

"Arguably."

We were silent for several moments, the Cardinal

staring balefully at his empty goblet and I no longer feeling any thirst for mine.

"Terrible," the Cardinal broke the silence. "It didn't have to go that way."

"But it did."

"Yes, Blackwood, it did."

Another long pause.

"Blackwood, do me a big favor."

"I'll try."

"I don't care what you finally uncover out there. Come back and tell me that she redeemed him."

And I'm supposed to be a romantic!

He was not so disconsolate that he did not say when he left my study, "See to it, Blackwood!"

CHAPTER 13

I PUSHED THE doorbell of the Reed house on Maple Street very gently. The house, American Federal rather than Victorian, white with crimson trim, was, as best as I could calculate, behind the Curtin safari station.

The rain had swept away the heat and the humidity and blessed us with a dry and pleasant Chicago August day, an excellent day on which to meet a lovely woman—or to search for one's winter coat that one will need soon.

"Come in, Bishop Ryan." Lynn skillfully kissed my ring. "This is my daughter Evie, Dr. Evelyn Reed Culhane. She has been visiting me as I think I told you, visiting me while her husband and daughters make their annual pilgrimage to his parents' summer home in Vermont. Evie, His Excellency Bishop John Blackwood Ryan."

She was still the j.g. from Korea. Of course she was older and there was a network of fine lines on her face and neck and her short, deftly coiffed hair was a discreet mix of gray and black, but the plain oatmeal (as I'm told the color is called) summer tank dress she was wearing (skirt above the knees) would have fit the Navy nurse of so many summers ago with only a few adjustments. Her body, which demanded immediate attention, was voluptuous but not quite full-figured, a compact, neatly packaged, and disciplined womanly form that was both aesthetically pleasing and erotically desirable.

You wanted to admire her all day long.

More erotic than her ingeniously carved body, however, were her bright smile and her glowing gray eyes, a smile and eyes that had not changed since the picture in *The Bridge*. A tragedian Lynn Reed certainly was not. She was not tall; rather she was several inches shorter than her rangy, handsome daughter. Yet she dominated the room with intense vitality and radiant sexuality. Every move of her delightful body, every change of expression on her appealing face, signaled sexual sophistication and self-confidence. Lynn Reed knew who she was and that part of who she was, surely not the most important part, was sexual prize. She did not flaunt it, but neither did she disdain it.

A very dangerous woman indeed.

The daughter, wearing the jeans and T-shirt that are required uniforms for academics (Her T-shirt was an outrageous purple affair that blasphemously proclaimed, "Go Wildcats, Beat Irish!"), shook hands instead of kissing my ring. "Hi, Bishop. I insisted to Mom that I stay here till you arrived. I'm leaving right away to pick up my husband at O'Hare. These visits to Vermont are always traumatic for the poor dear man. I wanted to meet you and tell you how much I enjoyed your book on Joyce."

"Really?" I stammered.

The unflappable Blackie Ryan was flapped, even flustered. Bad beginning.

"I use it in my graduate seminar on Irish literature. It's really about all twentieth-century Irish writers, isn't it? I thought you were particularly good on Seamus Heany. Do you think he's going to win the Nobel Prize? What are you working on now, Bishop?"

It's a question we academics always ask one another, even if the truth is that we hardly work at all.

"The Tenebrae liturgy in *Finnegans Wake*," I managed to say.

"How exciting! Working off Beryl Scholssman's book?"

"A fascinating study, pioneer I might say, and you, Dr. Culhane, what are you working on?"

"Early nineteenth-century songs among women in the cotton weaving factories of Ulster."

"Fascinating."

Mother and daughter hugged each other affectionately.

"Now remember, Mom, what I said. Everyone loves you."

"I know, dear," her mother replied in the tone of voice which women of our ethnic group and arguably of our species use when they are listening to but dismissing daughterly advice as something you would expect to hear from a child.

Evie was determined to get in the last word.

"Isn't my older sister totally gorgeous, Bishop?" she asked.

"Undoubtedly."

"Doesn't everyone love her?"

"I have heard no dissent."

"Your mother's a genetic freak," Lynn said, blushing furiously as her daughter left.

Then she turned to me and said, "I'll make tea, Bishop Ryan. Earl Grey be all right? Black of course."

"As midnight on a moonless night."

She sauntered toward the rear of the house, trailing a delicate scent that I could not identify and revealing appealing derriere and legs, the latter encased in nylon, though it was a summer morning. But then a bishop had come to the house had he not?

The room to which I had been led at the front of the house was more drawing room than parlor, but a parlor with a hint of the boudoir about it—the boudoir of a Balzac novel, which was still a great distance psychologically and physically from the bedroom, a place for intimate tête-à-têtes. The colors of the drapes and carpet were varying shades of gray to match her eyes and set off by color-drenched abstract paintings. The antique desk was also gray with red roses as a trim. The furniture, Louis Quatorze unless my memory on such failed me as it often did, was upholstered in yet another shade of gray fabric, soft to the touch and inviting to the weary and perhaps anxious body. Several prohibitively expensive vases were filled with freshly cut roses, perhaps taken from her extensive rose garden, just outside the window.

This was a room in which a woman presided, a strong, vibrant, and arguably imperious woman, but still every cultivated inch a woman.

Well, this morning she wouldn't preside and it wouldn't be a tête-à-tête.

Beyond the garden, partially obscured by trees, was a stockade of narrow wooden poles, an African kraal (not unlike an Irish ring fort). Clearly the Curtin safari station.

The kettle must have been near the boiling point because she was back in a moment. Even her motions as she poured the tea were erotic, lightly and tastefully and perhaps not intentionally so, but still powerfully appealing.

"You must excuse my daughter's ebullience, Bishop. She's naturally an enthusiast. But this morning we just finished an hour of exercise in my little gym downstairs and swimming. Hence the glow and the exuberance."

The mother was also glowing. It was time for me to launch my attack, though I was most reluctant to do so.

"She's a very beautiful woman," I said lightly.

"Thank you." Her mother beamed. "I think so too. . . . You don't use lemon like I do."

I must emphasize that Lynn Keating Reed's manner was anything but flirtatious. It was too matter-of-fact, too gentle even to be considered with that word as a possible predicate. Which made her all the more dangerous.

"She looks very much like her father."

She glanced up from her tea, frowning.

"No, Bishop, I don't think she looks at all like my husband."

"I didn't say your husband, I said her father."

Her lips tightened dangerously.

"I think you know, Bishop, that you are being gratuitously offensive."

"I'd rather say that my words are true and that you and I know that they are true."

"And who do you think her father is?"

Her eyes blazed with fury, her body was tense with rage.

"One glance at her leaves little doubt: Charles McInerny. Evie was conceived during your love affair in Korea. About that interlude I make no judgment, but I do insist that we speak candidly."

She closed her eyes and leaned back against the chair in which she had arrayed herself.

"I was debating whether to tell you . . . now it seems I do not have to decide. Is the resemblance that obvious?"

"To someone who has seen pictures of him as a young man it is indeed obvious."

She opened her eyes. No tears.

"As far as I know, no one in the parish ever noticed the resemblance. Maybe they have and were afraid to mention it. Did anyone suggest it to you?"

"No . . . did he know who she is?"

"I'm sure he did not. I never told him I was pregnant. It would have been too much for him to bear."

"Arguably." I sipped carefully from my tea.

"And I hardly need say that I never told her. Will this have to become public?"

"I very much doubt it."

"Not that Evie is not strong enough to absorb it. Yet I would rather she did not have to."

"I understand."

She leaned forward anxiously, all her elaborate defenses torn away and now more attractive than ever.

"I've led a terrible life, Bishop. I am certain I will go to hell for all eternity."

"You may count on this: you certainly will not go to hell."

She sat up straight. "How can you say that when you don't even know my sins?"

"Because everyone who knows you loves you. Why should God be any different?"

I made a mental reservation about Sister McGee.

"That's a very peculiar kind of theology, Bishop," she said dubiously.

"Very orthodox, however. I presume that you have often in your life held in your arms a neonate and been overwhelmed by that helpless and appealing little creature that you have brought into the world?"

"What woman has not?"

"You deny the possibility of that kind of love to God?"

She closed her eyes, reflecting on that challenge.

One might think she had conned the unflappable Blackie into putting on his priest hat. In fact, we were struggling now for a soul (using for the moment the old term) and that was more important than solving a couple of mysteries. Moreover it seemed highly likely that if I could win an initial victory in that battle, all other matters would fall into place.

"If only I could believe that."

Her normally luminous eyes were drab and dull.

"My dear woman, observe my pectoral cross . . ."

"Made by Catherine Curran, that's one of her sunbursts on the wall over there. And I hung it there months ago. She sells very well in our gallery."

In truth I had not noticed. Forgive me, beloved cousin.

"Indeed."

Her eyes brightened. The woman's vitality was irrepressible. Therein was the deepest secret of her appeal.

"I like her nudes, too. They sell very well. She . . . well, that's irrelevant."

"You declined to pose for her?"

"I said maybe. I'm afraid it would embarrass my husband . . . but I'm sorry, Bishop, I interrupted you."

"I was about to ask you what this cross stands for."

"It's St. Brigid's cross," she answered promptly. "It's a sign that you're a bishop."

"Successor in some fashion to the apostles."

"Of course."

"Then would I kid you about God's love?"

She smiled. "I suppose not."

"So?"

"So I suppose that God will not let me escape his love?"

"B minus. But we're getting there."

She rubbed her hands together watching the movements of her fingers.

"Can I tell you my story, Bishop? From the beginning? I don't know what you will think and I don't know whether it will help you solve the mysteries. But it will be a relief to me to be able to tell it to someone for the first time."

"Please do."

"I grew up," she began with a sigh, "on a farm near Lincoln, Nebraska, during the end of the Great Depression and the war. We were very poor, but my mother and father loved each other very much. I was the youngest of four children. The way I remember it, my brothers and sisters loved me a lot. I guess I was a spoiled little girl. My father was drafted and served in France. We had a great party when he came home.

"I did very well in school. I graduated from the parish school when I was twelve and went right into high school. One night when I was fifteen, there was a terrible thunderstorm, even tornadoes a few miles south of us. Lightning hit our house. I don't remember it very clearly. Just a terrible noise and an explosion of light and a horrible smell."

She stopped, utterly motionless for a moment.

"All the others were killed. I wasn't even hurt. I don't think I've ever recovered."

What does someone say to that?

Nothing. He continues to listen.

"I went to live with my aunt, my father's sister. She was all right. But she didn't really like me much because she thought I was prettier than my cousins. So during my senior year I signed up for a Navy nurse's training program. For some reason they thought they didn't have enough nurses, so it was an accelerated program, only two years. That was fine with me. I wanted to be on my own and independent.

"I probably wasn't cut out to be a nurse. I liked being nice to patients but I didn't like the suffering and the gore. I've wondered what I would have been if my parents had lived."

Her voice was level, matter-of-fact, almost as though

she were relating a story about someone else. But her fists were tightly clenched.

"So four months after I had graduated I was a brand-new and terrified ensign, going ashore with a field hospital attached to X Corps and the First Marines. It was horrible. I was seasick when we hit the beach and then sick from all the boys who were dead and dying. I don't think I was much help to the unit. But they were all nice to me.

"I guess I got used to it because no one sent me home. I had learned in training that a nurse who men think is attractive will be the target of a lot of what we now call sexual harassment. I was a completely inexperienced and innocent Catholic virgin. I learned how to fight them off, but it was a constant fight.

"Later we went ashore again at Wonsan in what was North Korea. I hadn't been very good at geography in school. So I had no idea where we were. We moved up toward what I now know was the Chinese border in early autumn. I never stopped being scared, Bishop. Every day I was afraid of the blood and the severed limbs and the thought of what the Koreans would do to American women if they captured them. Whenever I heard artillery, I wondered what it would be like to have your legs blown off by a shell. Every night I had dreams about the smell of lightning and the burnt flesh of my family.

"Then autumn went on and it got colder. We were about halfway up toward the Chosun Reservoir in late December when the Chinese counterattack began. The casualties came streaming in. The wounded men talked of swarms of Chinese. They said that the second and third waves didn't even carry guns, but picked up the rifles of those who were killed in the first wave.

"Then it got bitter cold, as cold as I have ever been in my life. We were ordered to redeploy, which meant retreat in a hurry. We loaded our wounded on trucks, no helicopter evacuations in those days, abandoned all our equipment, and drove without stop for thirty-six hours back to Wonsan. I was numb with hunger and fright and cold. They put us on a hospital ship and we got out of there two days before the Chinese arrived. They gave us some warm coffee and a few donuts and put us back to work. I went on automatic pilot and stayed there. I knew I was a coward, I knew I was going to die, I didn't care. I'd be with my parents and with a lot of the poor boys whom I'd seen die."

One hand now lay on her breast, its fingers unconsciously stroking her neck.

"Did your colleagues know you were so frightened?"

"I guess not. As time went on I realized that they were afraid as I was . . . then the lines held and the Eighth Army recaptured Seoul and the war settled down to artillery and assaults on hills, and thousands more casualties. Finally we got some rest, but that meant Pusan, which was the ugliest place in the world. Men kept making passes and I kept saying no, regardless of what other nurses were saying. But, funny thing, after I'd said no a lot of them seemed to become my friends. I asked them to teach me how an automatic weapon worked, so a couple of Marines taught me."

"Why?"

"I don't know. It was something to do. Maybe I had some glorious idea of fending off waves of Chinese rapists."

She drew a deep breath and then went on.

"I was still only eighteen. Then they moved us back up to the front and the usual routine of trying to save lives. We did save a lot of them. Once we got them their survival chances went way up. Spring was beautiful, I can always remember the smell of flowers as the guns thundered a few miles north of us at night.

"Then it was summer. That might have been worse than winter. The Korean weather seemed then to be like the worst of Chicago extremes all the time. It was hot and humid, day and night, and dusty and smelly and bugs were everywhere. I thought I was in purgatory and it would never end. I also was convinced that I would die soon. Later I found out that was only a passing fear for most of the men and women in the unit. For me it was constant. And there were always the dreams about the lightning every night. I could never watch that TV series *M*A*S*H* when it was on television. My husband has wondered a number of times whether I wanted to go back to Korea and see what it's like now, especially when we were in Japan only a couple of hours away. I would literally become sick at the suggestion. Still, maybe if I want to get rid of the bad memories. What do you think, Bishop?"

"Doesn't that depend on the answer to a lot of questions?"

"Like whether I believe you when you say God loves me the way I love Evie?"

"Arguably."

She resumed her story, her eyes now glowing with the narrative, despite her clenched fists and stiff body.

"In the middle of that summer, there was a kind of lull in the fighting. Peace negotiations had begun somewhere. There were fewer casualties. We were warned that the North Koreans were infiltrating guerrillas across the lines through tunnels. I guess they'd been building tunnels. No one paid any attention to the stories."

She stopped again, as if she was gathering courage. I knew the next part of the story, but it was an entirely different story when you heard it from the woman who was there.

"I was talking to a badly wounded Marine—shrapnel in the chest—trying to convince him that he would live, which he did, and helping him to write a letter to his girl back home. There was only one guard in the tent and he was there more to help control our men if they became hysterical than to keep anyone out. He had been talking to me and then had gone up to the front of the tent to calm down a delirious guy with a bullet in his chest and had told me to watch his weapon. I looked up and I saw six young men appear at the door of our tent. At first I thought they were ROK troops. Then I saw one of them slash at the guard and the others rush toward the patients."

She stopped for a couple of moments.

"Does this sound like a script for a late movie on Turner Broadcasting, Bishop? Colorized black and white? I know it does. But it's true. I can prove it."

"I have no doubt that it is."

I would have believed her even if I had not read *The Bridge* article or talked to my friend at the Pentagon.

"I don't know what happened to me. Suddenly everything happened in slow motion. I could see ahead of time exactly what was about to happen before it happened. As calmly as if I were about to skip rope, I picked up the weapon, flicked off the safety catch, and killed them all. I suppose it didn't take more than fifteen seconds. Then I went up to the front of the tent and made sure they were dead by firing again into each one of them. I thought that they were about my age and were as frightened as I was. But I kept shooting. Later I found out that they were armed only with the machetes they carried. Even if I had known that, I still would have kept shooting. Then, when I was sure they were dead, I put the safety back on the weapon and knelt next to the guard to wrap a tourniquet around his arm.

"Then the Marines finally arrived. There was a lot of shouting and confusion and the usual stupid officers saying stupid things. One of them complimented the guard on his shooting. He pointed at his arm and told him that he had been wounded and I had done the shooting. Then the same guy, a reserve major, turned on me and accused me of killing six ROK soldiers and told me I'd be court-martialed. I said some obscene words to him that I had never used before and rarely since. Then I finished my work with the tourniquet and gave the kid a shot of penicillin. The Major then screamed angrily that I wasn't supposed to know how to operate a weapon. I was still icy calm. I told him that if I hadn't known how he would have had twenty corpses on his hands, including mine. Then I said I was tired of their stupidity and was going to get some sleep and they should figure out themselves what had happened. I stopped by the bed of the kid for whom I was writing the letter and finished. I said to him, 'You're going home to her, understand? I don't want to hear any more of your bullshit.' He saluted me with his left hand and grinned and said, 'Yes, *ma'am*!'

"It's strange, Bishop, how it all comes back. As vivid as if it were yesterday. I never told anyone the story since I came home from Korea."

"Neither your husband nor your children?"

"No. I was ashamed of myself for some reason. Yet telling the story now I am astonished at the poise of that kid who was three days short of her nineteenth birthday. She became hysterical the next day. But that night she was . . ."

"Wonderful?"

"Arguably . . . anyway, they gave me the Navy Cross eventually. There was a lot of controversy about giving it to a nurse. Some of the medical officers said it should be an even higher award. By then I was such a basket case, I didn't care one way or another. I still have it as proof of my story."

She slipped off her chair and walked over to a gray "secretary" in the corner of the room that served as a desk. She took a key out of one door, opened a second door, extracted another key, then opened the glass-enclosed shelves above the desk, and opened a hidden compartment at the back. She removed a slender oblong box and brought it over to me.

"You're the first one I've shown it to since I came home. My husband knows I received it because somehow the news got into *The Bridge* at the time of our marriage. But he's never asked because, to be fair to him, he knows or rather knew that I didn't want to talk about it."

The medal was tarnished, the blue ribbon with the white stripe was tattered at the edges, and the citation, the same as the Admiral had read to me on the phone, was yellowed.

"I've often thought that it was poor pay for all that I lost over there. I've been bitter and angry and ashamed about that night. Now as I look at it for the first time in a long time, I think those reactions might have been wrong."

"Perhaps not at the time . . . you have never talked to a psychiatrist about that night?"

"Every day at Pusan where they were trying to calm me down. Not since then. Maybe I should. Maybe it's not too late."

"They sent you to Pusan, not to Japan or home?"

"The Navy was kind of ashamed, Bishop, that a mere woman had saved twenty lives. They wanted to keep me out of the papers. So I went to Pusan where I met, fell in love with, and lost my virginity to Major Charles P. McInerny, a chaplain in the United States Navy. . . . I'll get us some more hot water, Bishop, and try to pull myself together for the rest of my little story."

CHAPTER 14

"I DON'T WANT to seem to be blaming him for what happened. I was at least as much to blame as he was. Maybe more."

"Let us stipulate, as the lawyers say, that no one is to blame."

"Maybe you're right. I've often said that to myself as I studied psychology in school. Maybe I'm too easy on myself sometimes. I don't know. But Chuck could never forgive himself. Never. Sometimes I think that he saved my life and I ruined his. Now don't argue, Bishop, until I finish my story."

"Agreed. But before we go on just one question."

"All right."

"Does it not occur to you that you did something astonishing that summer night so long ago? Does not the story itself, ringing in your own ears as it does now, describe a truly extraordinary woman involved in an almost incredible act of bravery?"

She smiled, caught up for a moment in a mood of playfulness, a mood that probably lurked always at the threshold of her personality.

"What was it I said to your cousin about posing for one of her nudes?"

"Maybe."

"Same answer . . . now to my story."

"Which you enjoy telling?"

"Will you *stop* interrupting me? And yes I enjoy telling it. Maybe it is a good story . . ."

Instantly she was serious again.

"I was a wreck by the time I arrived at the base hospital in Pusan. Technically I was assigned for regular duty but actually the shrinks there were supposed to calm me down. The tranquilizer drugs were not in common use yet, so they tried to sedate me at night and let me talk a couple hours every day. I refused to take the sedation, but I talked my head off, mostly incoherent babble I'm afraid. When I wasn't talking I was reading every novel I could get my hands on in the base library—Dickens, Thackery, Scott, Balzac, Faulkner, Hemingway. I was determined to make up for the lack of literature in my nursing school program. I learned to think in that hospital, though it might have been the wrong time to think about anything.

"I had long fits of hysterical crying. When my shrink would ask me what I was crying about I'd scream at him that I was crying about everything. I went over the deep end a couple of times and turned into a screaming psychotic. My shrink said I didn't want to get better and maybe I didn't.

"Then one afternoon, when I was in the library reading *Pride and Prejudice* of all things, I started to sob uncontrollably. Then I was sobbing because I was sobbing. I knew they were all looking at me and that someone would call the men in the white suits. But I didn't care. Then this handsome officer walked over and took my hand. He didn't say anything, he just held my hand.

"I didn't go to Mass anymore. I figured that crazy people didn't have to. So I didn't know he was the Catholic chaplain. I saw the cross on his shirt but I didn't care. I stopped sobbing and began to talk. He never let go of my hand.

"Looking back on it, poor Chuck was almost as bad off as I was. He never admitted it to me, but the word was that he had broken down during the retreat from the Chosun Reservoir. Nothing wrong with that. It can happen to anyone. He didn't run, but just kind of got lost inside himself. He didn't want therapy so the Navy just reassigned him and pretended to forget about it. He often spoke of going regular Navy and becoming a career chaplain and I think he must have tried. But the Navy didn't want him.

"So we were two fragile, lonely people, looking for a little warmth, a little reassurance in a hellhole. The only difference—besides our gender—was that I could admit I was out of control and Chuck couldn't. He was so sweet, so kind, so gentle. I fell in love with him instantly. I don't know who seduced whom, probably it was mutual. We were lovers before the week was over, two innocent, inexperienced virgins. But it didn't matter. It was pure ecstasy. I forgot all my troubles and began to heal. In a world where such joy was possible, there had to be a reason for everything. He relaxed too. As Chuck said, it was the first time in his life that he had experienced happiness. The rest of the world drifted away, all that remained was our love and our pleasure. . . ."

She stopped and bit her lip.

"It is wonderful and sad even to remember those days."

"I assume that he found it difficult to talk about himself."

"Except when we were making love. Even then he could not be specific. He did say once that he had never wanted to be a priest but he had no choice. We didn't talk about the future, priesthood, or anything else. I didn't care about the future. All that mattered was now."

Cholly was six or seven years older than she was. Was he amusing himself at the expense of a mere child or had not only passion but love slipped into the arid desert of his emotional life. My guess is that it was the latter. Charles P. McInerny experienced love for the first time in his life. And the last. For him it was a much more critical turning point than for her, his last chance. He found an oasis and then ran from it. Perhaps he used the priesthood as an excuse. But that would not have been the real reason.

"Would we have married? I don't know even today what might have happened. If Chuck had asked me, I'm sure I would have said yes. I would have done anything to make him happy, to see that smile of peace and contentment which lit up his face after we had made love. Looking back on it, Bishop, I had developed a great capacity for self-destructive sacrifice, had I not?"

"Would it have been a happy marriage?"

"Surely not . . . Chuck was afraid of intimacy, though I didn't see it then. He would not undress completely for me and I threw off my things with reckless abandon. In the act of intimacy he was free, but neither before nor after. Of course that's all hindsight."

"How long did it last?"

"Three unbearably happy months, sweetness so overwhelming that sometimes I thought I would die. Even now the memories tug at my heart. Of course I was a naive little fool. And reckless. And wanton. Now I would say that I had become a bit of nymph."

"Arguably what in fact happened was that in most unusual circumstances you found the nymph which lurked within you, as she lurks in everyone."

"Oh, God," she cried out, a hand covering her face.

"Yes, that was it, Bishop. Later I thought I had been some kind of sex fiend, a heathen wanton."

Or a rare prize for the right man. But now was not the time to say that.

"I think I know better now . . . then one day Chuck told me that he had asked to be sent home and was leaving the next day. He said that we were both terrible sinners and we should spend the rest of our lives doing penance. I should join the Magdalens which was a religious order for fallen women because I had seduced a priest. He was very stern and distant, almost like a judge passing a sentence, almost like I imagine God will be on Judgment Day."

"No way."

"He said that we must never see each other again, that I was an occasion of sin for him, and that only if I lived a life of prayer and penance would God forgive me for what I had done. It was all my fault, you see."

Her lips became a thin line of anger.

"You are angry now. Were you angry then?"

"No. I was brokenhearted and felt terribly guilty, but I kind of assumed that Chuck was right, though even then, deep down, deep *deep* down a voice told me that he was all wrong. Only many years later did I listen to that voice.

"Chuck stood up at the table where we'd been drinking a cup of coffee and, shoulders squared like a real Marine, strode out of the USO hut. He never once looked back. I was surprised when he turned up at the altar for our wedding. He was full of all his old kindness and charm. Said he'd been passing through and noticed the wedding on the chaplain's bulletin board and asked permission to do it."

"I thought he had gone home."

"So did I but I didn't ask."

She stopped and then continued her story.

"I didn't fall apart when he walked out on me. I didn't even cry. My days of emotional pyrotechnics were over. My heart was broken, but my psyche was healed. I knew I could cope and I have coped ever since."

"Indeed. . . . You knew you were pregnant at that time."

"Yes."

"And, as I understood what you said earlier, you did not tell him."

"No . . . I thought about it while Chuck was telling me that I was a strumpet, but I didn't want to blackmail him. If he wanted to be a priest or felt he had to be a priest that was his decision."

She paused a moment to think. "A mistaken decision but fortunate for me."

Charles McInerny turned a corner that day. There were surely ways he could have remained a priest without the cruelty with which he ended the relationship. Milord Cronin wanted an ending in which Lynn redeemed him. No such happy ending. Jolly Cholly turned his back in terror on the possibility of redemption.

"In a way Chuck was right, you know, Bishop. It would never have worked. Yet I missed him. I would always miss him, at least the way he was in our best moments together, funny, charming, tender, sensitive. . . . So I knew I had to find a father for my child. No thought of an abortion and no thought of giving up the child. I'm glad I was stubborn. Where would I be today without Evie?"

I did not attempt to answer that question.

"I began looking for a husband. Gerry was kind of hanging around me. Most of the other men in Pusan were terrible. He was nice—funny and gentle and considerate. I was being very businesslike and sensible. I told him about my condition and asked him if he would marry me.

"He hesitated and then said he would be happy to. He told me that he wanted to have a child of his own, but that he was afraid he never would because he was incapable of sexual intercourse."

"What!"

"I was shocked. I didn't understand what he meant. I guess I didn't believe it. He said that he would try of course, but that he was not hopeful. He would always take good care of me and the child and would never be harsh with me. At the time I was disillusioned with sex. Maybe all men were like Chuck—arrogant, cruel, self-centered. Maybe a man who wasn't interested in sex would be a welcome relief. And, anyway, I needed a father for my child. What a fool I was!

"Gerry kept all those promises. I've had everything I wanted: college, travel, clothes, the gallery, the best of everything for my children. I know that people think he's a wimp, but I'm fond of him. He's a good man and a wonderful father. It was a stupid decision, but I didn't know any better then. I gave my word and I've stood by it."

"How terrible!"

"It's not that we didn't try. We tried everything; the only result was more humiliation for poor Gerry. I could do it to him. When the sexual dysfunction clinic opened at Loyola, I hinted that we might try it. He didn't say 'no,' he never did. But the pain on his face was too much. I forgot about it. I don't know whether he ever had any sexual pleasure with anyone else, male or female. I doubt it."

"It's not a marriage, Lynn," I gasped.

"That's what a priest told me in confession, but I'm not sure I believe in annulments. Even if I did, it would have destroyed Gerry. We're friends, Bishop, good friends, not the closest of friends and not best friends, but still friends.

We learned how to adjust to our situation. He loves me, Bishop. More than many a man who would sleep with me and make love. He loves me as best he can. What more could I ask of him? It's worked out."

But only at the cost of terrible suffering.

"His father destroyed him. From the day he was born, Gerald III thought he would be a useless son because he didn't look like a Reed. He did everything he could from that day on to make his prophecy come true. He even left most of the family money to me. That was the ultimate insult: I was a better man than his son. I wanted to give the money to Gerry, but there was something in the will that prevented that. Gerry wouldn't have taken it anyway."

"They accepted you then?"

She jumped out of her chair and began to pace back and forth, fury in her every move.

"Almost at once. His father said at the dinner for us when we came home that he wouldn't have believed it possible for his son to capture a woman like me. With a leer, I might add. Then he ridiculed Gerry when Evie was born. Not even enough of a man to produce a son."

"An observation which you accepted calmly?"

She laughed and relaxed and then sank back into her chair.

"You're getting to know me pretty well, Bishop. I slapped him, told him he was a mean-spirited son of a bitch, and that unless he apologized, I would never speak to him again. He apologized."

"The other children?"

She shrugged indifferently.

"You've read D. H. Lawrence, Bishop?"

"*Lady Chatterly*!"

"That's right," she said grimly. "Gerry wanted a son to sustain the family tradition and to please his father. He hinted at it for months and then in a very roundabout and indirect fashion he said that he would not object if I had more children. All he asked was that I did not tell him or them who their father was."

"And you were furious?"

"At first, sure. Then I was intrigued. The nymph who had been quiet for a long time leapt out of the pool, ravenously hungry. Why not? I had a right to sex, didn't I? I had kept my part of the agreement. Was I not entitled to some fun? Men liked me, didn't they? Would God mind? God was responsible for my being in the situation. Let Him worry about it.

"I became very wicked. I flirted with men just to see their reaction. I decided that I could have any man I wanted. I wanted Arnie. I'd always found him attractive. He was lonely and unhappy after his wife's death, poor woman. So I set about seducing him, just to see if I could. My hormones which had been dormant for so long took control of my life."

She sighed.

"It was disgracefully easy. He fell like a brick wall hit by a tractor. I got more than I bargained for, however. I wanted to play around and have a son as the result of the play. He wanted all of me and would not let me go. I tried to escape but I didn't seriously want to. He owns me body and soul as I own him."

"Both the other two children are his?"

She nodded.

"Gerry doesn't know who their father is. Or at least he pretends not to know. He would never say if he did. I don't know whether he realizes that the affair continues. Again he would never say if he did. I realize there are whispers, but no one has any evidence. It's remarkably easy to carry on an extramarital affair in this community if you are only moderately careful."

Not for the first time in my years as a priest did I marvel at the ease with which married women will entrust the most intimate details of their lives to a celibate priest.

"You've even enjoyed that part of it."

"It's an ongoing adventure. We'd both like to live together and we have occasionally for a week or so on vacations, but one accepts in life whatever one gets . . . of course I stopped going to Communion for a while. As did Arnie. He didn't think what we were doing was wrong under the circumstances, so he resumed receiving the sacraments. I didn't know what to do. I did know that I was obsessed with him and could not give him up. I wanted to talk to a priest about it. I knew that my situation was unusual. In a way I was married to two men, both of whom I loved and both of whom loved me and neither of whom I could hurt or give up. What should I do? I was afraid to talk to a priest here in the parish. I wanted to talk to someone I knew. On an impulse one day I called . . . but you already know whom I called, don't you, Bishop?"

"Charles P. McInerny?" I murmured.

"Yes. And he gave me permission to commit adultery."

CHAPTER 15

"HE WHAT?"

"It was after young Gerry was born. My husband was ecstatic. He has been as proud of him as though he were his own son. I sometimes think that the poor man has persuaded himself that he *is* his own son. I told myself that the reason for my love affair had ended. I must give up Arnie and become a virtuous Catholic matron again. But I was a prisoner now not only of Arnie's love but of my own desires. A touch and I became a wanton. A look across a crowded room was enough to arouse me. Even his presence in the room would turn my body on. I told myself that such reactions would stop eventually. They didn't and to be candid, Bishop, they haven't. Perhaps if we slept in the same bed every night I'd have better control of my passions and so would Arnie."

"I doubt it."

She looked like she might become angry.

"Is that a compliment or an insult, Bishop?"

"What do you think?"

She studied me intently.

"I think it's probably a compliment, but I've never expected to hear anything like that from a bishop."

"Look how much you're learning . . . now go on with your story."

She smiled briefly, blushed, and went on with her astonishing story.

"I knew he was on the Chancery staff then, so I called him. He was charming and warm. Delighted to hear from me again. Just like he was in Pusan before we became lovers. I told him I had a problem I wanted to discuss with him. He invited me to lunch at the Chicago Club. First time I was there. A very fancy place. . . . He was so sweet. Not a word about what happened between us. But nothing about me being a strumpet either. I told him the obvious things about my life. He congratulated me on my children, my M.A. degree, my role on the board of the Butternut Community Hospital, and told me how proud he was of what I had done with my life."

"I'm sure he was proud."

"He also said I was more beautiful than ever."

"Doubtless an accurate compliment."

"Then I told him about my problem. He listened sympathetically and then said that I could continue in my relationship with Arnie. That's what I wanted to hear, as you can imagine, Bishop Blackie. But I was shocked to hear it and wanted to argue. He told me that he was vice chancellor of the Archdiocese and would soon be chancellor and had worked for many years in the Matrimonial Tribunal. Thus, he insisted, I could take his word for it that he knew what he was talking about: I could and should continue in my relationship with Arnie and I should not worry about it ever again."

"So you followed the former instructions but not the latter?"

"I guess so," she said ruefully. "What do you think, Bishop? Did I believe Chuck because I wanted to believe him? Am I a victim of vincible ignorance? Will I go to hell? What do you think?"

"In the order in which you ask the questions: You did indeed believe him because you wanted to believe him. I don't think you are a victim of what we used to call vincible ignorance. I have already expressed myself on the subject of your eternal damnation and see no need to revise my position. Finally, why does it matter to you what I think?"

She shifted uneasily. "I need to hear again that I haven't been doing wrong. Please tell me."

The poignancy of her plea would touch hearts considerably stronger than mine.

"I think Chuck, moved by the affection he still felt for you, made a quick decision which combined two principles of canon law which were existent at that time and which could logically be combined in one case. Only rarely if ever at that time would anyone dare to combine them. Even now it would require a somewhat brave canonist to do so. But in fact both pertain to rights that a layperson enjoys as a matter of strict justice."

"Really?" Her eyes widened.

"I now cite canon law, though my own personal opinions are much less legalistic. But I assume you want legalism. The first is, as the priest told you in confession, an attempted marriage in which there is permanent impotency from the beginning of the attempted marriage is not a valid marriage. In ideal circumstances this matter should be adjudicated by a Church tribunal. In circumstances where that is impossible, the wife may nonetheless enter a new marriage which will be valid even if this marriage cannot be celebrated at a ceremony in church. Is that clear?"

"I read something like that in a pamphlet once but I didn't know that it applied to me."

"It did. And does. . . . The second principle is that

when the usual form of marriage—before a priest and two witnesses—is for one reason or another impossible—a couple marooned on a desert island or less fantastically no priest available for a month, then the couple may exchange permanent marriage vows between themselves and that constitutes a valid marriage. Impossibility may be physical or moral, the latter meaning that even though a priest may be physically present, it would be an extremely grave inconvenience for the couple to attempt such a public marriage. It is of interest to note that the mere exchange of consent was considered enough for the first thirteen hundred years of Catholic history, give or take a century depending on your notions about the Church."

"Oh," she said in a tiny voice.

Then she added with a chuckle, "You even look like a lawyer when you talk that way."

"I have many personae depending on the circumstances."

"You're telling me that Arnie and I are really husband and wife?"

"If one holds this theory that I have explained, one would say that since whatever time you pledged yourself permanently to one another, you have indeed been two in one flesh. Mind you, the theory is not ironclad and you will have to decide whether you accept it. I personally will not pass judgment on any residual doubts you may have except to say that they're stupid."

"That's what Chuck was saying when he told me it was all right."

The recording angel will note that, instead of responding "arguably" as I am wont to do, I merely said "yes."

Love had moved Charles McInerny to leap ahead thirty years in canonical practice. So maybe she redeemed him after all.

"I'll stop worrying," she said. "I promise."

"Most of the time . . . so now you have three men who loved you, each in his own way, and each with a remarkable degree of unselfishness."

"It cost poor Chuck his job. I saw him for lunch a few times after that. They were always pleasant lunches. He was sweet and nice. Nothing more. Then that terrible woman who knew me from Korea wrote those awful letters. Was God punishing us?"

"In fact," I sighed, "that was not why he was replaced. The then Cardinal showed him the letters and he told him the truth: you were a nurse who had a hard time in Korea and he met with you occasionally. He denied that there was any sexual involvement. Of course he meant at the time of the letters. The Cardinal believed him."

"But then why . . ."

"You knew him and I didn't. I suspect, however, that he need periodic reaffirmation, perhaps especially in his days here in the parish. He offered his resignation to the Cardinal pro forma because many priests were complaining that he did not accept the spirit of the Vatican Council. The Cardinal, much to Chuck's surprise, accepted the resignation because he agreed with the priests. . . . Did he blame you for his fall from power?"

She lowered her head. "Not exactly . . . sometimes when he was in one of his moods he kind of hinted at it."

I would leave that where it was.

"It must have been a considerable surprise when he appeared here as pastor."

She looked up at me.

"Yes it was. I was terribly uneasy. I need not have been. He rarely even alluded to Korea. Gerry and I knew that the three of us had been there at the same time, but we did not discuss it with people. We paid our respects to him when he arrived in the parish and again he was very friendly. Nothing more. We became part of the group of people that he rallied round himself. . . ."

"While he alienated the rest of the parish. And it became your duty through the years to calm him down, soothe his ego, heal as best you could the wounds he inflicted on others?"

She closed her eyes again and leaned her head back against the chair.

"That's a fair description of what I did. We brought the Curtins over to the rectory—Steve and Gerry were classmates all through grammar school and high school. Margie was a nurse like me and a lovely person in those days. Both were sane then. Poor Chuck was so depressed by what the Church had done to him. He hated Monsignor Cronin and because he did we did too. Gradually we built up a little group of Catholics around him so he wouldn't . . . wouldn't isolate himself completely. They were mostly very conservative, because Chuck had offended everyone else the first month he was in the parish. I told him that he ought not to take out his anger at the Cardinal and Monsignor Cronin on the people. He just stared at me and said that I just didn't understand what was happening to the Church."

"And you became a Catholic conservative yourself?"

"No . . . not really . . . I thought the Latin Mass was nice, but I certainly didn't agree about birth control or the rights of women. I kept my ideas to myself. I wanted to protect Chuck and prevent the anger in the parish against him from getting worse. I like the parish under Father Pete a lot more than I did the parish under Chuck."

"You still loved him?"

"Of course I did. Not the way I loved Arnie or my husband. I didn't want to sleep with him again—not that there was any chance of that. But he had saved me twice, once in Korea and once when he helped me about adultery. I felt I owed him something and I was sorry for him."

"You thought you might turn him around?"

"Yes. . . . No. . . . I don't know. . . . At first I kidded myself into thinking that there was still a chance I could make him a happy and successful priest. Then I saw that was impossible. So I realized, like the good nurse I still was, that all I could do was control the pain. For everyone involved. So I did that."

"Perhaps that's the story of your life?"

"That I've been a nurse for all three men? Surely not for Arnie."

"You said earlier that you felt sorry for him because he had lost his wife."

"I also said I wanted to try my hand at seduction."

"Still your target of preference was a man in pain."

She opened her eyes again and examined my face.

"Do you really think that's what I am?"

"It's not a bad thing to be."

She thought a moment, biting her lip.

"You know, Bishop, for years, decades I suppose, it all seemed like familiar and ordinary routine. I would kiss my husband good-bye when he would walk over to the bank at six-thirty. Then I would feed my kids and send them off to school. I might stop by the rectory to cheer up or calm down the Monsignor, perhaps to advise him on the long process of decision making about the organ or the tower bells, realities which he said would long outlast the present foolishness in the Church. I would feed my kids lunch with the help of a cook, perhaps attend a committee meeting at the hospital, and then meet Arnie, home early from the exchange for a romp. Then home for supper and reading or television. Isn't that what the affluent suburban matron does with her day. Maybe it was wicked and maybe I was a wretched person, but that's what I did and I had no choice about any of it and that was that. I might go to hell when I died, but I probably wouldn't die for a while."

"I see."

"The Monsignor and Gerry were easier. They required only patience and affection. Arnie was more difficult, more exciting, more challenging, the best part of the day and the worst. Pleasurable and scary. He is a demanding man, Bishop, and he demanded everything that was me. Everything. There was no hiding with him."

"You wanted to hide?"

"Certainly I wanted to hide. I still do. Doesn't everyone? Isn't a lover someone who won't let you hide no matter how frightened you may be?"

"Arguably."

Suddenly a drumbeat thundered just outside the window. Tense as I was I jumped out of my chair.

"Sorry, Bishop," she said with an amused smile. "It's only Margie Curtin pretending to be a Zulu witch. I think she's putting a curse on me. . . . They used to be such a nice couple. Too many drugs for too many years."

"Scheduled substances?"

"African stuff that neither that government nor the drug gangs have found out about yet. They grow the raw material in their own greenhouse."

"Why should she think you're having an affair with the Doctor?"

"Because she hates me and because when she's high she suspects everyone. Not without reason. Steve hits on every woman he meets."

"Including you?"

"He tried to rape me twice. Threatened that if I didn't go along with him he'd tell Gerry who the father of his two

kids was. After a meeting of the hospital board on which
we were both serving at the time. He was dropped soon
after that. I managed to fight him off, but just barely. He's
a big man. I screamed once and he was afraid someone
would come rushing in and catch him."

"Then you had him removed from the board?"

"I sure did. Even twenty years ago, you whisper that in
a couple of ears and every woman on the board turns
against him. He already had a terrible reputation among
the nurses on the staff. A few years later he was dropped
from the staff too."

"You were involved in that?"

"Of course."

"And he didn't follow up on his threat."

"I don't know. Gerry never said anything. But then he
wouldn't."

"You warned him not to try again?"

"I told him I carried a scalpel in my purse and that the
next time he tried I would cut off his testicles."

Oh, yes, a formidable woman indeed. Ready to heal
pain wherever she could, but hardly a doormat.

"Did you indeed carry the scalpel?"

"Not that day, but every day since."

She stood up, walked to the secretary, picked up a
fashionable brown Coach purse, opened it, and removed a
scalpel that she flipped open.

She grinned and returned the weapon to the purse.

"I think there may be just enough of that young j.g. in
me that I'd react the same way I did then."

"I wouldn't doubt it for a moment," I agreed as she
returned to her chair. "Did you use it the second time?"

"I waved it at him and took one swipe. Tore his slacks.
Second time I would have cut him. He knew I would. He
ran away screaming."

"Do you want to tell me the circumstances?"

"Sure I do, Bishop, since I'm telling you all my secrets. It was a hot summer night only three years ago, like the ones we've been having this summer. Gerry was at a convention in Los Angeles. Arnie was at some kind of Merc dinner. I was reading here in this room, Margaret Atwood, and on my chaise—removed from the room when there's a bishop coming to grill me—in, well, minimal attire and that mostly transparent, partly because it was hot and partly because I thought Arnie would stop by on his way home if it were not too late."

She was blushing now but not really ashamed of herself.

"I had turned off the air conditioner because, well, because a warm humid night is sexier, and opened the sliding door to the rose garden. He charged in from the garden with one of those bolo knives of his and told me in graphic detail what he would do to me if I didn't cooperate."

"He was on drugs?"

"Totally stoned as my kids would say . . . from then on it was all in slow motion, just like in Korea. I dived under his arm, grabbed the purse, which I never let out of my sight, opened the scalpel, and slashed his arm. He hollered and dropped the knife. Then I swung at his genitals. As I said, he ran through the garden, trampling some of my best plants and back to the little door over there in his stupid barricade. I returned the bolo to him the next day in a gift box."

"He required medical attention?"

She lifted her lovely shoulders indifferently. "I'm sure he did. Made up some crazy story. At the hospital they told me that a nurse had gone after him with a scalpel. That was true enough in a way."

"And you are still quite proud of what you did?"

"Isn't that terrible? I know it's wrong . . ."

"It is not," I insisted.

She smiled wryly. "Since nothing I say seems to offend or shock you, I might as well add that I learned later that night that aggression is as much an aphrodisiac for a woman as it is supposed to be for a man."

"I take that as a given."

The woman now trusted me completely . . . or arguably thought she had bemused me completely.

"And," I continued, "apart from other incidents like that, your life went on in its seamless fashion. You were loved by three men each in their own way and you loved them each in your own way. You protected the parish from complete collapse. You kept the late Monsignor on this side of sanity, but just barely. Perhaps there were times when you and he had tête-à-têtes, when he experienced interludes of happiness . . ."

"Never in this room, Bishop," she insisted primly. "That would have been inappropriate."

"Arguably. And perhaps a little dangerous."

"Maybe, but I doubt it."

"And you administered his finances for him?"

She smiled triumphantly.

"Now we leave the preliminaries behind, Bishop Blackie, don't we? The answer is that I paid no attention to his money until the week before he died."

CHAPTER 16

"MAY I GET you a peach, Bishop?"

She gathered the teacups and saucers and slipped out of the room. I glanced at my watch and told myself I had heard a fascinating story of an interesting life from a remarkable woman, but I was no closer to a solution to the puzzle than I had been when she had begun her story.

In fact, there were two peaches, the stones removed, cut into slices on a china plate.

"I thought you'd like the skin left on."

"I do . . . why did you withdraw from nursing?"

"You're not patient, Bishop Blackie. When Evie went to school and I'd finished my degree work I gave it a try. There were too many memories, I'm afraid. And too much conflict. If some people think a nurse is beautiful, she'll have problems at a hospital. The women will hate her and tell lies about her. The men will hit on her, especially the doctors. She's being hassled all the time. I like being president of the board because I have enough power to fight that stuff off, and maybe to help some young women defend themselves."

"I see."

"When I was cutting the peach"—she shifted uneasily in her chair—"I realized that I had gone back on my word."

"So?"

"I had given my word to myself that I'd tell you everything today exactly as it happened and not try to make myself look good. I realize now that all I've done is put myself in a favorable light that I don't deserve. I am really a terrible person."

"You actually believe that?"

"Yes," she said sadly, "I do."

"So you think you have deceived me?"

Her keen gray eyes bore into my Coke-bottle glasses, then turned away, and she blushed.

"I don't think many people deceive you, Bishop. I know I can't."

"Perhaps then you are not so terrible after all."

"You don't think I'm terrible?"

"I want to hear more of your story, but I doubt it."

"Then let's get to Monsignor's money."

"Fair enough."

She folded her hands in her lap, a novice reasoning with mother superior.

"I grew up in the Depression. I learned to be afraid of money problems. I have never wanted to think about money or worry about it. I'm careful the way I spend it, but though I'm a banker's wife, I never reconcile my checking account, the one thing Gerry has complained about. I'd tell him I've never overdrawn, but that wouldn't be enough. When I got all that money from his father, I asked Arnie for the name of an adviser who'd invest it. Arnie checks the reports for me so I know I'm doing all right. I don't like money."

"Indeed."

"I know it's neurotic, but I'm not sure I want to get over that neurosis. So I paid no attention to Monsignor's money. I signed some checks for him because he insisted

I have power of attorney. I'd carry the check over to Gerry. He and Steve are the trustees of the McInerny trust. I knew that we were investing it for him and I knew there was enough to buy the organ and the bells. I certainly didn't know that it belonged to the parish and not to him. Or that he should have sent it downtown. I did not want to know about that. He did ask me whether I thought he should give the parish checkbook to the new priest. I said that I thought that would be the right thing to do, especially since Monsignor had begun to like the new priest and to realize that he wouldn't throw him out of the rectory."

"The good Peter Finnegan is far too gentle and far too wise to do that."

"That's the only time we ever discussed money seriously up until a week before his death."

"Ah?"

"The club has installed an indoor lap pool that some of us use in the wintertime. I do my exercises here, throw on a jacket, grab a bag of clothes, and drive over there for my swim. It's usually deserted in the morning. So this day the week after New Year's, on a terribly cold, gray day, I came out of the locker room and walked by the bar on the way out. There were only two people in the bar, Steve Curtin and Father Joe, over in the corner by the lobby. I like Father Joe, but I can't stand being near Steve unless I have to. . . ."

"You were carrying your weapon, I suppose?"

"Of course . . . as I walked by them I heard Father Joe say something that paralyzed me.

" 'You guys had better be real careful what you're doing with that money. It belongs to the Church. The kid is an innocent but he's no fool. He might start making some calculations.'

" 'It's up to the Monsignor. Besides, we're cleaning up

on these exotic options. In a couple of weeks we'll be able
to give it all back.'

" 'Maybe, but what if the old man dies?'

" 'No one knows about the money. How will they ever
find out downtown?'

" 'You'd better make sure they don't.'

"And they both laughed, Bishop, and went on to
something else. I tiptoed away as quietly as I could. I was
devastated—confused, troubled, uncertain about what I
should do. I tried to talk around it with Gerry, though I
didn't tell him what I had heard. He told me about huge
profits they'd made for the Monsignor's trust through the
years and that it was all perfectly legal and honorable, a
very successful investment for example in the Butternut
Mall, a big profit during the silver run-up. I asked, trying
to seem innocent and curious, whether it was Monsignor's
money or the parish's money. He became nervous and said
that as far as he was concerned it was Monsignor's to
invest however he saw fit and that he'd turned it over to
the McInerny trust and it was all being used properly."

I listened in silence. The puzzle was beginning to sort
itself out and I didn't like what I was beginning to see.

"I wrestled with it for several days," she continued,
"tossing and turning at night and worrying all day. I told
myself that it was none of my business and that I'd make
trouble for everyone if I interfered. But I worried about my
husband, about young Gerry, about Arnie, about the
Fasios. What if Steve Curtin who seemed crazier by the
day was doing something that would cause trouble for all
of us? What if Monsignor without realizing it was helping
Steve to steal from the Church? I couldn't ask my son. I
couldn't ask my lover. I didn't know what to do."

She shook her head sadly. "I still don't know whether
what I did was wrong. I may have been responsible for

Monsignor's death . . . I hope not. I have created a lot of problems for all of us. But it isn't right to steal from the Church, even if this is a very rich parish."

"So you talked to the Monsignor?"

She opened her hands in a gesture of resignation.

"What else was there to do? I tried to be clever. I asked vague questions about parish money for the new school. He said there would be plenty of money without any new collections. I asked about the money that my husband had been investing as executor of the trust fund; was it his or the parish's? He said all that was taken care of and that he'd write a will sometime leaving it all to the Church so it didn't matter what belonged to him and what belonged to the parish, but he wasn't going to give a penny to Cardinal Cronin while he was still alive. I asked him what would happen if he died without a will. He said that he'd write up the will one of these days."

"He did not mind you talking about these matters?"

"Not at first. He was in one of his genial and relaxed moods, nostalgic about growing old and about Korea, though he said nothing about us. As I told you, he never did. Then he became upset with me. Why was I asking all these questions? When had I become interested in money? He thought I hated money. I felt backed into a corner. I wanted him to write up a will then and there and have me witness it. I thought, poor fool that I was, that it would solve everything. But I couldn't ask directly or I would have turned him off. So I took a big risk and told him about the conversation I had heard at the club."

"His reaction?"

"He became very stern and somber. He thanked me for telling him. He said it was typical of my generosity and love. . . . Yes, Bishop, he used that word. . . . He went over and opened a panel which revealed a large safe built into the wall. He wrote down the combination, gave it to me, and opened the safe. It was filled with files and boxes of checks. 'It's all in here,' he told me. 'If anything should happen to me, you clean this out and take it over to your son at the Butternut Mall. He's as honest as you are and he'll see that the right thing is done. Don't let anyone else know you've done it.'"

"You were frightened?"

"Terrified. It was all vague but I knew far more than I wanted to know. I was afraid we were all in trouble. But of course I promised to do what he asked."

"Of course."

"I begged him to make a will. To my surprise he agreed. He took out a sheet of parish letterhead stationery and wrote two paragraphs. I couldn't see what he was writing, but for a few moments he was not a sick and feeble old man but vigorous and decisive again. He signed the note, put his hand over the paragraphs, and asked me to witness it. I was trembling, but I did what I had to do. He folded the will, put it in a parish envelope, and addressed it to the Cardinal.

"'It's all business,' he said. 'No recriminations. The s.o.b. did me a favor by sending Pete. Let bygones be bygones. If anything happens to me, before I get something more formal done, take it right to the Cardinal. Will you promise me?' I promised. He put the envelope in the safe, spun the lock, and slid the panel back in place. There was nothing more for me to worry about. Then when I was leaving he put his arm around my shoulder, kissed me on the forehead, and thanked me for being the only loyal friend he ever had."

"But you continued to worry?"

"About my husband, yes. But not about anyone else. I didn't care one way or another about Steve. But at least we weren't stealing money from the Church . . . you know the rest."

"You removed the material from the safe the day after his death as he had told you to?"

"Everything but the will. It had vanished. I piled it in the trunk of my Mercedes and drove right over to the bank. Young Gerry was horrified when I told him what the three big boxes were. He became even grimmer when he glanced at all the material. He said we'd have to go over it very carefully before we decided. With tears in his eyes, he told me that we'd better not let Pop know what we were doing. Maybe we could straighten things out somehow and avoid trouble. I trusted my son and I'm proud that he lived up to that trust. We've finally figured everything out."

I looked at the peach plate. Some evil spirit, perhaps in response to the African drums that were beating again, had stolen all the slices.

"You're sure there was no will?"

"He had put it right on the top of one of the boxes. When I opened the safe it was gone. . . . Poor Father Pete hardly noticed what I was doing when I carried them out."

"Perhaps he trusted you, like you trusted your son."

"With less reason, Bishop. With much less reason."

"Do you think the Monsignor was killed?"

"I didn't then. I was too sad to think of anything but doing what he wanted. I knew he had high blood pressure. It didn't occur to me to question Steve's diagnosis. Besides, the doors to both the suite and the bedroom were locked. How could he have been killed? I didn't think that anyone I knew would kill him. There was no reason to even ask myself about murder then."

"Not even when you had the oriental rug repaired?"

She frowned, trying to recall her emotions from six months before.

"I suppose there was a little tickle of doubt in the back of my head. But how could anyone get into the room?"

"You didn't have a key yourself?"

She was not offended by the question.

"Oh, no. He never offered it to me and I wouldn't have taken it if he did. There were too many memories. . . ."

"I understand."

"As the weeks turned into months and Gerry and I worked our way through the documents and I thought more about the disappearance of the will, I began to have doubts about everything. But I can't honestly think of anyone who had the motive to kill Monsignor. Or the courage. Steve is off the wall, but all he can shoot is dumb animals. Not another human. The only one who might have a motive . . . and the experience . . . would be me. I didn't do it, Bishop. I didn't do it."

That remained to be seen but my tentative conclusion was that she was telling me the truth. Yes, she had a motive, yes, she had killed before. Yet . . .

"What do you think happened to the will?"

"Whoever killed him must have taken it."

"Arguably."

"I have it all here, Bishop."

She rose from her chair and walked over to a cabinet on the far wall. She knelt in front of it and opened it. I followed her.

"We finished it last week, Bishop. Before you came."

The sunlight that came through the window next to the cabinet cast a ray on her face and chest. Despite her skillful makeup, there was no doubt about the lines on her face. Yet the lines were serene and the face perhaps more lovely and certainly more haunting because of them. Several times as she leaned forward to remove the boxes, the tank dress, designed doubtless with such "accidents" in mind, disclosed generous breasts deftly captured in a silver bra.

A proper male reaction to that is to be quite over-whelmed by the cameo—and to envy Arnie.

She passed a series of documents to me.

"Here is a stack of cards for you to sign. They will give you access to all the funds. This is a consolidated statement of gains and losses for the trust through the years. You'll find that even with the money that's missing, it still has earned more than if the funds had been invested in the Dow average. This is a list of transactions with friends of ours for investment by my husband or of investments he made himself. Gerry and I could find nothing illegitimate in any of the deals with the Fasios or Arnie. They seem to be sound and very successful investments. The Archdiocese owns a nice proportion of the Butternut Mall and made a lot of money on silver. Nor is there any reason to believe that either man knew that the funds belong to the Archdiocese. Even though Arnie is my lover—my husband I guess I should say, shouldn't I?"

She paused and shivered.

"Are you sure?" she asked.

"Are you sure?"

"It will take getting used to and that might itself be a delightful experience . . . anyway, if he were cheating, I'd tell you.

"Some of the investments Steve was permitted to make are very dubious but eventually they were repaid. Young Gerry tells me that it may have been improper for my husband to have made those decisions, but that at this date nothing much would be done about them . . . do I have two husbands, Bishop?"

"In different senses of the word."

She thought about that and went on.

"Young Gerry also says that he believes that if we turn all the documents and the funds over to the Church, there will be little likelihood of legal action against anyone. He says we should be happy you came out here because that makes the transaction much easier. We could probably persuade a judge and jury that we thought in good faith that the money was his."

In the distance the bells of Saints Peter and Paul were tolling again. Ask not for whom the bell tolls . . .

"The elder Gerry would have a hard time with that explanation since presumably the Sunday collections were coming into his bank. But you're right, we don't want to prosecute anyone or to create any publicity."

She picked up a folder off the top of one of the boxes and moved to stand up. I extended a hand to help her. The tank dress fell ever farther forward as she rose. I'm sure I blinked (behind the Coke-bottle glasses of course) and swallowed.

"Thank you," she said. Then she strode back to her chair, terminating abruptly my delicious fantasies.

"There is just one problem." She sighed as she sat down in the chair. "In the last year and a half, my husband and Steve have been playing in the derivatives market, Steve for the hell of it, Gerry because he wants to make enough money so he won't have to sell the bank. . . . You know what a derivative is, Bishop? I didn't know until a couple of months ago."

"Basically it is a hedge against interest rates."

"Right. Against falling interest rates. They're called derivatives because the values derive from the underlying value of some other stock or bond or financial instrument or combination of many financial instruments indexed against one another. Thus you can agree to buy or sell a million dollars of some instrument or combination in three months without exchanging any money at all. At the end of the three months you earn or lose what someone who actually owned such a 'forward' as they call it would have earned or lost."

"Fascinating."

"What went wrong—and Arnie took my money out of this kind of investment before it happened—was that no one seemed to realize that what comes down can also go up and probably will. So when the interest rates went up earlier this year, a man named Sauros lost a billion dollars and Procter and Gamble lost a hundred and ten million and Gerry and Steve lost two million dollars of the Church's money."

"I see."

"One kind of derivative is called a swap, a kind of child of a forward. Typically one party agrees to pay a fixed interest rate in exchange for receiving a floating rate from another party. Then they can combine these in what they call 'exotic swaps' in which oil prices and interest rates and other indices are combined and sometimes 'multiplied' and 'leveraged' to use their terms."

"Which notably enhances the possibilities for profit and loss?"

"Exactly. So Steve finds some hotshot broker who is piling up money on these trades—which don't deal with anything real like pork bellies or wheat but only imaginary numbers. They get themselves involved in an exotic swap, the dynamics of which I don't understand and don't want to understand. They use two million of the Monsignor's funds and promise themselves they'll split the profit with the trust. That's a failure of a trust I'm told and an indictable offense."

"So I am given to understand."

She closed her eyes and rested her head against the back of the chair.

"They made lots of money, fifteen million dollars, enough to save the bank many times over. If they'd gotten out. Gerry wanted to. Steve begged for one more renewal. They lost it all and their investment too. Gerry also lost a quarter of the capital of the bank on a 'structured' note as they're called, issued by a federal government agency. The Feds were close to driving him out of business. It was a miracle that they didn't lose everything they own. Steve wanted to throw all of the trust into another throw of the dice, but Gerry said no."

"I see."

"We had a meeting two weeks ago, the four of us. Young Gerry laid it out. We had broken the law. First of all we had failed the trust. We had embezzled money. We had probably embezzled it from the Church. He and I were also guilty of obstruction of justice because we had not turned all these documents over to the proper authorities. We were under constant risk of disclosure because the Church would be certain to figure out eventually that there was a lot more money involved than it seemed to realize."

I did not tell her that if it were not for the supernatural phenomena, we might never have noticed.

"He insisted that his dad had to sell the bank to NBD immediately, as he would have to eventually because his capital was so low, and Steve his string of nursing homes. Immediately. He pointed out that both of them would suffer no appreciable change of lifestyle. They didn't want to do it. He asked Gerry if he wanted to see me sent to the Women's Prison at Dwight. That did it. Both sales are still secret, but there are documents in this folder assigning the appropriate amounts of money back into the trust. Gerry made them ironclad so they'll hold up even if we should all die. Gerry will be willing to work with your lawyers and accountants in straightening all of these things out. But promise me that you'll sign these cards and take this stuff away today."

She buried her face in her hands but she did not cry.

"Better I think that the Cardinal sign them. But I'll deliver them to him today. It is remotely possible that some of our lawyers, seeing billable hours in this time of law industry downturn, will want to carry the matter further. I assure you that won't happen. In this matter, if in few others, I can deliver the Cardinal's vote."

Especially since there was now an arguable possibility that she had redeemed Cholly.

"Thank you, Bishop."

She removed her hands from her face.

"I am a very vain woman."

Where did that come from?

"Indeed?"

"I spent a lot of time and money on my physical appearance. A woman my age has no right to look like I do."

"Who says so?"

"Everyone . . . I tell myself I do it to please Arnie and my family. They're proud of me. But I really do it to please myself. Isn't that terribly wrong?"

"No."

"It's vanity."

"Self-respect."

"What do you mean?"

"Do you not think that God, like any lover, enjoys your attractiveness?"

"Why should God care what I look like?" Her face was now flaming red.

"Because She made you to look beautiful and likes to

admire Her handiwork. Come on, Lynn. You know it's not wrong. You merely want reassurance that your guilts are not to be taken seriously."

"I suppose so," she said with a sigh. "I'll help you carry this stuff out to the car."

She made no move to rise and neither did I.

"And the elder Gerry? How did ending his family tradition affect him?"

"He had my son meet with NBD and signed all the papers over at Butternut. My son said that his father, as he will always believe him to be, wept bitter tears when he brought the papers back to him, like it was the end of his life. . . . May I tell you one last part of my crazy story?"

"Candidly, Lynn, I'd be disappointed if you didn't."

"Gerry told me the story of the sale at supper that night and thanked me for insisting that everyone do the right thing. He said it was all a big load off his mind and that he realized now that a bank like ours couldn't make it in the financial world of today. He said he should have seen that long ago and that now he'd enjoy his retirement. He also said how proud he was of young Gerry and how successful he'd be in a financial world at which he felt at home.

"I said some fool thing about starting a new family tradition and he smiled sadly and said I was probably right."

"A liberation for him, in a way?"

"I don't know, Bishop. Probably too late. He'll always be sad, but the pressure is off him anyway . . . and now we get to the strange part. Maybe wonderful. I don't know. I'm embarrassed to talk about it, but I haven't held anything back so far."

"It's your call."

She nodded briskly.

"I know it is. . . . That night Gerry came to my bedroom. In his pajamas. His bedroom is down the hall from mine. Obviously I don't lock my door. He wanted to spend the night in bed with me, like a little kid afraid of a storm wants to sleep with his mummy. Only this was more than that. He wanted to be with me in my bed. Not make love with me. But be with me. Almost his very words. Of course I threw back the covers and took him into my arms. If he wanted to make love, I would have done so, but it would have been cruel to embarrass him again when that really wasn't what he wanted. He lay in my arms and wept. He didn't say why and I didn't ask him. It was for everything. I was filled with love for him. I unbuttoned my sleep shirt and rested his poor, sad face on my breasts. He covered them with tears. Then he fell asleep and slept peacefully till morning."

What does one say to that?

"He came back the next night and wept in my arms and on my boobs again. We said nothing except that we loved one another because there was nothing else to say. It wasn't passion. Or if it was, Bishop, it was a different kind of passion . . . suppose that he wanted to have sex and could have—and I'm sure that's not going to happen— would it have been wrong? Would that be a sin of adultery against the man who you say is my real husband?"

No way I was going to field that one.

"Should it have happened, I'm sure you would have followed your instincts and that would have been all that God would have required of you."

She nodded. "I hope God is as understanding as you say He is."

"She. Mother as well as Father. Nurse too."

She puzzled over that one and then went on with her story.

"The third night he did not come to my room. I lay

awake waiting for him. Then I did what might have been a foolish thing. I took off my sleep shirt and went down to his room and snuggled in beside him. He sobbed bitterly in my arms but wouldn't let me go, not that I wanted to go. I've done that several times since. I think I've made him happy. I figure if he's not had sex with me so far, he won't."

Maybe and maybe not. But not up to me to say anything.

"Mind you," she went on, "this 'bundling,' as they used to call it in New England, has had no effect on my relationship with Arnie. I won't say I don't like it, however. I do."

She waited for me to tell her she shouldn't like it. I didn't. Instead I asked, "Have you told Arnie about the embezzlement?"

"No. I'm going to tell him this afternoon. I thought I ought to settle it with the Church. He'll approve."

"Of almost anything you do or say?"

She laughed happily.

"Certainly."

"He knows about Korea?"

"Only that I had some terrible experiences and came home pregnant."

"You should tell him about the Navy Cross."

I reached over and picked up the box in which her decoration had hidden for so many years. "And you should wear the ribbon or the lapel button on occasion. Perhaps have a pendant made."

"Do you think so?" she asked hesitantly.

"Yes."

"Should I tell Arnie about who Evie's real father was?"

"What do you think?"

"It's part of the story and I should tell the whole story."

"Fair enough."

I rose to leave. The Cardinal must have the papers as soon as possible.

She stood up too. We both lifted a box.

"I presume that next week young Gerry will call the Cardinal's office for an appointment?"

"I'm sure he will."

"You come too."

"Why?"

"The Cardinal will want to meet you."

She held the door open for me with her foot.

"I'd be afraid to meet him."

I put my box on the front seat and opened the trunk.

"Don't ever try to kiss his ring," I said, dumping the box in the trunk. "Otherwise he's quite charming. He'll insist on meeting you."

She carefully put her box in the trunk and, womanlike, arranged mine so that both were neatly ordered. In that effort she disclosed an even more extensive view of the silver bra and the lovely mounds of flesh within it.

We walked back to the house together.

"I'll bring out the last box, Bishop."

"No, you won't."

I carried it out, with some huffing and puffing. She brought the folder with the summaries and the signature cards and the promissory notes.

"What do you think, Bishop?"

"Of what?" I said, knowing full well of what.

"Of me?" she said, a flush suffusing her face.

"Why does it matter what I think?"

"You know more about me than anyone else."

"Only of your story which is not quite you."

"Then what do you think of my story?"

I closed the trunk and entered the T-bird. To hell with being nondirective.

"It is the story of one of the most remarkable women I've ever met. I'm sure God is very proud of you as a brave and resilient daughter."

This woman who never seemed to cry burst into tears and ran back to the door of her home.

Not bad, Blackie. Not bad.

Under the circumstances.

CHAPTER 17

I STOPPED THE T-bird near the railroad station. A couple of hours with Lynn Keating Reed had proved an exhausting experience. I hardly knew what to make of it, though the outline of a solution to the death of Monsignor Charles P. McInerny was taking shape.

That could wait. I must first deliver my treasure trove to my principal. I punched his Chancery number into my car phone. (Of course you must put a car phone in a rehabilitated T-bird!)

"Bishop Ryan for the Cardinal," I told the person who answered the phone.

"The Cardinal is eating lunch."

"Tell him I want to talk to him now."

"Yes, Bishop."

I can be authoritative on rare occasions, when it becomes absolutely necessary.

"Did you bring me home a happy ending, Blackwood?" he demanded.

"Arguably, but that remains to be seen. However, I am about to bring you home the records and access to all the funds from Saints Peter and Paul in Woodbridge. It amounts to rather more than we had anticipated. Have someone at the door of that house of horrors where you work in forty-five minutes with a cart to bring them up to your office, while I park our family heirloom."

"I'll be waiting. Call me when you're ten minutes away. . . . Do I get to meet her, Blackwood?"

"Arguably."

An hour later the relevant materials were spread out on the big oak table in the Cardinal's conference room. Wearing his "granny" half glasses (a retreat from vanity when the bottom line was important) and hands on his hips, Sean Cronin surveyed the layout grimly.

"The will is missing?"

"Indeed."

"An important clue for you, I should think."

"A suggestion."

"But we don't need the will?"

"Not when you sign those cards."

"You believe her?"

The Cardinal had picked up quickly the essentials of my story (which left out the personal details of Lynn Reed's life, including the full story of her relationship in Korea with Charles McInerny). His grasp of financial details exceeds that of most clerics and virtually all of his fellow hierarchs, perhaps a result of his father's financial acumen. Lynn was well advised to come clean now. If she had not, some night the Cardinal would have awakened and calculated how much money Saints Peter and Paul ought to have.

"In broad outline, yes. She is too smart not to have told the truth."

He glanced again at the fax of her Navy Cross citation that my friend at the Pentagon had sent me and shook his head in astonished admiration.

"I still want to meet her."

"That is within the realm of the possible."

"The money goes into the Saints Peter and Paul account here. Less the special collections he didn't report during all those years. Some of our lawyers will want to make trouble for her and her son. I won't let them. The kid is Cholly's by the way?"

As I said the Cardinal doesn't miss much.

"You will meet her and make your own judgment."

He grunted. "And Cholly thought I sent young Peter Finnegan out there to take care of him?"

"It would seem so."

"So he made peace with me in the end, at least in his own head?"

"Arguably."

"Never occurred to him that I might be concerned about the parish?"

"Apparently not."

"Poor bastard . . . without going into details, all of which I'm sure you possess and none of which you can tell me, she *did* redeem him, didn't she?"

"As in the woman in the film *Odd Man Out*."

The familiar manic Celtic grin illumined his face for a moment.

"As you yourself say, Blackwood, never argue with the Holy Spirit . . . now see to it that we put his soul at rest or whatever must be done out there."

"I am already on the way back."

I managed to escape the worst of the rush hour and arrived at Saints Peter and Paul in time for my scheduled pre-prandial sip with the Pastor. The chimes were playing "White Christmas" as I pulled up to the rectory. A crowd of grammar school kids were standing in front of the bell tower singing the song at the top of their voices. Thus does youth routinize and then ridicule the uncanny. The good Megan informed that the kids' behavior was "gross."

"He's really been on a roll today," Peter Finnegan told me when he offered me my drink. "It's going both ways, Blackie; the older people are furious when he wakes them up at night; the kids love the show; and the parish staff is going crazy. Even Emil D'Souza finds him a 'trifle disconcerting.'"

"And you?"

"I just want to learn who killed him and put his spirit to rest. How are we doing?"

"We progress."

"You saw herself today?"

"Indeed."

"What did you think?"

I rolled my eyes, I trust impressively.

"You don't think she killed him?"

"It seems unlikely."

"It's all crazy, Blackie. Crazy."

"Milord Cronin asks that I assure you that you enjoy his full confidence. He is amazed at how quickly you have turned things around here."

He shrugged off the compliment.

"It's easy if you give people a chance—and if you have some money. When the Cardinal said that it was all right to use the money Monsignor gave me to remodel the place and to forget about the bureaucracy downtown, I called the decorators and the contractors and told them to get to work."

"And they were?"

"The Fasios, naturally. Monsignor told me truly enough that she had wonderful taste and that he was an honest contractor, maybe the only one in the western suburbs."

"I did not know he was in the construction business."

"Sure is. He not only developed that mall and owns most of it, he built it."

"Remarkable."

"They were his friends and maybe I could have got a better price with someone else, but it made the Monsignor happy, so he didn't get in the way. He thought that most of the ideas were his."

"They must have had a hard time with the rectory."

"Only on the third floor. The electricity and the plumbing were all right down here. Monsignor had more or less closed down the third floor. The Croatian was next door and Father Joe down the corridor. My two rooms were used for storage. It seemed to me that we should open up the third floor so that the priests who were working here would have larger suites and use the rooms on this floor for guest suites for visitors."

"Wise."

"I still haven't figured what to do with the tower."

"When we resolve this puzzle, I may have some suggestions."

"I sure hope so."

We went down to supper. I felt more uneasy as the meal wore on. I should have been upbeat after my conversation with the remarkable Ms. Reed and the apparent recapture of large sums of money that belonged to the Church and more specifically to the people of the parish (who I felt sure would in due course under the gentle persuasion of Peter Finnegan want to use much of it to sustain inner city parishes). But there were storm clouds gathering someplace, and I did not know where or why.

I thought I was coming close to a solution to the puzzle, but I didn't like that much either. However, the sense of foreboding that was closing in on me was not the result, or at least not merely the result, of the picture I was forming in my head of how someone got into the two locked rooms.

Conversation around the table was as cheerful as ever. Emil talked about the Irish as Untouchables in Britain (half fun and full earnest as my mother would have said), the Pastor recounted how he had broken up a fight between two teenagers (girls) on the softball field. Tom Wozniak lamented the absence of a community-wide softball (sixteen inch, is there any other?) league of the sort in which he played when he was growing up and promised to organize one for next summer. Joe O'Keefe described the comedies of his latest checkup at Butternut Community Hospital, adding with what I thought was a dubious show of confidence that he had been given "a clean bill of health."

"What is eating you, Bishop?" Tom finally demanded. "You're not talking, you're not smiling, and your eyes are not twinkling."

"Blinking," I said.

"Close to a solution?" Joe asked lightly.

"Maybe."

"And you don't like what you see?" the Pastor asked.

"Not especially."

"Lynn isn't involved, is she?" Joe persisted.

"Not directly."

I was thinking about the missing will she had pushed the late Pastor to write. Who had taken it? Why? Where was it, if anywhere? Did she still retain it? What was in it?

Before I had a chance to answer the chimes began to play the Marine Hymn.

"Why that?" I asked, glad to change the subject.

"Cholly had it put on the chimes as an extra because he was proud of his days in the Marines," Joe explained. "Though actually he was a Navy chaplain. The Marines don't have their own."

"When we dedicate the new school to him," Pete added, "I'm going to have a wood carver make a statue of him in his fatigues. That should reassure the last of his hard-core admirers."

"A prudent decision," I agreed.

Not to say ironic, given all I had learned today.

"It was Lynn's idea."

"Indeed."

In my tower office, I thought long and hard about the case and liked less and less my conclusion. I also realized that I was in some personal danger, a fact that I also didn't like.

Pete had assured me that I had the only key to the tower suite. Before going to bed, I locked the door to the study and propped a large chair against it. Someone trying to enter would make enough noise to provide advance warning.

Then equipped with a glass (large) of Baileys and one of the large gold candlesticks with which the late Pastor might well have been killed, I descended to the bedroom floor. I locked that door too and propped yet another chair against it. Then I took certain other precautions.

I went to sleep with the candlestick next to me in bed, not as attractive a sleeping companion as the fair Lynn might be but under the circumstances a more sensible one.

I awoke with a start at 2:17, as the alarm clock informed me. I heard footsteps, careful, stealthy footsteps and not the noisy ones the shade of the former Pastor would normally make. I did not instruct the noise to stop, but waited, still mostly asleep, clutching my heavy weapon in my hand.

When I approached something like full consciousness I rolled out of bed, candlestick still in hand. The footsteps came closer. I raised my weapon to strike. I waited. The footsteps waited.

Half of eternity went by.

Then I heard a deep sigh. The footsteps began again, this time receding into the distance. Eventually, they stopped. I found that I was shaking and that sweat was pouring from my body. The makeshift weapon slipped out of my hand and hit the floor with a loud bang.

I retrieved it and brought it back to bed with me.

I did not sleep well, however. I was already half awake when Pete rang me on the house phone at seven.

"I have an emergency sick call, Blackie. Will you take the eight for me?"

"Surely."

As I would soon learn, the demons had been unleashed. Saints Peter and Paul and Woodbridge would be racked by disasters and scandals the next couple of days that I tell myself that I could not have been expected to anticipate.

But I am not sure.

CHAPTER 18

AT THE EIGHT o'clock Mass, I told my story about St. Colmn of Iona and the generosity stone. It is the story that certain Cathedral parishioners insist is my fallback when I don't have any other story for daily Mass. It was a pleasant experience to tell it to a congregation that had never heard it before.

I was not even greatly troubled by the fact that the organ went into an orgy of wild and discordant notes after I had finished the story. So what if the shade or whatever didn't like my story.

However, I knew something was wrong the moment I returned to the sacristy. Peter Finnegan was sitting, disconsolately on a chair by one of the kneelers (prie-dieu in an earlier day), oil stock in one hand, his eyes staring vacantly at the skylight.

"Bad one?" I asked.

His blank facial expression did not change.

"Doc Curtin blew off Gerry Reed's head with his shotgun this morning. The guard found the body when he opened the bank."

This was not supposed to be part of the program.

"Was the doctor apprehended?"

"He wasn't there but it was the big elephant gun of his with his name burned into the stock."

"Indeed."

Mechanically I removed the Mass vestments.

"It was pretty ghastly, Blackie. Somehow the killer got inside the bank and was waiting for him. Must have fired the shot from his left-hand side. Died instantly of course. Shot off his face and the whole side of his head. Apparently ran out the back door, which is the way he came in."

"Thus escaping the commuters who would be on an early train."

"The Woodbridge cops were there. What a bunch of assholes. They wouldn't tell Lynn when she could have the funeral. They have to determine the cause of death first, as if it wasn't obvious. She wants it on Monday with the wake on Sunday and tomorrow night if possible."

"How is she?"

"Badly shaken. Crying most of the time. Not out of control however. Cops wanted to know where she was at the time of her husband's death. She didn't know the time of his death. How could she?"

"Indeed."

The wheels inside my head were spinning—like tires caught in a snowbank.

"I never thought I'd see her cry. He was a wimp, but I guess he was her wimp."

"Her son there?"

"Gerry showed up just after I did. Calmed her down, talked tough to the dumb cops who stopped harassing her. They won't even admit that it's the Doc's gun, though his name is on the stock."

"I think I'd better make a few phone calls," I said.

As it turned out the calls came to me in my tower suite before I could make them.

The first from Milord Cronin.

"Blackwood, what the hell is going on out there?"

"Regrettably people are killing one another."

"Judging by the radio news, one of our embezzlers killed another."

"Only if one assumes that the killer is so distraught as to leave a weapon with his name on it at the scene of the crime."

"There is that," he agreed.

"Moreover, I was given to understand that the deal with us holds even if either or both of them dies. In any event we have the document. I would advise that you sign those cards and messenger them to Gerald Reed V at the Butternut Bank."

"Did it yesterday. . . . Can we keep our name out of it?"

"That remains to be seen. The local police are apparently not very competent. The media will be swarming through the neighborhood within the hour, if they are not here already. I assume that your good friend Zack O'Hara, the State's Attorney for the County of Cook will be on the scene with his entourage in time for the five o'clock news if not the four-thirty, making his usual vigorous statements about the evils of crime. In the scripted playing out of the paradigm of murder on the media who is to notice a haunted rectory or a haunted parish."

"There'll be hell to pay if they find out that ten million dollars of Catholic money is involved."

"You are aware that I have serious questions about the hell metaphor."

"In fact," he continued, "money pertaining to the Catholic Bishop of Chicago, a corporation sole."

"Which he in effect took possession of yesterday or possibly even today."

"They are not to find that out, Blackwood. See to it."

He hung up before I could say that this would not be an easy task.

The phone rang again. Once more it was the aforementioned Cardinal Sean Cronin.

"Same killer, Blackwood?"

"Possibly."

"Not arguably?"

"Nowhere near that."

He hung up without instructing me again to see to it.

Not that it was necessary to repeat the instruction.

I prepared to dial another number. Before I could the phone rang for the third time.

"Blackie, what the hell is going on out there?"

It was Mike the Cop.

"People are killing each other, Michael. I assume your associates have Ms. Reed well protected."

"Of course, someone with her every hour of the day."

"Triple that . . . I also assume that they are in a position to testify that she was in her home at the time of the murder?"

"I've already talked to them. She's clean. So long as it's not a contract job."

"Excellent. You should perhaps inform the local police who are not rated too highly even by the gentle Pastor here. If only they don't mistakenly try to, I believe the term is draw down on your colleagues."

"What if Annie and I can find a suite at some decent motel out there. Do you want us to come out?"

"The sooner the better. Stay at the Butternut Marriott, by the mall. We may own part of it."

Then there was another phone call.

"Gerry Reed here, Bishop. Gerry Junior."

"My sympathies to you and the family."

"Thank you, Bishop. We are all in shock, as you can imagine."

"Your mother?"

"Taking it very hard. But she'll be all right. She's a brave woman."

"Indeed yes."

"Those damn-fool cops are hinting that she might have killed Dad."

"They will not be able to do that," I said flatly.

"I know but it makes it all the harder. . . . Anyway, she wanted me to call you to assure you and the Cardinal that this will not interfere with our project. It will delay it a few days, nothing more."

"I will relay the information to the Cardinal . . . and the wake?"

"We're going ahead with tomorrow night and Sunday whether the police release the body or not. Our lawyer is fighting them now and leaning on the State's Attorney's office, but they're awful blockheads. It's not as though we could have an open coffin anyway."

"Indeed not. I will see you at the wake."

"We'll be looking forward to it, Bishop."

Would they? Had it occurred to no one that if I had not come to Woodbridge, there would have been no murder?

I thought about that, as I would think of it for some time after the case of the haunted parish was resolved.

The next impediment to my breakfast was a call from Lisa, already on duty.

"The cops are here, Bishop Blackie, the Chief and the Chief of Detectives. Yucky!"

"Tell them I'm having breakfast and will be available after breakfast."

I heard her repeating these words to the two police officers in a voice dripping with sarcasm.

I thereupon went to the dining room, ate a long and leisurely breakfast during which I read the *Tribune, The Sun-Times, The Wall Street Journal,* and *The New York Times.* Carefully and thoughtfully.

I then went to my room and vested in regalia I rarely don—cassock with purple buttons and a cape lined in purple and a purple cummerbund. I thought about the zucchetto (skull cap to the uninitiated or perhaps even yarmulke), hesitated, and then decided there was no reason not to.

Glancing at myself in the mirror as I added Catherine's pectoral cross, I concluded that I looked utterly ridiculous, but no more so than most other bishops and indeed less so than many.

Having nothing else to do, the police were still waiting for me, not overweight blustering cops from films about white sheriffs in the South, but lean, hard-jawed cops from movies about state police in the North. Khaki uniforms, drillmaster hats thick with gold braid, Sam Browne belts burdened with large revolvers and walkie-talkies. One of them was wearing the star of a brigadier general, the other the silver eagle of a chicken colonel.

Well at least they weren't carrying billy clubs.

"Reverend Ryan." They stood up as I entered the room. "We'd like to ask . . ."

"Gentlemen," I said, "in our metropolitan area that title tends to be reserved for African American clergy. I can properly be addressed as 'Your Excellency,' 'Bishop,' 'Father,' 'Doctor,' 'Sir,' or even, as John Carroll the first American Bishop was pleased to be known, 'Mister.' But not 'Reverend.' "

Patently I was being contentious.

They introduced themselves as the Chief of Police and the Chief of Homicide.

"How many officers are there in the Woodbridge force, gentlemen?"

They admitted that there were twenty of them.

I did not call attention other than my rolling my eyes to the absurdity of their insignia and titles.

I sat down and fingered my Brigid cross, the way I had seen real bishops do when they're being tolerant of fools and bores.

"What can I do for you gentlemen?"

"We've been informed that you have been here this week, sir, and we're investigating any possible link between your presence and the murder of Mr. Gerald Reed."

I wanted to laugh out loud. Instead I said, "Really?"

"It has been called to our attention that you spoke with Mr. Reed on Monday morning."

"By the worthy bank guard, no doubt?"

"We are not at liberty to say, sir."

"So?"

"Can you tell us what you discussed with Mr. Reed?"

If they had bothered they could have learned that I had spoken to a lot of other people, including the presumed killer.

"No."

"Why not, sir?"

"Because it is none of your business."

"We're investigating a murder."

"Are you really? Tell me, have you taken fingerprints from the murder weapon on which I am told a name has been burned by its maker? Have you taken fingerprints from the man whose name is on the gun? Have you even talked to Stephen Curtin, M.D.? And, since I suspect you haven't, what are you doing in a Catholic rectory on the morning of the crime?"

"With respect, sir, you know nothing about the principles of criminal investigation."

"But I do, Chief . . . or should I call you General. . . . I have read Michael P.V. Casey's book *Principles of Detection* from cover to cover several times. I know good police work when I see it and I know bad police work when I see it."

I also know when cops are covering their asses when I see it.

"You absolutely refuse to discuss the nature of your conversation with the deceased?"

"Absolutely."

"We could hold you for obstruction of justice."

I was losing patience with these clowns.

"Make my day."

"You're not being very cooperative, sir."

"All right, Colonel, I'll tell you what you want to know. Yes, the Catholic Archduke of Chicago is very interested in the death of the late Monsignor Charles P. McInerny which you failed to investigate though the circumstances ought to have been dubious enough for you to question Dr. Curtin's death certificate. We do indeed doubt that the Monsignor died a natural death and we propose to find out how he died. If our investigation turns out to be an embarrassment to you, that would be unfortunate, but we have no particular desire to embarrass you. We want only to know the truth. If you think you can intimidate either Cardinal Cronin or myself, then you have made a very serious mistake."

I find it useful on occasion to cite the Cardinal. The title tends to awe certain people who are easily awed.

"We demand to know if you have any evidence linking the death of Mr. McInerny with that of Mr. Reed."

"No," I said flatly. "But then I know nothing at all about

the death of Mr. Reed. And will not know anything about it until you or the State's Attorney leak it to the media."

Whereupon, lamenting in murmurs my "lack of cooperation," they took their leave.

"Totally cool, Bishop Blackie." Lisa applauded me after she had with only the faintest hint of civility slammed the door on them.

"You weren't eavesdropping, were you, young woman? And don't answer me because if you do you will tell a lie!"

"Of *course* I was listening! See, I didn't tell a lie!"

I went back to the tower and removed my finery and began to pack. I wondered about the footsteps I had heard early in the morning. Had the creator of the footsteps, either changing his mind or encountering my precautions, decided to dispose of Gerald Reed IV instead of me?

It was altogether possible.

Who, I wondered, might be next?

Nothing was to be accomplished by my remaining in Woodbridge until after the funeral of Gerald Reed and the smoke cleared. I would be needed at the Cathedral over the weekend in any case. If I vanished, the killer would feel less threatened. If the killers were the same person, about which fact I was by no means sure. I would come back Sunday night for the wake and begin the week after the funeral with what would be the last phase of the investigation.

If I were lucky.

The mystery of the missing will remained. Or missing wills because it seemed to me for any number of reasons there might be more than one.

If I had any sense at all I would have known where to look.

I told Peter Finnegan my plans, bade a temporary farewell to Lisa, and departed to the Butternut Marriott.

Mike the Cop, whom I'd summoned on my car phone, was waiting for me in the lobby.

A lean, silver-haired man with piercing blue eyes and a face like the late Basil Rathbone playing Sherlock Holmes, Mike had turned to painting watercolors of Chicago neighborhoods after his retirement and his marriage to the wondrous Annie Reilly. But he still loved the scent of an occasional hunt.

"Not a bad getaway for a weekend with your woman," he said as we shook hands. "Not as nice as Grand Beach, but a lot more private. Annie's at the poolside already."

We went into the coffee shop where he had a glass of water and I had a pot of tea and two cinnamon raisin rolls. I filled him in on the details of the case, including my suspicions and hypotheses.

"Don't take any more chances like last night," he warned me.

"There was very little risk, Michael. It confirmed my suspicions about what happened to the Monsignor."

"You'd still need the will."

"It would help. But it may well have been destroyed. We must wait the proper time."

"Why kill Reed?"

"I'm at a loss frankly to explain that."

"I talked to the idiots in Woodbridge. They found two sets of prints on the gun. One is probably Dr. Curtin's. Though they won't know until they get around to finding a copy of his prints or asking him for them. The other?"

"That is the question, isn't it? My guess is that nothing will happen till Monday. The news will carry clips of the funeral Mass and then before the afternoon is over the State's Attorney will announce the arrest of Dr. Curtin."

"They'll start messing with the financial records and

that could mean trouble for the Church, couldn't it, Blackie?

"Arguably," I sighed. "It would be our own fault for permitting the situation to go on out here as long as it has. Or rather the Vatican's fault. But I suspect the scenario will prove to be a bit different."

That afternoon all four channels carried stories of the "Suburban Bank Murder," as they called it, as their lead story. It was our own O. J. Simpson case. There were, as one familiar with the paradigm might have expected, shots of High Street; of the tree-lined streets of Woodbridge; of Stephen Curtin, famous doctor for the rich and world traveler, whose shotgun was alleged to be the murder weapon, emerging from his car and running the gauntlet of reporters; of the Reed home, of Lynn, pale and dressed in black emerging from the house; of reporters pushing microphones at her asking how she felt about her husband's death and who she thought had killed him; of the Police Chief trying to talk like a character from *Hill Street Blues* and *NYPD* combined and assuring the viewers that his officers were pursuing the several promising leads; and finally as the pièce de résistance, State's Attorney Zack O'Hara proclaiming that crime happened in affluent suburbs too and that his office would prosecute the criminal responsible for this senseless murder with all the vigor it had prosecuted other crimes. As O'Hara's voice rose toward a roaring crescendo, the listener who didn't understand the paradigm might have thought that the State's Attorney already had the perfidious criminal in his grasp. There would be more such ringing proclamations of righteousness and integrity should an arrest be made and indictment obtained. If neither happened, one would never hear another word on the case from Mr. O'Hara.

Everything that an eagerly drooling public had come to expect of the TV murder of the week.

There were hints from a couple of the anchorpersons that the "beautiful Lynn Reed, many years younger than her husband," might also be one of the suspects. It was known, they said, that the Reeds and the Curtins were very close friends.

None of the reporters or anchorpersons said what was patently true and ought to have been said—there was every reason to believe that the investigation had been badly botched by a police force that had never dealt with murder.

The same clips would be played over and over through the weekend—before clips from the Bears' training camp at Plattville—to prepare for a possible denouement on Monday afternoon.

None of them seemed aware of the haunted rectory and the haunted parish.

When there's bloody murder, who cares about ghosts?

CHAPTER 19

"IT'S BEEN HELL, Blackie, pure hell."

Thus spoke Father Peter Finnegan at a quarter to nine on Sunday evening in front of the Woodbridge Funeral Parlor, an old Queen Anne house just off High Street. Dusk was slipping toward darkness but the heat and the humid haze of the day persisted, a veil over grief if there happened to be any. Men and women were standing outside the funeral parlor, talking and joking in soft tones as the Irish always do at wakes. Most of the mourners, if one could use the word, were young, friends of the Reed children rather than of their parents. High Street and Elm Street were jammed with traffic as those who were coming to the wake tried to find a parking place and those who were leaving tried to extricate themselves from the diagonal parking by the station. Woodbridge police, with apparently no other serious business at hand, were issuing warning citations to the cars that were parked along Elm Street, citations that the drivers contemptuously tore up and threw on the parkway in defiance of the litter law.

Woodbridge, which approved of only small and quiet wakes, did not like the invaders and the invaders didn't like Woodbridge.

Peter Finnegan and Tom Wozniak, in full clericals, were walking up and down Elm and directing cars to the parish parking lot, to the apparent chagrin of the cops who seemed to think they had a monopoly on traffic.

"What can you expect of cops," Tom had exploded, "whose top salary is thirty-five thousand a year in a village this wealthy."

"You get what you pay for," I sighed, "and usually less."

Then Pete had groaned about the wake being a weekend of pure hell.

"The press people are everywhere, poking, snooping, prying, even bribing. They're fixated on the idea that Lynn and Steve had a 'relationship.' They hassle her whenever she appears. Look at them over there at the corner, waiting for a last shot at her when she leaves the wake. She just looks straight ahead and pretends that they're not there. There's a couple of very smooth guys who are fending them off. Otherwise I'm afraid her son and sons-in-law would take a poke at them. The women are the worst. They really seem to hate her. Then when Steve and Margie Curtin showed up tonight they were all over them. They even asked Margie if she knew about the 'affair' between her husband and Lynn. Steve broke a TV camera and hit a woman radio reporter—which is just what they want of course!"

"They will assert that they are only doing their jobs in service of the public's right to know—by which they mean the public's right to drool over tasty scandals. . . . How did she react to the Curtins?"

"As grateful for their sympathy as for everyone else's. Do you think Steve did it?"

"Perhaps."

"The cops are bumbling and stumbling around, asking the wrong people the wrong questions. They haven't even taken Doc's fingerprints yet. The rumor is that they're going to arrest him tomorrow."

"In time for the five o'clock news."

"Some women reporters are snooping around the hospital. They're digging for dirt from the Doc's past. I guess he had a reputation for hitting on nurses. If they can find any evidence of sexual harassment, he's a goner."

"Possibly."

"Aren't you afraid the reporters will recognize you?"

"One of the advantages of being unimpressive in appearance is that often no one notices you. They don't even see you. It can be very useful."

"The Monsignor is going crazy," Pete continued. "It's not just the organ and the bells. Now he turns the air conditioner and the lights off in church—on a day like this. The parishioners are furious at him. And even the Catholics in the village hate the publicity. We're trying to calm everyone down, but the hot weather has made tempers short."

"Yet the geniuses of the media have yet to learn of the haunt?"

"Who's interested in haunting when they have illicit love and murder?"

"I had better go in and pay my respects."

Through the weekend I had worried, and not about the Bears first exhibition game either (which they won). Amid the alarms and excursions on television—with more hints that Lynn was under suspicion and more clips of her coming out of church and pictures of her from *The Bridge* and the *Trib*, I had continued to ponder the matter of the will or wills. How would I obtain them from the putative killer without tipping my hand?

No way.

And I also had worried about the murder of Gerry Reed IV. It didn't fit the puzzle at all. It seemed not only senseless, as Zack O'Hara had said, but unnecessary. Nor could I see how my bumbling investigations might have occasioned it. Yet it could not have been a coincidence, could it?

In any event, I would have to await the arrest on Monday to take my next step. Would they dare arrest Lynn, knowing that Mike's colleagues had been watching her every day? Maybe the Woodbridge cops, under pressure from the media and the State's Attorney, would simply ignore her alibi.

More likely they would go after Dr. Curtin. Maybe he would be sufficiently high on drugs or sufficiently down after coming off the high that he would blurt out all we needed to clear up the puzzle.

My guess was that they would mess it up more than they already had.

Just inside the entrance of the funeral parlor, Mike the Cop confirmed Pete's report.

"We are surrounded, Blackie," he confided to me, "by all the assholes of the western world."

"Their name is legion," I agreed, alluding to the Scriptures. "This might be useful."

I gave him a copy of the Navy's citation of valor for Lt. (j.g.) Evelyn Keating.

He glanced at it, folded it, and put it in his inside jacket pocket.

"You always come up with the most interesting women, Cousin Blackie."

"Arguably . . . the arrest of Dr. Curtin will presumably be tomorrow afternoon?"

"Almost certainly. He was high on something when he came by here, not really high, kind of lightly stoned. They finally got around to comparing fingerprints and, sure enough, his are on the gun. It's his gun, of course, so what else would one expect."

"And . . . ?"

Mike grinned. "And as you suspected another set of prints. The killer's, do you think?"

"Perhaps."

"They'd like to arrest Lynn as an accessory if they could find any evidence. That would make a great sound bite for Zack. But they have nothing on her."

"They are aware of course of the alibi provided by your associates?"

"Vaguely, but it doesn't seem to compute."

"It will when her lawyers sue for defamation and false arrest."

Having said that, perhaps with more glee than was appropriate, I joined the line to the bier, ignoring as do both the Cardinal and the Mayor, the traditional prerogative of priests and politicians of going to the head of the line (most pols have given it up but, alas, not most priests).

Despite its high ceilings and elaborate moldings, the Woodbridge Funeral Parlor was like all of its kind: hushed voices and the smell of flowers and other realities about which one would not like to speculate. The casket of course was closed.

Arnold Griffin, who had been standing unobtrusively in the background at the head of the line, not quite a member of the family perhaps, but not quite distinct from them either, spotted me and glided, skillfully for such a tall man, to my side.

"You shouldn't have to wait in line, Bishop."

"Yes, I should."

"Thank God you spoke with her before this happened."

I was not altogether sure why the Deity should receive gratitude for a visit that might have led to the murder.

"Ah?"

"She feels that he was at peace knowing the problem was on its way to resolution . . . it is, isn't it?"

"Oh, yes . . . I would advise you to see that the family hires the best lawyer it can find. There is solid reason to believe that they will attempt to charge her as an accomplice."

"I'm told that's all over the media. I can't believe it."

"Believe it . . . you have perhaps seen the tall man at the door?"

"The one that looks like Sherlock Holmes? A cop, isn't he?"

"Oh, yes."

"We didn't hire him."

"I did. His associates have been guarding Ms. Reed for several days. They will testify that she was in her home at the time of the murder. The authorities have been told this but somehow haven't comprehended it."

"You take good care of your own," he said with a smile, "don't you, Bishop?"

"We try."

"She told me about Korea. Everything. I'm not surprised about either aspect of the story. If I were a wounded Marine under threat from guerrillas, I'd want her in the tent."

"Indeed . . . I urge you to keep a very close watch on her in the next couple of days. We will continue our protection, but she can't have too much."

He hesitated, embarrassed at the possibility I knew about their relationship.

"She feels that we should be, ah, restrained for the immediate future."

"I can make no judgment on that matter. However, I adjure you, do not let her out of your sight."

"If you say so, Bishop."

"Good-looking kids." I nodded toward the mourners.

"Like their mother."

The two younger children, Jill and Gerald V, did indeed look like their mother, but were much taller than either their mother or their putative father.

"You must think of it as not the end of life for him," I told a red-eyed Lynn, "but the beginning of a new and better life."

In some fashion that goes beyond the power of human eyes to see and human ears to hear and the human heart to contain.

She hugged me and leaned briefly against me.

"I believe that, Bishop," she whispered. "I really do. He was a good man. They made his life miserable. I loved him. More at the end of his life than at any other time, as you know."

She then introduced me to her children and to their attractive spouses and to the four grandchildren who were present. They all smiled properly at "Bishop Ryan," hardly aware of what a devious person he actually was.

Young Gerry took me aside. "Legally and for our part, Bishop," he murmured, "this will make no difference. Will it for you and the Cardinal?"

"Only that we see no need, in the present circumstances, for you to hurry to consult with us."

"We want to begin the process of getting it over with. I'll call the Cardinal's office on Tuesday for an appointment."

"Bring your mother."

He smiled despite his grief. "You bet!"

As I walked toward the door of the funeral parlor, I glanced back at her. Even in a longish black dress and black hat with a partial veil, she was still a gorgeous woman. Lucky Arnie. Lucky Gerald. Even lucky Charles P. McInerny.

I waited at the door for the media circus that would accompany the family's departure. It was worse than I had expected. Although she was surrounded by her family and six of Mike's finest, three of them women (and all of them naturally off-duty Chicago cops), Lynn was still the target of shouted questions:

"Are you and Dr. Curtin lovers?"

"Did you sleep with him the night before he killed your husband?"

"How long have you been unfaithful to your husband?"

"Do you expect to be arrested tomorrow?"

One of them, a shrill young woman, managed to sneak though the cordon and corner her at the entrance to her Mercedes.

"Have they taken your fingerprints yet?" she demanded.

Lynn turned toward the TV camera that followed the journalist and spoke slowly and confidently.

"I served in the United States Navy in Korea. I'm sure they have my fingerprints if anyone wants them."

"In combat?" the startled young woman demanded.

"In a manner of speaking." Lynn turned and entered the car. One of Mike's young women closed the door and eased the journalist out of the way.

Think about that, guys.

Back in my tower suite in the rectory, I pondered the problem of the wills, performed my usual precautions, and retired to the bed with my candlestick firmly clutched in one hand. I hoped that the footsteps would appear again. But did not expect that they would.

They didn't.

The next day was, if anything, a worse nightmare.

An allegedly cool weather front that had dropped down

from Canada into the Chicago area overnight and dumped several inches of rain on the city changed its mind, stalled, and then eased its way imperceptibly north again as a warm front with yet more rain and humidity and a steady barrage of thunder showers, which provided news channels with the opportunity to interrupt their programming with the panicky warnings of hail, lightning, heavy rain, and possible tornadoes.

Like the boy crying wolf.

They were right about the storms, however, though at the wrong time. Thunder that had been reverberating in the distance all morning turned continuous as the funeral cortege pulled up to Saints Peter and Paul, lightning flashes crackled almost without interruption across the glowering sky, and rain fell in thick sheets. None of these manifestations of nature's displeasure prevented the press from swarming around the funeral party and the casket and blocking their entry to the church. Watching from the vestibule (a bishop in full choir robes would have raised too many questions with too many people), I took some joy in the observation that rain was drenching the working press, which now included network as well as local correspondents. The uncharitable and unchristian thought occurred to me that if lightning should electrocute some of them, it would be no great loss to the world.

The Woodbridge police—in ponchos of course—did not intervene. Mike's squad of twelve was pushed back against the pallbearers and mourners as journalists swarmed around Lynn. I found myself wishing I had brought my beloved candlestick from the tower.

Peter Finnegan and Tom Wozniak saved the day.

In the full white vestments for the Eucharist of the Resurrection (as we properly call the old requiem Mass these days, though I hear that some liturgical purists are trying to mess with that title), Pete appeared at the door of the church, heedless of the rain.

"All TV cameras on me please."

Every camera and mike in the mob was turned on him instantly.

"I hope that every news director who has someone in this riot which is disrupting a funeral service has the common decency to carry what I am about to say. Never in all my years as a priest have I ever seen such a blasphemous and obscene display of disrespect for the dead and contempt for the living. I now ask all of you to step back and permit this liturgy to continue."

I reflected that I could not have said it better myself.

Slowly and grudgingly the media pulled back far enough to permit the funeral party to enter the church.

Then the shade took over. Wresting control from the organist (as she later reported) by physical force, he played the Marine Hymn as the funeral procession entered the church and walked slowly to the front.

For a moment I believed in the shade. Who else would know how insulting to Lynn and her late husband that music would be. Then I realized that "Anchors Aweigh" would have been a more appropriate insult.

Having finished the hymn, the shade then struggled to take control of the Eucharist from the clergy. He knocked over candlesticks, pounded the organ, rattled the windows, and stomped on the roof. It was as though he were trying to make more noise than the storm (on which, thank heaven, the disturbances would later be blamed).

Peter Finnegan read the Gospel in contention with both thunder and rattling candlesticks, with an occasional protest from the organ.

"This has gone far enough," I insisted loudly from my

secret position in the sacristy. "Stop it now! And don't interrupt the Eucharist again!"

The noise subsided. It might, however, have stopped anyway.

I had quite had it with psychic phenomena.

Competing only with the thunder and the crackling lightning, Pete preached effectively about God loving us like a parent who protects us, not from every evil, but from ultimate evil, and praised the late Gerald IV for his dedication to his family and community. Pete, it turned out, is that kind of Irish rhetorician of whose efforts at a funeral liturgy it could be safely be said "left not a dry eye in the church."

High praise.

After the final benediction, I slipped out of the sacristy and unobtrusively walked to the mourners' pews to extend my sympathies to Lynn Keating Reed and her family. Since I am rarely noticed (when I'm not talking) no one observed in any practical sense of the word the funny little priest who materialized at the pew and then dematerialized.

The representatives of the fourth estate were more restrained at the end of the Eucharist, mostly because the Pastor still in full robes despite the now diminishing rain led the procession all the way to the limousine. They could get at Lynn only by knocking him down.

Instead of tolling, the chimes pealed in celebration.

I drove with Pete to Mount Carmel Cemetery which was only fifteen minutes away.

"I hope this is the end of it," he said.

"I'm afraid it isn't," I said grimly. "There's more evil that must out."

Lynn wept bitterly at the cemetery, her first show of emotion of the day. Her children clung to her in support but also for support. I offered my sympathies again, was hugged again, and adjured Arnold Griffin in a discreet whisper again not to let her out of his sight.

I wasn't quite sure what the danger was—though in retrospect I should have been—but I knew there was danger.

"This isn't the Reed family plot, is it?" I asked the Pastor on the way back to Saints Peter and Paul. "Where are Gerald I and II?"

"Buried in Ravenswood Cemetery in Chicago, with the five brothers of the great-grandfather who was the only one in his family to survive the Civil War. They were Protestants up till Gerald III if you remember."

The deceased's father, horrible man that he was alleged to be, must have loved his wife very much to abandon the family tradition of Methodism and become a Papist. When had he gone wrong?

"They're buried right next to the Crawfords," Pete continued. "General Moses Elias Crawford was the founder of Woodbridge and the man who built the rectory. His family and the Reeds were great friends on the north side of Chicago before they both moved out here. Colonel Reed and General Crawford were great drinking buddies according to the legend, Methodists or not. The Crawfords died out at the end of the century and the house and all the land was sold cheap to Father Kelly."

"Any tradition of it being haunted before?"

"None that I know of."

But a tradition of a tower suite. Interesting. Perhaps useful.

I went back to my suite in the rectory, made a brief report to Milord Cronin, and began to search the shelves of the late Monsignor's study for a book of Woodbridge history.

I found *A Brief History of the Early Years of Wood-bridge* by one Ellen Prudence King after about an hour of poking around, tucked behind a shelf of old missals that might well have dated to his predecessor.

Inside the front cover was a faded sticker proclaiming the book to *"Ex Libris* Patrick Flynn."

It was little more than a bound pamphlet of fifty-eight pages, published "privately" in 1910 by the "authoress" and printed on thick, yellowing paper that flaked off at the touch. Very early Woodbridge.

Ms. King must have been an early feminist or "suffrag-ette," a name that today is, needless to say, as politically incorrect as a word can be. She spent half the book attacking the vices of General Crawford, most notable of which was his "exploitation" of women. He built his "hideous house of horrors" in such a way that he could "keep" a respectable wife and family in the main part of the family home and maintain a "disorderly house" in the adjacent tower. At all times, she reported in horror, he held as prisoner in that tower two young women ("usually of *foreign* origin") to "slake his unspeakable appetites and those of his equally evil *friend*, Colonel G. T. Reed."

Aha.

After the General would tire of his prisoners, he would dismiss them ("or perhaps do even worse things to them") and bring in another pair of "poor, *pathetic* victims."

As proof that there was a just Providence, "according to unimpeachable information available to the present writer, General Crawford died during an *unspeakable* orgy, though whether of his own evil or at the hands of his victims or murdered by his foul friend Colonel Reed cannot be said with any degree of confidence. The writer fondly hopes the second explanation is the correct one."

Right on, Ellen Prudence!

"In subsequent years, there have been reports of *supernatural* disturbances at night in the tower. Lights are said to flash in the windows, shots are heard to ring out, the screams of tormented women are said to be heard. The author has in fact heard these screams herself."

So the place might have been a locale for psychic experiences almost a century ago. That might clear up some puzzles.

Then came the kicker:

"Small wonder then that the unfortunate children and grandchildren of this evil man did not want to live in this house of horrors and that it fell into disrepair. No one wished to live in the house, much less purchase it and the land around it until the first Roman priest assigned to Woodbridge purchased the house and land as a base for his *foreign* invasion of lovely Woodbridge. One imagines that the *superstitions* of the Church of Rome would be well received in such a terrible place. The author knows for a fact that the Roman priest has closed up the tower and no one lives in it now."

As a frontispiece, the good Ellen Prudence had drawn a "personal sketch" of the "Crawford Manse," which exaggerated the structure of the house to make it look more ghostly than your average Victorian haunted house.

She also provided a crude sketch of the inside of the tower, "based on information of those who have had the frightening opportunity of actually *investigating* it."

The sketch added little to what I had already known or surmised.

So Paddy Flynn, wondering where he might stash his peculiar brother Dr. Flynn, must have come upon the book, been unimpressed by the Nativist bigotry of its author and the spooky tales she had told, and rejoiced at the opportunity the tower provided him.

Had Charles P. McInerny read the book? Did he know about the past uses of the tower and the labyrinth within it? Had he told anyone else about it? Arguably showed them its passages?

Perhaps Lynn? Or his various cronies and buddies?

Then I realized that he wouldn't have had to read the book. Had he not ejected Dr. Flynn on arrival? So he must have been aware of the design of the tower if not its past history.

I called my friend who had served in the declining days of Monsignor Flynn.

"Did Paddy Flynn believe in ghosts?"

"Ghosts? Shit, Blackie, he didn't even believe in God!"

"There were no ghostly manifestations during your term there?"

"Only that bastard Doc Flynn appearing and disappearing and he was alive, unfortunately."

"Indeed."

"Hey, Blackie, what the hell's going on out there?"

"A number of people have asked me that question. I may be able to answer it soon. Don't believe what you see on television."

Those who were psychic perhaps would be tuned in to emanations of past horrors, memory traces still lingering long after the people involved had gone to their respective rewards, such as these might be. Those who were not psychic would sense nothing.

And as for Blackie Ryan, who in this area of behavior (as in so many others) was neither fish nor flesh?

Well, he heard footsteps in the night.

CHAPTER 20

ZACK O'HARA SOMEHOW missed a step. The news of the arrest of Dr. Stephen E. Curtin was announced on the five o'clock news and not the four-thirty. The slower-moving Woodbridge police force was edged into the background.

The broadcasts began, as the paradigm demanded, with brief clips of a securely handcuffed and very angry Dr. Curtin after he had been taken into custody at Butternut Community Hospital, "where he is on the staff and the wife of the victim, Lynn Reed, serves in an administrative capacity."

Chairman of the board!

Then the focus turned, as it was supposed to, on the State's Attorney for the County of Cook. His square jaw set, his round face taut, his hair smoothly slicked back, Zack assured the lovers of the TV "real murder" paradigm that crime was not limited to the city and to the poor and that his office would prosecute this crime with the same vigor and integrity that it would prosecute any similar crime in any other place in Cook County.

I laughed aloud at the words "vigor and integrity." Zack wasn't much interested in either, unless they provided an opportunity for a press conference.

"Zack, are there any other suspects?"

"We are investigating all aspects of the matter fully."

"Is Ms. Reed under suspicion?"

"We are investigating all aspects of the matter fully," he said in a higher tone of voice that was supposed to imply that he was losing his patience with the questions, whereas in fact he was delighted that the questions were being asked.

"Were she and Dr. Curtin lovers?"

"I said that we are investigating all aspects of the matter fully!" he bellowed at the top of his very loud voice.

"Are her fingerprints on the gun?"

He lost his cool this time, hot-tempered cement-head Irishman that he is. No one was supposed to know about the second set of prints on the gun, not until the FBI had a chance to check on Lynn's prints.

"I said that we are investigating all aspects of the matter fully!" he screamed.

The reporter covering the press conference, no matter on which channel (I was channel surfing rapidly), said that his channel had learned from sources close to the investigation that the shotgun that was believed to have been the murder weapon was the property of Dr. Curtin and his fingerprints had been found on it.

Brilliant! It was known as soon as the dead body of Gerry IV had been discovered that the gun belonged to Dr. Curtin because his name was on it. If it belonged to him, it would have been astonishing had his fingerprints not been on it.

Only two channels showed Peter Finnegan remonstrating with the press riot and only one had the integrity to report his words. He was, I thought, every bit as impressive on tape as he was in person.

The rest of the murder story focused on the funeral and almost exclusively on Lynn, subtly emphasizing the curves of her body that the cotton knit black dress could not hide and did not attempt to hide and her lovely and carefully made-up face. Somehow neither tears nor rain had marred the makeup so she looked even younger than she would have if her cosmetic efforts had not been so effective.

The journalists discussed the long and close association of both of them with Butternut Community Hospital and implied that they also had a long and close association with one another. All four channels featured her response, which each channel termed 'defiant,' from the previous night about her fingerprints.

Two anchorpersons summed up with the observation that "sources close to the investigation" had informed their channel that State's Attorney O'Hara was actively seeking those fingerprint records from the Navy Department.

FBI, you idiots, I murmured.

Mike the Cop called. "Saw it all, Blackie. Can't believe it. O'Hara is over the top this time."

"Nothing defamatory yet. The courts would find that there was sufficient reason for arresting Dr. Curtin because the gun was his."

"Yeah, but at some point the public is going to grow weary of the show."

"Of murder and adultery? Mike, gimme a break!"

"That poor woman," he said.

"But now at least half the women who soak up these cases will be absolutely sure she did it because they hate her for her good looks. Nothing will ever change their minds."

"She'll have to live with that for the rest of her life, Blackie."

"Possibly, though she is a tough woman."

"Zack may go too far this time and be forced to apologize."

"A consummation devoutly to be wished, nay prayed for."

"Speaking of beautiful and interesting women, the one I sleep with insists that we take you out for supper."

"An excellent idea. They'll probably be serving baked yogurt here tonight."

After a good Irish meal of steak and potatoes and a leisurely evening of basking in the approving smile of the beauteous Annie, I returned to the now certifiably haunted tower, feeling mildly less dyspeptic about the condition of humankind than I had been after the evening news.

Pouring myself a large glass of Baileys (the one at the restaurant did not count), I pondered the matter of the will once again. Was there any reason to suppose that whoever took it—and it might have been removed before, during, or after the murder—might have refrained from destroying it?

There was one reason patently: the thief, who in principle might or might not be the killer, could not be sure whether Lynn had seen the contents of the will. In fact, she had not because according to her report the late Pastor had covered the written paragraphs with his hand when she signed the will.

Would a woman who had been so honest about so many things fib at a matter like this?

Perhaps to protect someone, though that did not seem likely.

If Lynn had seen it and if somehow the thief was mentioned (and if he/she were implicated in the alienation of Church funds and inappropriate use of them, then he/she knew it since by definition the thief had the will) in what the late Pastor had written, the thief would have had excellent reason to destroy it. But should Lynn report what the will had said, the thief would be immediately implicated as a killer. Better that the will show up spontaneously in some fashion so that the thief, perhaps accused of malfeasance, would not also be suspected of murder.

On the other hand if Lynn had not seen the contents of the will, the thief was home free and could destroy the will. Since there had been no mention at all of the will, the thief by now probably thought that it was safe to dispose of it and most likely had done so.

Yet the behavior of the shade might have given the thief pause. The will and possibly other wills might still exist somewhere.

Fine. But where.

The answer, pathetically obvious that it was, almost blasted its way into my thick skull. But I was too tired to grasp it.

I made my usual preparations for fending off the footsteps. But they did not materialize that night.

I had resolved that I would stay at Saints Peter and Paul until the final piece of the puzzle fell into place. At the moment I would have to wait out the criminal.

So, after I had made a number of calls to the Cathedral to make sure my staff had not rolled it down State Street to Lincoln Park, I set to work on my Aero in my task to sort out the *Tenebrae* mysteries in *Finnegans Wake*.

In midmorning Mike the Cop was on the phone.

"Did you hear the news, Blackie?"

"Almost certainly not."

"They've released Dr. Curtin."

"Indeed!"

"Apparently he had an alibi, a young woman is what they're saying, with all that implies. He also passed a lie detector test. The investigation is continuing, we're told."

"They're up against a dead end until they get a match on the second set of prints," I observed, "which could take a while, especially if they're not Lynn's, as we know they're not."

"O'Hara will need something soon. She's the only target available. He might go for an arrest without the prints. They may never find matching prints if the person who made them is not in the FBI files."

"You think that he will have her arrested?" I asked.

"Probably just brought in for questioning. Not tonight, but maybe tomorrow night. He can't risk two mistaken arrests. That might be enough publicity to get him through the week. Next week everyone will have forgotten about the case."

"You are in touch with her lawyer?" I asked.

"Sure. As soon as he has a press conference, we'll have one. For the six o'clock news so he'll already be in the record and will have been the lead. Then we cut the ground out from under him."

"Admirably devious," I said and returned to my work, which, needless to say, is essential for the continuation of human culture.

I was interrupted by a call from my principal.

"Remember me, Blackwood?"

"I'm afraid not."

"I'm the Cardinal Archbishop of Chicago."

"Really?"

"You work for me."

"Indeed?"

"I was afraid you might have forgotten. . . . Would it be all right to ask what the hell you're doing out there in that lunatic asylum for the new rich?"

"Some of them are not so new."

"Was Jolly Cholly murdered?"

"Oh, yes."

"Well, that's somewhat more confident than just 'arguably.'"

"Perhaps."

"Do you know who did it?"

"Of course."

And in saying that I did.

"Have him arrested."

"No evidence yet. I'm waiting the matter out."

"Waiting it out!"

"No other choice just now."

"I see . . . well finish it up. Get evidence!"

Hoping to distract him from this rather simplistic approach to reality (which he adopts for my benefit, if that is the proper word) I told him the story of the past history of the rectory and of Monsignor Paddy Flynn's adaptation to it.

"Tell Peter Finnegan to tear the tower down!"

I remained silent. He really didn't mean it, though for reasons that there was no need to explain to him at the present, it might not be a bad idea.

"Incidentally," he continued, "young Gerry Reed phoned me for an appointment. Friday. They want to get things cleared up as soon as possible. His mother is coming."

"If she's not in jail."

"What!"

I explained our calculations about the likely strategies of those who passed for law enforcement officers in the County of Cook.

"Blackwood, that's altogether unacceptable. It is, in fact, intolerable. It must not happen. See to it."

He hung up before I could comment. That was the equivalent of his striding out of my room.

There were excellent reasons for both winding up the case of the haunted parish and for protecting Lynn Reed.

We had been fortunate so far. No one knew about the problem of parish money and the media had not yet caught on to the haunting. If Lynn were charged with murder, it would be most difficult to keep the misappropriation of parish funds a secret. Under such circumstances there would be more focus on the parish and hence on the local friendly shade.

In the event the news directors that night faced an apparently difficult challenge. There were three pieces of news:

1. Dr. Curtin had been released, but no one was free from suspicion. Naturally, all one required for such an announcement was the State's Attorney's spokesman. Zack O'Hara was doubtless busy elsewhere.

2. Lynn Reed had been questioned at the Woodbridge police station for several hours in the presence of counsel. The Police Chief said she had been "uncooperative." Her lawyer said that the police had been "incompetent and unprofessional." There was but one clip of Lynn in a black summer suit with silver buttons and a silver scarf at her neck walking out of the station in the company of her son and the lawyer under the now soft August sun. The woman liked silver. Nothing wrong with that. I noted with some anxiety the absence of Arnold Griffin. I had told him not to let her out of his sight. Perhaps he was out of camera angle. I hoped so.

3. Several women associated with Butternut Community Hospital had "come forward with sexual allegations against Dr. Curtin," made anonymously and off-camera or with faces protected. The doctor was charged with everything from the use of offensive language to actual rape.

Those who are familiar with the values of those who manufacture the news for consumption by TV audiences will have no doubt which item won the lead. I had little doubt Steve Curtin was guilty of a long life of sexual misconduct. But his right to his reputation and to be innocent until proven guilty had been destroyed.

Go ahead, sue if you want, Doc.

Mike the Cop called me just as the network news came on to tell me more about the morality tale being worked out in the case of the people of California against O. J. Simpson, the networks having lost interest in our vest-pocket scandal.

"We decided to hold back on our cards until tomorrow. No point in using them till we have to."

"A prudent decision."

"They wanted to take her prints and she wouldn't let them."

"Why not?"

"Because she found the suggestion offensive under the circumstances that they already know about her alibi. I add that the woman I sleep with strongly endorses that position. Which means that it is unassailable."

"Patently."

"How you doing?"

"Getting closer to the heart of the matter."

"*Finnegans Wake* or the case of the haunted parish."

"Both."

I still had to find the will. Or wills perhaps. I could move without them. I would by the weekend regardless. But it would still be most useful to have the wills. Especially because fingerprints would seal the matter.

What would happen after that?

I didn't want to think about the answer to that question.

Supper at Saints Peter and Paul was a glum affair.

"This stuff has got to stop," the young Pastor said, his face twisted in an untypical scowl.

"Driving everyone nuts," Tom agreed. "He was messing around with the softballs and bats over on the field today."

The meal was not baked yogurt, but, alas, something worse, a tuna fish salad that might have been made of recycled paper. Indeed, probably was.

"A most unusually prolonged and varied display of psychic pyrotechnics," Emil D'Souza, S.J., observed. "I'll admit it would cause me some concern."

"At least your test results were all good, huh, Joe?"

"Great," said the elderly priest. "And they didn't find any spooks inside me."

More tests?

The laughter was less than hearty.

"What about you, Blackie?" The Pastor turned to me. "Have you solved the mystery yet?"

"Oh, yes," I said blandly. "There are some obscure little details to be cleared away, but that shouldn't take more than a few days."

I was besieged with questions, but putting on my most owlish face, I begged them to wait a few more days.

There were, in fact, a lot more than a few details to be cleared away. And they were not little.

"Was that stuff on TV tonight a hint that they might go after Lynn?" Joe O'Keefe asked anxiously.

"The worthy State's Attorney needs something to get him through the weekend."

"Why don't they leave her alone?" Pete demanded.

"Because she is caught in a symbiosis between an amoral criminal justice system and an amoral media system."

"Surely," Emil said, "they will not be able to charge her with the murder of her unfortunate husband?"

The desert for which I had been hoping turned out to be fresh pineapple slices, as much a problem to me about God's goodness as was the mosquito to St. Augustine.

"They may charge her, even get an indictment. They'll never be able to bring it to a trial."

"What are they waiting for?" Joe grumbled.

I nibbled one slice of pineapple and eased the plate away as though I were virtuously denying myself something I truly loved.

"Her fingerprints. She won't let them print her and thus forces them to wait for the FBI to dig out her Navy record. They'll have to charge her to take her prints."

"Why is she being stubborn?" Pete scowled again.

"Because she is a tough woman who won't be intimidated by anyone."

"Can you be certain that the other fingerprints on the shotgun aren't hers?" he persisted.

"Oh, yes. Quite certain."

Everyone wanted to ask why but no one did.

"I didn't know she'd been in the Navy." Pete stirred uneasily. "Much less in Korea."

"I believe that's where she met her late husband. There is an article about their marriage in an issue of *The Bridge*."

He wondered patently whether she had known Charles McInerny in Korea. He had the sense not to ask.

"What did she mean"—Tom wrinkled his forehead—"when she said that in a manner of speaking she'd seen action."

"A field hospital of some sort, I suppose. Near the front lines, I imagine."

That ended that segment of the conversation.

I was still hungry when we adjourned. I found the ever faithful Megan in the office and produced my book of free Thirty-One Flavors certificates.

"Could I interest you and the wondrous Sean in some ice cream?"

"Oh, great! And maybe a steak sandwich?"

"A wonderful idea."

So I managed to eat a decent meal.

And to learn that "everyone" was hoping and even predicting that Lynn would marry Mr. Griffin who, poor man, had been a widower for such a long time. I declined to speculate on that possibility.

Moreover, "everyone" in Woodbridge also still thought that Dr. Curtin was the killer. Anyone who suspected Lynn was wise enough, I was assured, to keep his opinion to himself.

Back in the tower, after another hour of wresting with the problems of the case, including how my suspect could have gained possession of Doc's elephant gun, I gave up on the mystery and prepared for bed. With my usual tumbler of Baileys in my hand (the first of the day, be it noted), I made my usual precautions for the advent of the footsteps. I hoped as I lugged the heavy candlestick into the bed next to me that it was not becoming a fetish.

I suspected that I had heard the last of the footsteps. If they don't come tonight, I told myself, they won't come at all. And I don't think they'll come tonight.

I could not have been more wrong.

It was earlier, one-thirty, that I heard them from a great distance. I almost rolled over and went back to sleep. Then, realizing where I was and what I was hearing, I bounded out of bed and in the dark groped for my pike. Or was it my battle ax? Knights errant carried some such weapon did they not?

In the dark and in a room that was still unfamiliar I could not find it.

The footsteps came closer. And yet closer. They were almost next to me now.

I searched frantically among the tumbled bedclothes for the candlestick.

The intruder shoved hard against the barrier I had constructed. It wasn't very solid. Did not the intruder know the enormous risk that was being taken?

I found the candlestick and raised it above my head.

I imagined the headlines proclaiming that a bishop had killed an intruder in a rectory, indeed a reputedly haunted rectory. The whole story would pour out.

So I would only break a shoulder or two. I had the advantage of surprise, didn't I?

I thought of Lynn describing how reality flowed in slow motion. That wasn't happening to me now.

The intruder continued to shove. The candlestick grew heavier in my slippery hands. One more shove and the intruder would be on me.

Then the shade intervened.

All the lights in the tower went on, as did the television and my computer upstairs, and the microwave in the kitchen. The chimes rang out a Brahms chorale. Solemn high cheap tricks. Moreover the crowds of people that Megan had reported poured into the room and with them a winter chill, a new phenomenon.

No tormented women from the past however. Unless they were part of the crowd.

The intruder's footsteps, beating a rapid tattoo, rushed in the opposite direction.

What was that all about, I wondered.

"Go away," I said aloud. "I need some sleep."

Almost reluctantly the crowd dispersed, the chill lessened, and the lights and electronic instruments turned themselves off. So apparently had the chimes.

Fun rectory.

Peter Finnegan awakened me at seven on the house phone.

"Just back from another one, Blackie. I'm too sick to say Mass. Will you take it for me?"

"What happened?" I demanded uneasily.

"Cops found Doc Curtin in his Porsche under the viaduct about four this morning. Called me right away, oddly enough. Someone had slit his throat with a scalpel. Cut off his genitals too, probably when he was still alive. Blood everywhere."

CHAPTER 21

I REALIZED AS I groped over to the church that both nights the footsteps had visited me, someone had died violently. I also was fairly certain I knew where the wills were. I must retrieve them and have Mike the Cop dust them for fingerprints. The case could be drawn to a conclusion before Thursday was history.

My case. But how could the evidence from my case, secret as it still was, help explain the violence rending Woodbridge.

I barely noticed on the way into the church that the tenacious weather front had drifted back from which direction I had forgotten. It was raining again.

I told my story of St. Brigid's visit to hell, hoping that none of the congregation would see any link between the story and Dr. Curtin's death—if they had turned on the morning news and heard it.

Before I went into the dining room for my breakfast, I called Mike from the rectory office.

"It looks bad for our friend Lynn," he told me.

"She was not under your surveillance?" I gasped.

"Of course she was. And of course she never left her house. But Zack needs something to carry him through to the Friday night news. That means speculation today and an arrest on Friday. By Monday, he figures, it's all forgotten."

"He figures wrong, doesn't he?"

"Sure he does, but he's not exactly a genius if you take my meaning."

"I need some fingerprint work," I told him. "Delicate stuff."

I told him what I wanted.

He whistled.

"Are you sure?"

I hesitated before answering. I had something more than a guess and something less than certainty.

"Sure enough . . . you can do it?"

"Yeah, no real problem. Maybe get it done by noontime. You think it will be the same set of prints that are on the shotgun and probably on this scalpel?"

Again I wasn't sure. But why shouldn't they be the same?

"Maybe."

"I'll have to keep an eye on Zack's latest moves."

He did indeed take the prints off the wills. The hardest part in a neighborhood now swarming again with the locusts of local news was not to be seen doing it.

"Only a crude comparison, Blackie, but nothing that more careful inspection will reverse. You're dead right again. Astonishing."

"Elementary."

"On the other matter, the word I'm hearing is that Zack, not having the prints from the FBI yet, is going to stage another session at the police station today and promise an arrest for tomorrow, even if he doesn't get the prints. A big risk, indeed, as we know an insane risk. But that's how criminal justice works in a lot of places in our country."

"You should be aware, as should Ms. Reed's lawyer, that as a point of fact Dr. Curtin, the late Dr. Curtin as we must now call him, tried on at least two occasions to sexually assault Ms. Reed and that she has carried a scalpel in her purse for many years as protection against him and similar attackers. I presume she will tell him. If she does not, you may well want to pose such questions to her. I assure you, by the way, that this information falls well within the purview of matters in her life I am free to discuss."

"I take that as a given."

Why do most people steal my lines?

The wheels inside my head continued to spin, still stuck in the mud.

"She knows presumably that you and your colleagues have been assigned to guard her. She wonders why this protection?"

"Sure."

"I trust you did not tell her."

"I didn't tell her but she guessed. Looks like you've made another conquest, Blackie."

Damnation. We couldn't let the fact that she was being protected by the Catholic Bishop of Chicago, a corporation sole, leak out. Especially since the said Bishop was not exactly aware that he was paying for the protection.

Zack's performance at five was vintage. The bitter winds, more appropriate for autumn than for summer, ruffled his neatly cut hair, making him look even more boyish. The clips had just been shown of Lynn and her entourage leaving the police station.

"We questioned Ms. Reed for four hours," he confided to the world, "and candidly found her answers less than forthcoming. We are continuing our investigation. We expect to have something more definite tomorrow."

"Zack, is it true that Ms. Reeds claims that Dr. Curtin attempted to assault her sexually?"

"My staff has found evidence that she has made this claim."

"Last night or previously?"

He hesitated. "Previously."

The questions were plants, arranged beforehand to make it look like the zealous reporters were prying information out of the State's Attorney that he didn't want to reveal.

"Is it true that she has carried a medical instrument like the one which was found at the crime scene in her purse?"

"My staff has found witnesses that are willing to testify that she has shown this instrument to them."

"Did you search her purse for such a knife?"

"She would not permit us to do so."

Another decision that Annie Reilly Casey would doubtless endorse.

"Zack, we've been hearing rumors that she was involved with a killing when she was in Korea. Any comments on that?"

I gasped. The woman over at the hospital who had blabbed to Zack's gumshoes had confused the story.

"We're thoroughly investigating that rumor. Obviously a murder several decades ago has no direct relevance to present allegations. But it does tend to establish something about the suspect's character."

"Something about the murder of a Korean soldier, Zack?"

"As I said, we're investigating every possible angle on the case. We expect to have more tomorrow."

Almost immediately Mike the Cop was on the line.

"You saw it, Blackie?"

"Oh, yes. As you say, he is not the brightest South Side Irish cement-head in history."

"I couldn't believe it. . . . Do you want to come over for our press conference, live at six. Same venue?"

I would have loved to.

"It would be indiscreet I'm afraid."

House phone. Pete no doubt.

No, it was Lisa.

"Bishop Blackie . . ."

"Tell the kids to watch the six o'clock news. All the kids."

Then Pete.

"Did you . . ."

"I did, Peter Finnegan. I sure did. Postpone supper for fifteen minutes and gather all interested parties in the community room for the six o'clock news. I'll join you."

The live broadcast, in the fading light in front of the Woodbridge police station, featured the attractive woman in her middle thirties who was Lynn's lawyer and Mike the Cop.

The woman began. "Even by the usual loose standards of the State's Attorney's office, the allegations against my client are outrageous. They are also defamatory. Tomorrow we will go into court with a defamation action against Mr. O'Hara and the Woodbridge Police Department. We will contend that they have made their outrageous allegations with full knowledge that they could not be true. Standing at my right is Mr. Michael Casey, former police commissioner of Chicago. Mr. Casey, will you explain the information you have imparted to the police and the State's Attorney's office on repeated occasions?"

Mike looked more like Sherlock Holmes on camera than he did off camera. You almost expected a British accent.

"I am associated some of the time with an elite private security group. For over a week we have been guarding Ms. Lynn Keating Reed, without her knowledge up to the time of her husband's unfortunate death. Our client must remain nameless except to say that the client is a friend of Ms. Reed's. At all times there was at least one of our highly trained operatives—off-duty members of the Chicago Police Department in fact—watching her around the clock. Since the time of her husband's death, we have had three operatives protecting her. We have affidavits stating that she was inside her house, sleeping, at the times of both crimes. Indeed, one of our women operatives was also in the house all last night. We are not prepared to say who murdered Stephen Curtin, M.D., or Gerald Reed IV. That is not our job. But we are prepared to assert that Lynn Keating Reed was *not* the criminal."

"You also have a comment to make, I believe, Commissioner, about the allegation that Ms. Reed may have killed a Korean soldier during the war in that country, do you not?"

"Yes, I do. In point of fact, it was six Korean soldiers, *North* Korean guerrillas who were attacking a field hospital at night when she was on duty. If I may I'll read from the citation for the Navy Cross she was awarded for gallantry in action. Perhaps I should add that it is the Navy's second highest decoration after the Medal of Honor."

As he read the citation, the parish staff cheered. I heard echoing cheers from the office where the porter persons and a large teenage mob had doubtless gathered.

Lynn was a hero now, all over Chicago, whether she wanted to be or not. And the Navy Department would know where she was whether she wanted them to or not.

And she was now safely out of danger.

That was as foolish and as dangerous a conclusion that I had ever drawn.

CHAPTER 22

I REALIZED JUST how dangerous as I was pouring myself my end-of-the-day sip of Baileys.

I filled the glass and poured a sizable amount of the cream on the marble table against which Charles P. McInerny was alleged to have hit his head.

How could I have been so stupid? Why hadn't I seen the obvious before? Lynn was now in mortal danger.

I bumbled around searching for my glasses. It always takes me a while to find them, especially in a strange room. They turned out to be where they usually are—right in front of me. In this case they were covered with Baileys. Not so badly that I couldn't see through them, however.

I punched in the number of the Butternut Marriott. Mr. Casey was not in his room.

Perhaps he was over at Lynn's house. With Annie in the car waiting for him when he went off duty.

I did not know how to communicate with the guard unit.

So I called Arnold Griffin's number.

"Griffin," he said in a sleepy voice.

"Father Ryan. Didn't I tell you not to let the woman out of your sight?"

"She wants a little space for a while, Bishop. I don't think that's unreasonable. Especially since after that press conference she is absolutely safe."

"Has everyone forgotten that there is a killer on the loose in this community? I don't care what she wants or what you think? *I* want you over there tonight. Now. At once. Immediately. Do you understand? Keep her away from windows. Don't argue with me. She's in mortal danger."

I slammed the phone down, grabbed my White Sox jacket, and, struggling to clean my glasses with an inadequate piece of tissue, charged down the stairs, out of the rectory, and into the front seat of my T-bird.

As might be expected in such circumstances, the relic refused to start, perhaps because I had neglected to treat it with the respect it usually demands. To judge by the gas fumes, I had flooded the engine. I jammed the accelerator to the floor and turned over the key with all the authority to which my office entitled me. Slowly and reluctantly the T-bird came to life.

I roared out of the rectory parking lot and turned the corner at top speed. I remembered to flick on the headlights only when I passed a Woodbridge police car that had been hiding on the other side of the church, doubtless laying in wait for some curfew-violating adolescent.

Their headlights went on, the colored lights on top began to spin, and the siren started to wail as they turned around to follow me. The tolling bells in the church tower joined in the chorus of sound.

I figured it was just as well they were following. We might need them too.

But true to their incompetence they lost me as I turned down Maple Street.

I ground to a halt in front of the Reed house, bounded out of the car (as I almost never do), and began running.

I had no reason, other than strong instinct, to suspect

that the danger that might engulf Lynn was about to strike. But I trust my instincts.

"Mike!" I cried.

"I'm right here, Blackie," he said, emerging from behind a bush. "What's going on? Griffin just showed up saying that you had ordered him to come over."

"Backyard, rose garden," I gasped. *"Now!"*

I dashed around the side of the house and pulled up short. The garden was illumined by light. Floodlights?

No, the moon. Oh, yes, I remembered the moon. It was a full moon, harvest moon. The clouds must have moved on. The roses gleamed in the soft silver light, the lawn glittered like a bed of emeralds. Nothing moved. The only sound was the expressway hum far away.

Mike Casey caught up with me.

"What's wrong, Blackie?"

"A haunt."

"Dead?"

"Very much alive and very dangerous."

"But not tonight?"

I peered around the garden.

"Apparently not."

"Like I said, Griffin came by a few minutes ago. Said you'd ordered him not to let her out of his sight. He seemed a bit bemused."

"I would imagine that he did."

I glanced back at the house. A light was on in Lynn's "office." The sliding door was open, a transparent drape stirring in a faint breeze. Had I not ordered that the windows be closed?

No, I had merely told him to keep her away from the windows. Who would worry about a door to a backyard? I should have been more explicit.

Through the curtain I saw two people, standing some

distance from one another, apparently in a serious discussion. Lynn was wearing a robe, Griffin a T-shirt and slacks. A quiet end of the day in Woodbridge.

They were sitting ducks.

I spun around and surveyed the garden again. Nothing. Absolute peace on a lovely late summer night.

"Nothing stirring," Mike said softly. "False alarm?"

"Certainly not . . . Michael, will you ring the front doorbell and tell those people that I said they should close the sliding door in that office and draw . . ."

Suddenly the peace was shattered by a bloodcurdling screech. A figure with impossibly elongated arms rose from a bush and charged toward us.

"Look out"—I pushed Mike away—"she has Zulu spears!"

Margie Curtin stopped dead and, still howling like a wolf or a banshee or a Zulu warrior, heaved a spear at me. I tried to duck, fell into the rose beds, and felt the spear rush over my head. It banged into the house and fell a few feet away from me.

Bad shot. Too stoned.

I scrambled to my feet and saw Margie a few yards away. She was closing in on Mike, the spear aimed right at his belly. He was backed up against the house. He feinted left and then right. Where the hell were his backups?

Margie, dressed in some kind of lionskin dress, continued to howl. The world did not go into slow motion as it is alleged to do for others.

Nonetheless, I picked up the spear she had heaved at me and charged her. She heard me coming, turned to face me, and prepared to plunge the weapon into me.

In such circumstances I do not play fair. I swung my spear like a baseball bat against her right arm.

Her howl turned into a cry of pain. She pulled a long

knife from a sheath and rushed not me but the open door of the house. Lynn and Arnie Griffin, surprised by the noise, had come to the door.

"Close the door," I shouted.

Margie Curtin was at the door just as Arnie slammed it shut. She must not have realized that it was closed. Determined to kill her hated enemy who was only a few feet away, she charged right into it.

The glass shattered. Margie fell back on the ground, blood streaming from her face. She struggled to her feet and began another attack. Lynn and Arnie stood transfixed by the awful screaming, bloody apparition that was about to plunge through the shattered glass.

I reached out with the butt end of the spear I was still clutching and tripped her. She fell on her face just short of the door.

Mike fell on top of her, pulled her arms behind her back, and, after a fierce struggle, locked the handcuffs. His two associates and Arnie Griffin joined in the task of subduing her. The blood from her bleeding face spattered all of them. Finally, she gave up and went limp. The drug, whatever its nature, had run its course.

While we waited for an ambulance, Lynn wiped the blood from Margie's face, stanched the flow from her broken nose, and soothed her with the gentle crooning that might calm a troubled baby.

"Who would have better access to a doctor's shotgun than his wife?" I asked no one in particular. "Or his scalpel? Or his drugs? And Lynn wasn't the only nurse in the Monsignor's crowd."

CHAPTER 23

"ONE WOULD LIKE to be able to say that the mystery of the haunted parish is now resolved," I informed the group assembled in the tower study on Saturday morning. "Poor Margie Curtin may be in detox for the rest of her life, unable to stand trial for the two crimes she committed and the one she tried to commit. That she committed them we may take as proven because of the presence of her fingerprints on the gun, the scalpel, and the Zulu spears—though it may take some time before the State's Attorney closes the case. Presumably in a small story on page eleven of the *Tribune*.

"We may never know her motives. Whether they are in any way connected with the events about which we are concerned today remains problematic. Arguably she killed Gerald Reed in a rage over his insistence that her husband sell his chain of nursing homes. She may have killed her husband because of his infidelities or because they had at last become public. She tried to kill Ms. Reed perhaps because she saw her, wrongly, as the ultimate rival. As I say we will never be able to be certain. What is certain, however, is that she had been ingesting extremely potent African drugs, of whose origin forensic experts are still in doubt. She had been over the top as they say for a long time."

I looked around the room at my audience—Pete Finnegan, Joe O'Keefe, Tom Wozniak, Mike the Cop, Arnie Griffin, Lynn Reed and her son, the Fasios. I had locked the door to the tower to exclude nosy teenage persons who would otherwise want to eavesdrop.

"One might contend," I continued, "that she *could* have been the one who murdered Monsignor McInerny—and oh, yes, he was murdered—on a previous binge with hallucinogenic drugs. There are a number of reasons why such an explanation would be convenient and a number of others that would make it inconvenient. Therefore it is necessary to put the mystery of the haunted rectory to rest this morning, even if very little is done as a result of our solution. Any questions?"

I looked around the room. Everyone was grim, troubled with their own thoughts and emotions and guilts.

"Do we know," Lynn asked hesitantly, "why Steve Curtin falsified the death certificate. He must have known that Monsignor was killed with a blunt instrument."

"I think we can surmise that he was afraid that a police investigation would reveal the existence of the trust he and your late husband administered and, more dangerously, the recent borrowing from that trust."

She nodded, biting her lip.

She was still wearing black, this time a black dress with white cuffs and collar. A miniature blue and white Navy Cross ribbon rested contentedly above her breast. No reason to deny anymore what everyone knew.

Peter Finnegan hesitated and then spoke. "Will we have to avenge the Monsignor?"

"He has no right to demand vengeance. That right, as you may remember, is reserved to God. The Monsignor does have the right to truth."

There were no more questions.

"There can be no reason to doubt that the two trustees of the Charles McInerny Trust, as it was called, knew that the money came from parish collections. After all, the collection money was deposited in the bank every Monday morning, having been counted by careful and responsible ushers. From their viewpoint it was parish money and Monsignor's money and he could do what he wanted with it. Since he had turned it over to them for investment, they had the right and duty to invest it well. There is every reason to think that they did so. Indeed they made a very nice profit for the trust. Admittedly some of the money went to friends of theirs, but these investments were remarkably successful. It would appear that on occasion they made small loans to themselves from the trust account, which was perhaps a dubious practice, but the loans would appear to have been paid back with appropriate interest. I do not question that at the end of the day as our British friends say they would have turned the money over to the Church. However, Monsignor's death, which they had not anticipated, left them with a number of dilemmas. The first was what to do with the trust. I can only speculate that they would have turned it over to you, Peter, and accepted your gratitude gracefully. You would then presumably have informed the Cardinal who would have been delighted and hardly inclined to take action against what from his viewpoint was a manifest case of alienation of Church property.

"Unfortunately, they were also faced with the prospect of charges that they had misused and lost large sums of money from the trust in the last year to finance ill-advised speculations in the so-called derivatives market. The speculations were clearly in their own self-interest and not that of the trust, though presumably they would have shared their profits, should these have survived the interest rate run-up, with the trust itself according to some rate that they would have thought equitable. The Monsignor's death and the disappearance of his records terrified them. While they knew he paid no attention to such trivia, as he saw it, they also knew that the records could cause them grievous trouble."

Lynn closed her eyes. Her son scowled grimly.

"In a manner which need not detain us at the present, the funds have been returned to the trust and the Church in the person of the Catholic Bishop of Chicago, a corporation sole, has taken possession of it. You will find, Peter, when you next call the Cardinal that you have a huge surplus in your Chancery account."

"Wow!" he said softly.

He did not, however, ask how much.

"I mention all of these facts because it is necessary to understand them as background in order to understand the incidents that led to the death of the Monsignor. The essence of that mystery has always been the locked room. How did a killer penetrate into Monsignor's sanctuary, hit him with a heavy candlestick, and then escape undetected, even though the bolts on the locks were secured from the inside?

"I submit that it is patent how the killer entered. The Monsignor admitted that person. The problem is the escape. To address that question it was necessary to investigate some history of the rectory. It was built by General M. E. Crawford—the initials stand for Moses Elias—in the years after the Civil War and called Wood-bridge, a name later extended to the whole village. General Crawford was a cavalry officer with a substantial reputation for courage. Also, as I have learned, a reputation for brutality to his own men and to prisoners of war.

"According to a history that I have here at hand"—I

lifted Ellen Prudence's opus—"he used this tower part of the residence as, to use her words, a disorderly house for the amusement of himself and his friends . . ."

"Dear God!" Ms. Fasio exclaimed.

"It would seem that he died here one night, either by his own hand or more likely by the hand of someone who was here with him. Certain phenomena began to occur, lights at night, screams of tormented women, that sort of thing, shortly after his death. The house acquired an unsavory reputation. The heirs of the General did not choose to live in it and were unable to sell it until Father Kelly bought the house and the land around it as the site of Saints Peter and Paul."

"Did he encounter any of the phenomena?" Pete asked nervously.

"We have little in the way of information from that era. There is no evidence of any manifestations, however. Monsignor Patrick Flynn had a different problem. For reasons that are not recorded he had assumed responsibility for his brother, a certain Dr. Flynn. The issue seems to have been how the 'Doc' as he was called could live in the rectory and yet not be in the rectory. Eyewitnesses report that the 'Doc,' who was not popular with the curates as they were called in those days, lived in this tower and had a habit of appearing and disappearing at other places in the rectory."

"A real live spook," Tom Wozniak said with a grin.

"Those words are kinder than the ones used by priests who shared the rectory with him. . . . When Monsignor McInerny arrived he promptly banished the 'Doc' and took possession of this room and the suite below. As far as I know there were no hauntings in his day either, were there, Joe?"

"I don't think so, Bishop. Not that he mentioned. I do

know that he was jealous of the privacy this place provided. There was only one key."

"Still is only one key." I held up mine. "At least as far as I know . . . now may I suggest we go downstairs to the dinette and bedroom."

I led them down the stairs to the next level.

"Dark," I heard Gerry Reed murmur.

"Decidedly." I flicked on the lights. "The windows here are portholes unlike the large windows upstairs. I note that we are now opposite the third floor of the rectory, where all the resident priests except the Pastor live. At this level the tower and the rest of the house are structurally separate. One floor beneath the tower merges with the rest of the house, though the only link of which we are aware is the stairway which is entered from a door at the other end of the corridor from the present Pastor's suite. . . . Does anyone see anything unusual in what I have just described?"

"Too small," Lynn said wearily. "These two rooms together are much smaller than the study upstairs."

"There are only nine windows in this room," Al Fasio added. "I noticed that when I was rebuilding the rest of the rectory. The blind side is the one facing the third floor of the rectory, so there would not be much to see, but it's hard to understand why windows were not added when the place was built; they would have added some much needed light. Or, if in existence once, why were they eventually eliminated."

"I've always wondered," Joe O'Keefe mused, "why the stairway up to the study is so narrow. What happened to the rest of the, let me see, second floor?"

"When you were remodeling the rest of the rectory, Al," I asked, "did you notice anything unusual about the tower, in addition to the missing porthole windows?"

"To tell the truth, I didn't pay much attention to it. We weren't supposed to disturb the Monsignor, an idea of which I approved. I thought it was a curious old edifice and it might be fun someday to remodel it. Nella said it looked haunted, and that was when Monsignor was still alive."

Nella shivered. "It's an ugly, evil place. *Maybe* you could change it by redoing it, but I'd almost be afraid to try."

"Did you ever notice before, Lynn, that these two rooms were too small."

"I never came down here. Even when Monsignor was sick, he'd meet me upstairs."

"Joe, do you remember where the 'Doc' lived?"

He seemed startled by the question. "Never met the man. Cholly had banished him before I arrived. I guess I assumed he had one of the rooms on the second floor, maybe the one in which I lived for a quarter century."

"So what do we conclude?"

"That's easy," Peter Finnegan said promptly. "There are secret rooms here someplace. Why didn't anyone think of that before?"

Because anyone isn't Blackie Ryan, specialist in locked room mysteries as well as James Joyce and David Tracy, that's why.

"I will provide one more datum. In the basement where the drains from the tower join those from the rest of the house, there are four drains."

"One from the bathroom upstairs," Lynn counted, "one from the bathroom over there, one from the kitchen, and one . . . well, I suppose from the room behind the bed."

She looked and sounded so very tired.

"Well reasoned. Then all one has to do is to find the passage into the room behind the bed. I won't bother you with an account of all the panels I pushed and pulled, all the knobs I tried to turn, all the levers I searched for. It was a random walk. Eventually, I found this simple but ingenious mechanism."

I pulled the drawer on the bedstand next to Monsignor's—and more recently my—bed three times and then slammed it shut. A soft whirring hum briefly filled the room and then stopped. A panel between the bed and the kitchen slid open.

Gasps from all present.

"The proverbial secret door. I do not know whether it is part of the original arrangement as conceived by General Crawford or a subsequent addition by Monsignor Flynn. If I had to guess I would suspect that the structure was already here, that the Monsignor discovered it after he read Ellen Prudence King's book, and improved on the original work."

"It's so dark," Gerry Reed murmured.

"Only," I said as I flipped a switch, "when the lights are turned off."

Another gasp from the group.

"It's like this bedroom in miniature," Nella said softly. "Same furniture, same carpets, same drapes on the wall. Creepy."

"It occurs to me, Lynn," I said, "that you had a hand in remodeling the study for Monsignor but he barred you from the bedroom."

She nodded, a tired, discouraged nod. "Mrs. Raftery, his housekeeper, took care of these rooms. I bought the microwave a couple of years ago. She set it up."

"We pensioned her off after he died," the Pastor explained. "She didn't want to stay, though I would have kept her on."

"The furnishings in that room look a quarter century old," Lynn said.

"More like almost a half century," Nella corrected her. "Post-war, World War II that is. Rich and expensive and not all that tasteful."

"Cholly didn't like change unless it was forced on him or"—Joe smiled and nodded at Lynn—"charmed into it."

"It's scary," Nella said, "or am I the only one who feels that way?"

"Terrifying," Pete agreed. "Sinister."

Lynn hugged herself.

"Can't we close it, Bishop Blackie?"

"In a moment . . . note the doorway over there where the wall of the Monsignor's bedroom meets the curve of the tower. It leads to a stairway that goes down to the second floor of the tower, which as I have said is an integral part of the rest of the rectory. It's basically a large parlor, about the same size as the one above us, furnished in the style of this bedroom. There are electric lights but no phone or books or papers or television, an empty and uninhabited room."

"But, Bishop," Nella cried, "this room is clean!"

"Someone has lived in it," Al agreed. "Recently."

"Clean?" Tom Wozniak protested. "It's covered with dust!"

"Six months of dust, Father," Lynn explained, "not twenty-five years of dust."

"Anyone who wishes may go down the stairs," I announced, "and examine the parlor or library or whatever one wishes to call it."

"Want to have a look, Father?" Arnie asked the Pastor.

"No, but I better, I'm responsible for it. Coming, Al?"

"If you say so, Father. I'm the general contractor."

"As you will anticipate," I observed, "the study below is

somewhat smaller than the study above because it was necessary to yield some room to the spiral staircase from which we first obtained entry to the top floor of the tower. Of course it has no windows. When you are finished with your explorations, we'll meet upstairs in Monsignor's study."

"That poor man lived down here for twenty years?" Lynn asked as she climbed back to the third floor. "The 'Doc' I mean?"

"Almost certainly. It was a lonely life I suppose."

"Though no more lonely than Monsignor's."

"Perhaps less so . . . why, Lynn, did he keep the hidden suite clean?"

"I don't know," she said slowly, "unless he had someone living there or visiting often. I can't imagine who it would be."

"He was kind of a neatness freak in a funny way." Joe O'Keefe joined the conversation. "He abandoned the third floor of the rectory almost completely and let the rest of the place go to seed. He let the school and the convent and the church deteriorate although the chimes and the organ were his pride. But he insisted the organ console be polished every week, wore tailor-made black suits, had his hair cut every two weeks, and would send back shirts to be pressed again if they were slightly wrinkled. Most guys wouldn't have noticed. Navy training maybe."

"You can see him wanting to keep the room next to his spotlessly clean even though no one lived there?"

"I wouldn't have anticipated it," Joe said thoughtfully, "but somehow it doesn't surprise me."

"Was there someone living there, Bishop?" Lynn whispered to me, her face pale and sad, a pieta in the medieval mural.

"I'm not sure and we'll probably never know for sure, but I doubt it."

"Daylight!" Nella exclaimed as we returned to the late Pastor's study. "I love it!"

Within a few minutes we were all assembled once more in the light of day.

"I agree with Nella," Arnie Griffin commented, "the whole setup is creepy, scary, a little sick. But, look, Bishop. For your theory to hold, the killer had to have escaped by coming down to the now dead Monsignor's bedroom, slipping into the lower suite, and then escaping somehow. If there is no other way out, he'd have to come up the stairs just like we've done and he'd be back where he started from. What's on the first floor of the tower?"

"A laundry room and storeroom."

"I redid that, Bishop," Al agreed. "No sign of any connection with the rest of the tower."

"Patently."

"But there is another door," he continued. "In the guest room on the second floor, the one right at the head of the steps, there's a closet with a solid oak wall. And there's a solid oak panel downstairs. I bet if you poked around enough down there you could make that wall turn into a door."

"I get the picture," Tom Wozniak agreed. "Someone, the Doc a long time ago, the killer six months ago, could slip out at that door, rush down to the first floor and out into the driveway."

"Especially," Arnie said, "if it was night and no one was awake in the house."

"Provided, Arnie," Lynn cautioned, "the person had a key to the rectory and knew how the oak door worked."

"I was pastor by then," Peter said. "Everyone in the parish seemed to have a key."

"Where does that leave us?" Gerry Reed asked. "We know how the murderer could have escaped, but we're not sure that is what he did."

"I think I can reconstruct the matter with some ease," I told them all. "Let us assume that the late Monsignor becomes aware that in addition to the bank accounts he has turned over to his successor, there is another and much larger sum of money held by McInerny Trust. He has paid no attention to it and has no idea of its size. No one has told him about it, though, to be fair to them, he wouldn't have been interested in it if they had. Now, however, he knows he doesn't have all that much time to live. Moreover he thinks that the Cardinal has done him a favor by sending young Peter here to take care of him during his last days. He does not want to return that favor by leaving the Cardinal a financial mess. Finally, he has reason to believe that someone is misusing the funds in the trust. He rewrites his will in the form of a letter to the Cardinal in which he thanks him for Pete, deeds to him all the money in the trust so that there will no problem when he dies, and warns the Cardinal that there has been malfeasance and names the perpetrators of the malfeasance and one of their allies. Then he signs the will and asks Lynn, who is present in the room, to witness his signature, but, so that she won't be able to read it, holds his hand over the rest of the autographed document—a valid will in this state, is it not, Mr. Casey?"

"Certainly."

"Were you able to read any of it, Lynn?"

She was biting her lip, trying to hold back tears. "If he didn't want me to read it, then I wasn't going to try to read it."

"Now, then," I continued, though not inexorably because I am incapable of that manner, "let us suppose that the Monsignor summons the culprit to visit him late at night. He denounces, excoriates, ridicules said culprit. He waves the will, the new will he probably would have said, and then reads it. He taunts the culprit to the point where the culprit's high-strung emotions can no longer tolerate it. Said culprit grabs a candlestick and strikes the Monsignor over the head with it, not intending perhaps to kill him, but only to silence him for a moment."

There was a solemn silence all around the room. Tears were forming in Lynn's eyes. Gerry put his arm around her.

"The culprit realizes what he's done and then begins to behave with an almost preternatural cleverness, calm and devious now instead of insane with rage. The culprit rubs prints off the candlestick, because that is what killers do in a mystery story. Both wills go into the culprit's pocket because they could, especially in combination, be incriminating. The culprit thinks about escape and realizes the possibilities in a locked room situation. The culprit reasons through the scenario a couple of times and can find no flaws in it. There will be a small risk, but it is really very minor.

"Are there any traces left? No. All right, downstairs. Almost out the door. Wait? The wills! If there is an investigation, they will mean doom if they are found in the culprit's possession. Where to leave them? Of course, in the suite itself. The culprit rushes upstairs to Doc's bedroom and hides the wills in a place which he will easily remember. . . ."

"Why hide the wills instead of destroying them?" Arnie Griffin demanded.

"The culprit, who as I say is now preternaturally devious, reasons that perhaps someone else has seen the text of the newer will. If that has happened, then the culprit would be at risk of a murder charge, if the will has vanished. If on the other hand the will is somewhere else where it may be discovered eventually, then there is less risk that the culprit will have to face such a charge, whatever other charges may arise. The will remains hidden for a time, until the culprit can be sure that no one has seen it. Then the culprit will destroy it and plant, perhaps in the parish baptismal records, the older will which will not threaten the culprit but will quite the contrary be a benefit."

Lynn was sobbing. Arnie took her hand.

"So having hidden the wills," Peter Finnegan said, trying to puzzle out the mystery, "your culprit escapes through the secret door in the closet on the second floor, runs down the stairs, and out into the night."

"Not quite, Peter," I said grimly. "He runs upstairs to his suite of rooms on the third floor. Didn't you do that, Joe?"

"You're crazy," the old priest said sadly. "You can't prove a word of it."

"Although you live on the third floor now, your former suite was on the second floor. It included the closet with the oak wall which was the passageway to the tower and to the hidden stairway. You explored it long ago because you were curious. It provided you with a hideaway from which you could spy on Monsignor McInerny, though much to your disappointment you never found him doing anything wrong except wasting twenty-five years of his life in aimless consumption of books and television."

"How could you possibly know all of that?"

I couldn't but I could guess. Judging from the surprise on his face, the guesses were accurate.

"Where would a clever criminal hide the wills so that he could easily and quickly find them, I asked myself. It occurred to me that one convenient place would be the bed table that is the equivalent in Doc's bedroom, if I may call it that, to the one in the Monsignor's room which opens the secret panel."

I opened the folder that I had earlier placed on the Monsignor's luxurious oak desk and removed the two letterhead stationery sheets.

"In the first he assigns all his possessions to the McInerny Trust and expresses his confidence that the trustees will see that it is used for proper purposes. He also earmarks a half million dollars for his lifelong friend Father Joseph O'Keefe who has shared his long exile. In the second, in addition to the substance about which I have already speculated, he denounces the same Father O'Keefe to the Cardinal for taking bribes from the embezzlers and recommends that he be sent either to jail or to a monastery to spend the rest of his life on bread and water. Incidentally, these are copies. Mr. Casey's associates have removed prints from the originals among which prints are, as you well know, Joseph, yours. You were too clever by half. Still the clever gambler who loses by outguessing himself. You should have destroyed both wills immediately."

"I could have killed you twice," Joe wailed, "and now you do this to me!"

"It would have been unwise of you to try, Joseph. I was waiting for you with a candlestick. The Monsignor would have been avenged rather more quickly that he will be now."

I motioned Gerry to take his mother downstairs. She would never forgive herself if she became hysterical in the presence of a crowd. Arnie raised an eyebrow and I nodded. He went after them.

Joe O'Keefe's personality went through a transformation. The injured child beneath the wise old priest persona appeared.

"I didn't mean to kill him," he said, his eyes childishly searching among us for pity and understanding. "He had been pushing me all my life. He made the twenty-five years out here a living hell of humiliation. I put up with it all. Then that night something snapped inside of me. At first I was glad. The bastard had got what he had deserved long ago. Then," he began to weep, "I realized what I had done."

"You were taking payoffs from Curtin and Reed?" Al asked.

"Small tips, nothing much, a few dollars here and there, that's all."

"Twenty-five thousand dollars since Christmas?" I asked. "The elder Gerald Reed kept accurate records."

"I earned it all during the last twenty-five years, and more than that too."

"You hung around at the club listening to the conversations, picking up dirt, mostly just for the fun of it, and also for the sense of power it gave you. Then you found out about this and began very subtly to blackmail Reed and Curtin. The Monsignor found out. You killed him."

He hid his face in his hands, a hurt, bitter, and very clever old man.

"You'll never be able to put me in jail, Blackie."

"I'm aware of that."

He looked up at me. "You would be!"

"Pancreatic cancer. A month to live."

"I don't want to know how you found out."

I didn't offer to explain that I had called the doctor as a representative of the Cardinal and wondered how serious Father O'Keefe's cancer was.

"Why did you bother then?" he said as his sobs racked his sick body.

"The truth had to be told, Joe. The truth that makes us

all free, the truth which enables God's love finally to break into your bitter heart."

Apparently it did because I received a deathbed letter thanking me.

Lynn recovered her equilibrium later that day.

"I can't be a nurse to everyone, can I, Bishop Blackie?" she said to me through her tears.

"You can't take away their free will. Not even God tries to do that."

I thought about that line for a moment and then added, "But She does have Her sneaky ways of winning us over."

"God really is a nurse?" She smiled at me. "Like you told me last week?"

"So She was often described in the Middle Ages. And so She is."

CHAPTER 24

ON A BRISK Saturday in October, Lynn Reed and Arnold Griffin were married at seven-thirty in the morning in the Blessed Sacrament chapel of the Church of Saints Peter and Paul in Woodbridge, Father Peter Finnegan presiding. Or, as I told them in a whisper before the Eucharist began, they were in fact renewing vows they had made to one another long ago and obtaining the Church's blessing on their union. Another example, I insisted, of how long it takes the Church to catch up with God.

The bride wore a pale gray dress with a hint of the flouncy, fluttery 1940s fashion that was once again in style. A miniature Navy Cross hung on a pendant around her neck.

The ceremony was supposed to be private—for the family only. But in addition to children and grandchildren (one of them a babe in arms who seemed to find my pectoral cross a delightful toy) there were four other guests, uninvited. Three of them, as any sensible person would have expected, were the faithful porter persons, Megan, Lisa, and Jennifer who giggled quietly in the back of the chapel. The fourth was, naturally enough, the Cardinal Archbishop of Chicago.

He presented the bride with a papal decoration—membership in some obscure order, which, as he pointed out, made her a papal dame. She could properly insist on being called "Dame Evelyn."

"I will leave it to Bishop Ryan," he chortled, "to make references to the song from *South Pacific.*"

Disrespectful giggles from all.

Driving back to the city in his Buick Park Avenue, he said, "That tower where we vested is a terrible place. Pete should tear it down."

"I believe he is going to gut it and convert it into a combination of offices, meeting rooms, and a parish gallery."

"Parish gallery!" he snorted. "Well, I hope they douse the place with high quality holy water."

"Perhaps from a holy well in Mother Ireland."

"Blackwood," he continued after some thought. "What the hell was that haunting about?"

"It was a well-known psychic phenomenon, as I've tried to explain before," I said with my customary west-of-Ireland sigh. "The tower was infested with memories of past horrors, psychic traces, if you will, of the rage and the evil and the pain which had once existed there in full reality. When these traces, and I suspect that they were the remnants of events in the distant past as well as of the more immediate past, interact with the, uh, psychic propensities of someone who is attuned to such phenomena, a vast variety of phenomena may occur. The person who is the catalyst may well be unaware of the link between his psyche and the phenomena, as was patently true in this case. But the more deeply concerned this link person is with the suspected horror, the more powerful the phenomena will be."

"Pete?"

"Patently. He knows when hitters are about to hit home

runs and the target of Chicago Bear quarterbacks, even before the quarterback does."

"Figures . . . he doesn't know?"

"If he does, the knowledge is so remote that he does not notice it."

"Now that the money is in the right hands and the murder has been solved and poor Joe is in the ground, all the phenomena have stopped."

"Precisely."

"We're not going to move Pete out of there, are we?"

"Heaven forbid."

The Cardinal smiled happily as we blended into traffic on the Congress (oops, Eisenhower) Expressway. He liked happy endings with all the loose ends neatly tied up. The events of the morning have given him the neat, happy ending he wanted.

I saw no point in telling him that as we had left the tower ten minutes before, the room was filled with sensations of relief, peace, and gratitude.

And the scent of orange blossoms.

I did not know, and did not want to know whence came the emotions and the aroma. It was, I told myself, none of my business.

But the smell of orange blossoms lingered in my nostrils until we were well inside the city.